Tall Jerry

The Crown

TALL JERRY
AND THE
DELPHI FALLS TRILOGY

Post War
Historical Fiction
CLASSICS

ECHOED LEGENDS

Legend One

TALL JERRY

in

Summer of Shadows,
Bodies and Bridges

First Edition

JEROME MARK ANTIL

SCENE: RURAL AMERICA
TIME: POST WAR 1953
(Summer vacation to Halloween.)

Historical references offered by
Judy Clancy Conway; Marty Bays; Dale Barber;
New Woodstock NY Historical Society; Cincinnatus NY
Historical Society; Pompey NY Historical Society; Cortland
NY Historical Society; Cazenovia Public Library; Carthage NY
Historical Society; Binghamton NY Historical Society

Some characters are from combinations of Jerry's siblings (James,
Paul, Richard, Frederick, Michael, Dorothy, and Mary)

PRINTED IN AMERICA

TABLE OF CONTENTS

To Wyatt, J.O., and Hudson

12-year-old Tall Jerry, his mom and dad. 1953

Tall Jerry in the Delphi Falls Trilogy are of a time filled with characters that show true heroism. Of legends that happened after the war and before there were cell phones and an internet, and not every house had a telephone or television. Of a time when a full, hot meal at school cost a quarter. It was a time when you could leave the house and go off to play without having to ask. The people are real, and the fictionalized legends are based in truth, give or take a stretch or two. The Delphi Falls with its shale-crusted cliffs, big white rock, my boyhood home, campsite and barn garage are there to see today if you have a mind to head on up to the town of Cazenovia, New York—near the hamlet of Delphi. Both waterfalls are magical to this day, I promise. Oh, they may not grant a wish or turn tin into gold, but they will make you feel good about yourself and give you confidence.

JMA

The cliffs at Delphi Falls tower sixty-feet high.

Spring in 1953 – a boat crafted from a creamery tin.

CHAPTER 1

EARLY SPRING 1953

The name is Charlie, and I'm a guardian angel.

You'd have no cause to know me lest you've read a book, *The Pompey Hollow Book Club,* by Mr. Jerome Mark Antil. That book was mainly the truth about a place in 1949, after the war ended. That story was about the year his momma, Missus, and his daddy, Big Mike, moved Jerry and his brothers, Dick and Gourmet Mike, from a house on sleepy Helen Avenue in Cortland, far out into a hinterland of wilderness, as eight-year-old Jerry chronicled it at the time. The twist was young Jerry never got to see where they were moving until after his family plumb upped and moved.

"Get in the car, son."

"Where we going, Mom?"

"Get in the car, son."

We'll get to the myth soon enough, but imagine you're eight years old and you've just climbed from the back seat of a car filled with cookware, shoes, and moving boxes at a house you've moved to only to look up and see your house setting in the middle of two sixty-foot tall stone cliffs as tall as high-rise city buildings with even taller pine trees, maples, and rotting elms on top.

"Where are we, Mom?"

"Carry a box into the house, son."

Trees on top of cliffs, doubling their height. If you can imagine that, imagine the lonely chill and shadows of darkness those giant stone walls laid on the house below. If the cliffs alone weren't enough to scare the lad, the house was smack in front of two giant sixty and

JEROME MARK ANTIL

seventy-foot rock waterfalls, the Delphi Falls, one on top of another, water roaring day and night, crashing down like thunder.

Young Jerry made new friends in the country who, like him, grew up during World War II. They wanted to emulate war heroes, the brothers, sisters, fathers, and mothers they knew or had learned about. Jerry and his friends wanted to make a difference. When he was eight and his friends were nine and ten, they started a club of valor, to do good by catching a crook or two or save a farm animal from meeting up with an axe blade. Best you know the club wasn't about books, as the name implied.

The name was about the only lie in it, truth be told.

Jerry and his friends had saved rabbits from being slaughtered for food.

"Holbrook, I'm in big trouble," young Jerry said.

"Why?"

"I forgot to latch the doors on the cages."

"For what?"

"Three rabbits."

"What's the problem?"

"Now there's thirty-eight."

"Where'd they all come from?"

"Hell if I know."

Young Jerry and his friends were celebrating their bunny- saving victory in the hamlet's cemetery on an Easter morning when young Barber first dreamed it up.

"We need to start a club," Mayor said.

"For what?" Mary asked.

"We'll save more bunnies like we did and maybe catch crooks and stuff," Randy said.

"So, let's start one," Barber said.

"What do we call it?" Bases asked.

Barber climbed up on a cemetery stone.

"Barber, what are you doing?" Holbrook asked.

2

Barber raised his arm, pointed at the sky.

"Ain't a mom in the county would stop us from leaving the house for a meeting, even on a school night, if we call ourselves The Pompey Hollow Book Club," Barber proclaimed.

"Who can join?" Holbrook asked.

"How about anybody who shows up?" Tall Jerry asked.

Kids standing around favored the notion, spat, making the name official.

It was Mary who stood up and offered an afterthought. "With a name that literary we might consider stopping using the word 'ain't.'"

Not only could she spell, she could hit a homerun.

Mary was named president.

And here's the good part.

Truth be told, the Delphi Falls are mythical waterfalls. That's the legend, it surely is. Jerry didn't know it at the time, as he couldn't give much thought to such notions trying to sleep with his concentration being perplexed by a window frame that rattled from the sounds—wind howling through trees and water crashing down shale rock cliffs in his back yard.

It took months for him to get accustomed to the noise.

"Will somebody close the back door, please?"

"It is closed, son. Go back to sleep."

As with country kids those days, young Jerry and his brothers were given chores. His was walking a mile regular on Saturdays, first down to Maxwell's mill on the corner of Cardner Road then right and up the steep hill to my place to fetch a basket of eggs for Missus. That was when he still feared the country, and he'd walk the mile up and the mile back with sulks and moans, near scared to fright.

"Do I have to, Mom?"

One day ole Charlie here thought I'd set him down to explain just how lucky a boy he was, moving in front of the Delphi Falls that would protect him by giving him strength so he never had to worry

3

about critters like hoot owls or foxes or the night winds howling through crackling cold tree leaves, while ole Charlie here was stuck up on this side hill on a half-acre bog with a patch of reeds, an old barn, and a chicken coop. I remember like it was yesterday, young Jerry and me setting there on my porch while I was trying to calm his nerves. The boy turned and studied me straight in the eye, as if he was thinking of how he could stop feeling sorry for his own self and make ole Charlie here feel better about my lot. He reached in his pocket and pulled out a wrinkled road map. His daddy had marked his house with an X and mine with an X to keep him from getting lost. I'll be switched if the boy didn't take a pencil from his shirt pocket, lick on the point and start connecting the hamlets and villages on the map—looking up from time to time to be certain I was taking notice. He began at Cazenovia and ran a bold pencil line from it down to his house, Delphi Falls, then a line up to Pompey Center, then one down to Shea's corner near the school, then up to Pompey, down to Apulia Station, up to Lafayette, down to Tully, then a long line back through Gooseville Corners down the hill to Cardner Road and the Delphi Falls then on up to Cazenovia where he started. He sat back, taking a gander at his work. Then he held it up for me to see.

"Look," Jerry said. "The map looks like a crown. We both live in a crown, Mr. Pitts. Maybe you're a king, living up here so high on this hill."

In one breath an eight-year-old boy took his own fears and carpin' about his two-mile walk and turned them into an old man's coronation, just to make the point a body was consequential.

That happened in 1949.

I died before that book ended. Who better than me, ole Charlie here, their guardian angel to tell this Delphi Falls trilogy? I'll begin the trilogy with the first spirited yarn that began in the spring, just before their school summer break and led to a Halloween filled with spine-chilling valor.

It's the year 1953 I'll be telling you about.

Taking after his six-foot, six-inch daddy, Big Mike, and his six-foot momma, Missus, Jerry was twelve but had grown taller by more than a foot, but he was still a boy at heart. In the day most kids had nicknames for each other, and his friends called him Tall Jerry. His friends had grown, too—Bases, Mayor, Holbrook, Randy, Mary, and Barber, teenagers from thirteen to fifteen, Tall Jerry being the youngest at twelve and tallest at six foot two—but nobody much counted back then. I reckon you'll know the character in each of 'em early enough, as I tell you legends you won't soon be forgetting.

I'd been laid to my rest in the hamlet cemetery in Delphi nigh on four years by the time this one happened. Naturally not being a person any longer, I could be there only as a spirit, and I surely was. And just for the record we angels prefer *spirit* to *ghost,* thank you very much—although we can be ghostly when riled. As an angel I can see around and I can be just about anywhere I need to be at any time I want. Don't need specs no more, and my hearing's better than it ever was when I was alive. I see and hear everything. I can see and hear through eleven houses at the same time. I promise I won't miss nary a detail or blemish in my telling of it.

The club met in the cemetery. Tall Jerry could be seen climbing down from Farmer Parker's hayfield hill with the kerosene lantern I gave him when I was alive. He'd carry it like it was an old friend and set it on my gravestone to light their meetings. I joined them in spirit. They couldn't see me, but I would rise for the occasions. Their sitting around the glow of the lantern warmed the cockles of my heart like a golden yolk of the morning sun warms my cloud.

And bless my buttons, in their secret meetings, whichever wanted to take the floor to make a point over the others, they would stand up taller on my headstone just to give them the muscle their shout might need to make their point.

This spring the kids were coming to an age of leaving childhood ways behind after living through a war they were born into—the war that taught them more about death and hate than people see in a lifetime.

Most of the kids, except Tall Jerry, who was still growing, were near full grown in body, near as tall as their folks. The boys' voices were changing; the girls blossoming, their brains playing a tug-of-war as they rediscovered the world through young adults' eyes and ears for the first time.

"Why is it I get one pimple right on the end of my nose?" Mayor asked.

Puberty ain't pretty, but if they must get stretched out, gangly, pimply, awkward, and tripping over their own selves, best early sprouting happens somewhere close to home, or as in this case near the Delphi Falls, with friends around.

This story happened just as I'm about to tell it.

CHAPTER 2

OLE CHARLIE BECOMES AN ANGEL

With a world at war, the '40s was a frightful time for kids to grow up in. Now in '53, it's summer vacation for my flock, with no more fears of Nazis in Germany, only thoughts of being high school freshman in the fall. Oh, there was the two Nazi escapees, but most folks had forgotten them by now.

Pine Camp was an army military base in upstate New York that held prisoners of war captured in battles in Germany and Africa and places ole Charlie here can't spell. Story was two varmints escaped daily work release while workin' a farm. POW escapees could be scary stuff to a twelve-year-old during the war.

Tall Jerry's dad was Big Mike. Six-foot-six inches tall, smilin' and happy, wearing suspenders and nice ties. The nicest man a body could ever meet. People liked the adventure yarns he'd stop and tell. He had bakeries in Homer and Carthage, and he and Missus owned a barn dance hall over in Cincinnatus, at the Y in the road where there'd be dancing on Saturday nights when the guitars and fiddles would play while caller Wayne Schram would sing out.

"I like mountain music, good ole mountain music, played by a real hillbilly band. Give me rural rhythm..."

Missus had her boys, Dick—the scallywag I'll be tellin' you about—and Jerry, selling soda pop, boiled hot dogs, and chips from behind the snack counter while they watched the dancers twirling and spinning about.

Life was good with the war bein' over, but then Big Mike caught tuberculosis in '51 and had to be alone in a TB sanitarium for more than a year. Jerry grew a whole foot before his daddy got to come home.

Tuberculosis was a disease in the '50s what laid a mean curse. The others were polio and cancer.

Most folks were dying of TB.

Cancer was what ole Charlie had. Like termites in a fencepost. Got it from the sun, they said.

Now I was an old man and had my life and two wars to learn what a friend was, so I'll tell you what a friend is. Big Mike (or Missus if he was out of town) knowing I had the cancer, came up the hill to my farm every other week and drove me, setting right next to them on the front seat of his Oldsmobile or her Chevy, to the University Hospital in Rochester to be treated. Every other week for seven months, one of 'em would come, and I'd be setting next to them talking normal. Right up until the week I died.

Sometimes it's hard to best describe people—like trying to find the right chaw of tobacco—but that pretty much describes Big Mike and Missus. They had hearts as big as Big Mike and Missus were tall.

I sensed when ole Charlie's time come, from my heartbeat the night I lay watching lazy ripples of moon shadows on my bed sheet in the dark. I hankered to waste no time helping Jerry get over his city fears of country night winds and dark howling wood's noises before I left, so I'd talk with him best I knew about taking charge and showing critters who's boss at night outside in the chill and not being afraid of what's natural—snakes, owls, foxes, and the like. While I was able, I showed Jerry how to proper care for chickens and geese and gather eggs—not telling him why he needed to know soon. I gave him my carrying lantern, a full bottle of kerosene, kitchen stick matches, a few wicks, and my hunting knife, case he run into the escaped POW prisoners.

Ole Charlie here died the day I walked out to my barn, stood and gazed at it a spell, the way a body might if they know they were leaving a place forever. I thought of times when Jerry and his friends would play in the hayloft and tell me all smiles how my barn reminded them of hand-painted Christmas cards, the certain way it glowed with golden straw hanging over the loft and the bright blues and yellows flickering off two lanterns. It wasn't much of a barn—only had one stall for my horse, Nellie, another for my cow, Bessie, a corn manger in the middle—but memories were tucked away in those old rafters. Standing there, I had a feeling come over me that this ole farmer's eternity was about to begin from whatever made me the happiest during the times I was hurting most with the cancer and packing up to go to another place, as be said.

My understanding now, as an angel, is, if something can make a body happy while the body is in pain and the mind knows it's failing, that special happiness is a special kind of heaven-sent sedative for the soul. And that's when I got the big message, saw the light and figured my destiny was going to be guardian angel for Jerry and his friends from the moment that thought came to me. I smiled and said goodbye to my old barn one last time, to my Bessie, promising her someone would come milk her soon enough. I walked to the back gate to say goodbye to my horse, Nellie, and that's when my heart give out.

Ole Charlie's Barn

CHAPTER 3

SCHOOL'S OUT, SUMMER VACATION STARTS

There were two horses at Delphi Falls this summer. Jack, a tall frisky gray stallion—gentle in nature but he liked to run full out. A new horse at the place was Major, a retired New York City Police horse, a well-behaved chestnut gelding about the size of my mare, Nellie. Tall Jerry and Holbrook rode bareback and walked barefoot most times around the place under the waterfalls like the native Indians they'd read about. The horses carried them up the back hill behind the alfalfa field to their camp by the spring above the first falls. That was most times, but as they began looking across this school's summer vacation to their starting high school in the fall, the thinking of girls was capturing their imaginations a bit more than usual, obliging their wearing shoes on a regular basis.

Mary, the president of the club, asked Barber, the meeting caller, if he'd kindly call a meeting before vacation started. Just wanted to see what everyone was up to for the summer. As usual, Barber telephoned every member but Holbrook—he still didn't have a telephone—but he'd call Tommy Kellish.

"Hello?"

"Tommy?"

"Yes."

"Barber."

"Is there a meeting?"

"Saturday."

"At the cemetery?"

"Ten o'clock."

11

"I'll go tell him."

Some farm folks in the day didn't have telephones, and most that did couldn't use them when they wanted to because of what was called a party line, meaning it was a one at a time wait your turn for making a telephone call. You'd have to pick up the receiver to see if someone was already talking on it before you could make your call.

"Harriet, have you heard Bessie-Mae was putting saltpeter in her tomato preserves?"

"Whatever for?"

"Her Frank told her saltpeter might calm down her growing boys, if you catch my meaning."

"Isn't saltpeter what they put in gunpowder, Florence?"

"Oh, my stars."

Telephones were not all some folks didn't have. Outhouses were common in the country. In-house necessaries, as a privy was called in those days, and bathtubs were scarce in homes.

"I'm going out back, Ma."

"Take paper, son. You'll need paper."

"Where's the paper, Ma?"

"There's a Montgomery Ward catalogue on the tinder box. Take that. Use the pages."

"Okay, Ma."

Some had to wash their hair in the rain barrel.

Mary's meeting was called the week Tall Jerry and Holbrook were settin' on a log up at their campsite on top of the cliff by the lower falls.

"If you were a POW escapee, where would you hide out?" Tall Jerry asked.

"You still thinking about that?"

"We've got nothing else to do this summer."

"They probably hitched a freighter or cattle boat back to Germany or someplace."

Flippin' twigs into the campfire, Holbrook eyeballed a chipmunk scampering from the mouth of the spring and decided to follow it.

"Hey, look," Holbrook said.

"Where?"

Crawlin' on all fours, Holbrook found a two-foot, shale-stone ledge around the corner on the face of the cliff and a cave at the end of it, big enough for two people. Somethin' came over them sitting in the dark cave the first time. They'd sit up proud, taking in the sights below—masters of their new domain. They could see Dick's treehouse across the way and see if he was up to no good.

"This is a mighty inspirational spot for personal reflection, for thinking. It's a perfect spot for putting the mind at ease," Holbrook said.

Tall Jerry had never heard Holbrook being quite so insightful before.

"I wonder if they hide out in a cave like this," Jerry said.

"They're long gone by now," Holbrook said.

"I wonder if anybody knows about this cave," Jerry said.

"Don't matter," Holbrook said. "It's ours now. First come, first serve."

Now ole Charlie here ain't no authority, but I'm thinking basic logic isn't Holbrook's strong suit.

"When's the meeting?" Holbrook asked.

"Barber said noon," Jerry said.

"I'd be afraid to sleep in here. I could get killed falling over the cliff," Holbrook observed.

"That'd be a fall," Jerry sympathized.

"We going to walk or ride?" Holbrook asked.

"We can ride if you want," Jerry said. "I'll take Jack, you saddle Major, or we can go bareback, or we can double up. It's all good."

"Does Dick shave?" Holbrook asked.

"I think he borrows my dad's razor. He does—sometimes."

13

"I found whiskers under my nose. I'm thinking we should maybe start smoking," Holbrook said.

"What?" Jerry snapped.

"Whiskers," Holbrook said. "It means we're men now."

"Smoke cigarettes? No way am I doing that!"

"And why not?"

"Mom caught Dick smoking in the barn garage—yanked his ear, led him to the back stoop and stood over him with a fly swatter."

"Did she whup him?"

"Made him smoke the whole pack of Chesterfields to teach him a lesson. Folks have a way of knowing."

"Ain't that the truth."

"Don't ask me how, they just do."

"Did he smoke them?" Holbrook asked.

"Every one. He told me guys his age smoked in the war fighting Japanese in the Pacific and German Nazis in Europe. Why couldn't he?"

"I know they smoke, him and Duba," Holbrook said.

"He and Duba smoke all the time they work on their cars or drag the Oran Delphi. It wasn't any big deal his finishing off a pack of Chesterfields."

"You think your dad knows Dick and Duba smoke?"

"My dad is Big Mike. He knows everything."

"That's the truth, he pretty much does."

"I think he feels sorry for guys like Dick and Duba," Jerry said.

"They weren't old enough to fight and become heroes in the war," Holbrook said.

Holbrook had a brainstorm. "What if we only smoke in this cave and what if we puff, let's see—what's say we puffed on corncob pipes, maybe?"

"They're not cigarettes," Jerry affirmed.

"Can't be bad like cigarettes, can they?" Holbrook asked.

14

"And we wouldn't have to lie about not smoking cigarettes," Jerry said.

"Our lips would never touch a cigarette or tobacco making us smell," Holbrook said.

The lie was taking shape.

"What's it going to be?"

"You mean what do we smoke?"

"No, the cemetery—are we walking Parker's Hill or riding through the hamlet?" Holbrook asked, looking at his watch.

"Walk—but let's walk through the hamlet so we can go to Hasting's store first and get corncob pipes," Jerry said.

"We have time," Holbrook said.

"We'll come back here and smoke after," Jerry said.

"Think Hasting will sell us pipes?" Holbrook asked. "We're too young if even Dick got in trouble for smoking."

"We'll figure what to tell Hasting, so he'll sell us pipes. Besides, I'm taller than he is now. How will he know how old I am?" Tall Jerry offered.

Getting around obstacles was in the boy's nature.

"Like what will we say?" Holbrook asked.

"I have to think," Jerry said.

"We could ask the older guys. They make up stories better than almost anyone," Holbrook said.

"Dick and Duba?"

"Yeah, Conway and Dwyer too. Did you hear about when the school principal was punishing Conway for skipping chemistry class last winter?"

"No."

"While he was sitting in detention in the principal's office Conway started brown-nosing and told the principal he saw him walking to school because of the snow and asked if he could walk over to his house and put snow chains on his tires for him."

"That was nice."

15

"Principal thought so, too. It was right after the January snow. He thanked Conway for the offer, gave him a quarter to do it and told him that right after he got them on, he was off detention and could go back to class."

"Did he get them on?"

"Conway got the chains on all right, but then he got in the car, started it up and drove to Tully."

"Maybe he wanted to see if the chains were on the tires good," Jerry said.

"Conway didn't even have a driver's license. He put the chains on in the principal's driveway, got a hankering for an ice cream sundae, skipping another class and a shiny quarter in his pocket, so he started her up and borrowed the car without asking. The principal saw him drive past the school and near had a heart attack. He put him on a week of detention."

"I wonder sometimes if we'll ever have their daring—the older guys," Jerry said.

"Sometimes they don't think what they're doing," Holbrook said.

"Maybe that's the secret."

"What are we going to tell Hasting?"

"We'll come up with something," Jerry promised. "Let's go."

The cave overlooked Tall Jerry's Delphi Falls house below.

CHAPTER 4

THE STARE-DOWN WRESTLE

The two crawled around the ledge from the cave, back up to the spring and doused the campfire. They made their way to the edge of the cliff above the big white rock and down the cliff from there. Holbrook went into the bathroom to check his latest count of whiskers and to comb his hair in case they saw girls.

"If Hasting sees my whiskers, maybe he'll think I'm old enough to smoke," Holbrook said.

Tall Jerry opened a mason jar and poured its contents onto his bed.

"A dollar thirty-three is pretty embarrassing."

"I've got thirty cents," Holbrook said.

"It may be enough to get us pipes," Jerry mumbled to himself stuffing the change into his pocket.

They started down the long gravel driveway.

"I'm tired of being broke all the time. I need a real job, not mowing a lawn for a buck-fifty," Tall Jerry said.

"Like full time?"

"Yeah, for the summer."

Holbrook had been working part time at the Tully bakery since he was ten. Big Mike got him the job.

He kicked at a pebble and missed.

"I'll ask my dad. He'll know. Guys our age need money for stuff we never needed before," Jerry said.

Jerry kicked a pebble onto the pavement. Holbrook caught it with the side of his shoe and plinked it a good eight feet closer to the hamlet.

"Want to walk to Syracuse sometime to see the new Scenic Cruiser?" Holbrook asked.

"What's a scenic cruiser?"

"Greyhound bus."

"I've seen Greyhound buses."

"Not like this, these are amazing one and a half story super-buses. They're supposed to give the passengers a better view of the sights than the bus driver has. Want to walk up with me?" Holbrook asked.

"I'll walk it sometime."

"I wonder what it would cost—a Greyhound ticket to Chicago?" Holbrook asked.

"Do you know where the bus depot is?"

"Somewhere in Syracuse, on Erie Boulevard maybe, not sure. My dad will know."

"I'll walk it," Jerry said.

Jerry kicked the pebble one last time into the hamlet. Holbrook pulled the paint-chipped door open, and the lads stepped in and split up in the one-room store, busy with customers settling with Mr. Hasting for the few gallons of gasoline they had pumped, or canned goods and vegetables they had gathered on the counter and might need for supper.

The boys combed the store for a display of tobacco items. By the time the store settled down, Tall Jerry had worked his way around the center table piled with early melons and over to the cash register, only to find Holbrook already in conversation with Mr. Hasting.

"Holbrook here says you two are looking for pipes," he said.

"You got 'em?" Jerry asked.

"Only the best," Hasting said. "We get them shipped in from St. Louis."

"Wow!" Holbrook said. "Imported."

"We're looking for corncobs," Tall Jerry said.

"Meerschaum makes a mighty good corncob," Mr. Hasting said.

"Mr. Hasting, do you ever get wanted posters here, like for the POW Nazi escapees?" Tall Jerry asked.

"That'd be at the Manlius post office, and just what might you be doing with your pipe, Tall Jerry?"

Mr. Hasting had the advantage the lads completely forgot to consider. He knew how old they both were. His daughter, Marie, was in their grade.

"Same as Holbrook, Mr. Hasting, I need it for a school play about Huckleberry Finn and Mark Twain."

Holbrook's eyes began to cross, one eyelid trying in vain to twitch a signal to Jerry while his face was contorting and about to turn a lighter shade.

"That's interesting," Hasting said. "Most interesting indeed."

"Why? Huck smoked a corncob," Tall Jerry said.

"Your friend Mr. Holbrook here was just telling me how he needed a pipe for blowing bubbles at his sister's surprise birthday party coming up."

"Huh?" Tall Jerry grunted.

"You boys forget to get your stories straight?"

"Well ah…" Tall Jerry started.

"Seems you have. Which might it be, boys?"

The boys stood there, contemplating a next move.

"Or is there something else you want to think up? Think it good, now."

Holbrook's eyes twitched and crossed as his mind wandered in thoughts of how good he felt sitting in the cave, being above it all there, and in a second of inspiration– like a skilled Shakespearean stage actor – he removed his thick glasses, wiping them with his front shirttail, as would an Einstein or President Roosevelt about to speak to Congress. He looked with an exaggerated, near-blind stare in the general direction of Mr. Hasting's face. Holbrook was relying on the sight of his four whiskers to make him look older. Oh, the lad was good.

"What'll it be, fellas?" Hasting nudged. "Which one you sticking with? You goin' with Tall Jerry's Huck Finn story, or you going with Holbrook's girl's birthday bubble story?"

Hasting folded his arms with a wry *gotcha* smirk on his face, waiting for either boy to throw in the towel and give up.

"Which one will it be, gentlemen?"

"Both," Holbrook blurted, his eyeglasses in hand.

The lad shut his mouth, bit his lip and stared Mr. Hasting down without so much as a blink of his near blind eye, hoping the one single word *both* and his four whiskers might turn the tide.

Mr. Hasting winced at first and then tried to get an eyeball fix on what he guessed might be Holbrook's best eye when his own began to marble and roll, like he was trying to keep the lids open from dozing off. He saw the whiskers for the first time, wondering if they were whiskers or what Holbrook had for lunch. Hasting started running it back through his head—their stories and exactly what got them to this moment in time. Out in front of the store was commotion—cars backed up, a farm tractor pulling up to the gas pump, his hay wagon blocking the drive.

"We have customers, Ralph!" Mrs. Hasting barked.

"They're forty-nine cents apiece, fellas, but I won't be selling you a whit of tobacco lest I hear from your fathers first. Both of 'em, ya' hear?"

Mr. Hasting had given in.

The boys made it to the cemetery up the cinder drive to the tombstones, passing the time talking about how they would solve various world issues, the general economic conditions of boys their ages, their wants and needs now they was older, and which swimming holes might best draw the prettiest girls this summer.

Barber was on my headstone, waiting for the meeting to gather while flipping mumblety-peg with his jackknife into a patch of grass.

"Randy and Bases aren't coming," Barber said. Bases was Bobby Mawson from the hamlet. They nicknamed him Bases because he never did much without a baseball glove on his hand, including eating. He spent Sundays fetching baseballs out of the creek at the quarry for a dime apiece when the hamlet team played.

Barber was sporting his freshly cut summer vacation Mohawk haircut. Other than an inch-tall patch of hair down the middle of his head like a beaver tail, the boy's head was shaved bald as a hard-boiled egg.

"Mary's dad went to pick Mayor up," Barber said.

Mayor was Bobby Pidgeon's nickname. When he was little everyone thought he had a determined disposition and a happy politician's look in his eye, like he would grow up to be mayor someday, so Mayor stuck.

Waiting for folks, the lads passed time throwing pine cones over a high hanging tree limb.

Meeting about to start, ole Charlie here lifted onto a branch to observe. Mary walked up with Mayor, took a gander at the smoking pipes sticking out of back pockets and Barber's Mohawk. Taking a second look she turned and rolled her eyes, shaking her head. She stuck out her lower lip and puffed away a curl hanging over her eye.

"Who's doing what this summer?" Mary asked.

She wanted to get down to business.

"How often do you want to meet?"

"What say we only meet if there's an SOS comes up?" Barber asked.

"Works for me," Holbrook said. "I'm working at Tully bakery."

"We can start back meeting regular when school starts again in September," Mayor said.

Mary was agreeable. She had her peddle cart with popsicles to sell and morning papers to deliver, and she knew summers were long days and heavy workloads for a farmer's son. Church potluck suppers or a barn dance now and again was about the only times a farmer might break a spell for all summer.

Best you know now, going back to the war, SOS could mean only one thing: *Save Our Ship*. It was a ship's distress signal when they were at sea. It was tapped out in Morse code as: *dot dot dot—dash dash dash—dot dot dot*. That translated into SOS abbreviation for *Save Our Ship*…three dots being an *S* and three dashes being an *O*.

If the younger kids saw trouble and needed the spunk and daring of their older mates to help, calling an SOS would get the older guys to at least listen. The older guys loved challenges, weren't afraid of snakes, and they had working knowledge of both sides of the law, as be said.

"Did anybody write for pen pals?" Mary asked.

"I've got to get a job this summer," Jerry said.

"Was writing a pen pal homework?" Holbrook asked.

"It was a suggestion," Mary said.

"An assignment or a suggestion?" Tall Jerry asked.

"A suggestion for something interesting to do this summer," Mary replied.

"Swimming with girls is interesting," Holbrook said.

"Camping out is interesting," Tall Jerry said.

"We're in high school now, ninth grade, and soon we'll be going out into the world," Mary said. "Things we need to know."

"We need to know more about girls," Holbrook said.

"Writing letters to somebody we don't know and may never meet could be fun," Mary said. "Maybe we can learn about different cultures, different parts of the country or world."

Holbrook threw a pine cone over the branch.

"Are you doing it?" Tall Jerry asked.

"Yes," Mary said.

"Who you gonna write?"

"I haven't decided. I'm thinking of sending an air mail letter to some people."

"Air mail?" Mayor asked.

"Air mail letters go fast, you know. I think they get delivered in a week instead of longer."

"How do you know who to write to?" Barber asked.

"I'm thinking of writing a girl my aunt knows in Alaska, or a boy my mom read about in Pennsylvania, or maybe somebody in the army someplace, maybe Japan."

"How will you pick?" Holbrook asked.

"I'll guess which one will write me back."

The boys sat on the ground, impressed that Mary had thought of these places around the world.

"Pennsylvania? Alaska? Japan?" Barber asked. "How do you know what to write to those places?"

Mary allowed that the cool spring air had affected Barber's newly shaved head and ignored him.

"Do you know any of them?" Jerry asked.

Mary leaned down, picked up a pine cone and threw it a branch higher than the branch Holbrook, Jerry, and Barber were throwing at when she walked in, leveling the playing field.

"That's the point of having a pen pal," Mary said. "You're not supposed to know them. I don't know two of them but I read about one. I know his name is Eisenhower."

Now, ole Charlie here ain't a teacher, but if you know'd the war, Eisenhower was a world hero for masterminding the D-Day invasion that helped end the war in Europe. Ike, as he was better known—was every American kid's World War II hero who had since become our president.

"Ain't but one Eisenhower," Mayor said.

"You nuts, Mary?" Holbrook bellowed. "It'd be like there's more than one Superman, man of steel, or more than one Dick Tracy, police detective."

"It couldn't happen—more than one Eisenhower," Mayor said.

Holbrook started the ruckus by falling backward onto a grassy spot holding his stomach, laughing with guffaws and gasps for air.

"Let me get this right, Mary. You're going to ask the president of the United States of America to be your pen pal?"

He chortled. He turned and rolled on his stomach, giggling with his face in the grass for full effect.

Mary had a sense Mayor was about to get his two cents in. She puffed a curl from her eye and tapped her toe, waiting for the two of them to settle down.

"Oh yes," Mayor chided in, not letting her down.

He opened one hand flat palm up using his other hand's first finger like it was a pen writing a note and began dictating a loud mock-presidential letter to Mary.

"I can just see it now.

'Dear Pen Pal Mary,

How are you? I am fine. I've had a busy day today. First, I had tea with the Queen of England, and then I dropped a bomb on Russia. How was your day? Busy running the Pompey Hollow Book Club, I suppose.

Signed, Your Pen Pal, President Eisenhower.'"

Mary was maturing, too. She didn't slug either of them.

"If you're both finished, this Eisenhower I'm writing to just happens to be the president's grandson," Mary snapped.

"What?!" Holbrook said, bolting upright, picking pine needles from his hair.

"David Eisenhower," Mary said.

"He's just a kid," Holbrook said.

"Well, he's not Ike," Mayor said.

"President Eisenhower has a grandson—or don't any of you read the newspapers?"

"He's not Ike," Mayor said.

"I'm writing the president's grandson."

"Well I'll be," Holbrook said.

"His name is David. He goes to school, just like us. He's normal just like—(Mary looked down at Holbrook and over at Mayor)—well, like some of us."

"I'll be," Holbrook repeated.

"It's not his fault he's the grandson of the president."

"Where's he live?" Barber asked.

"He lives on a farm with cows and horses, just like normal people in Gettysburg, Pennsylvania."

The lads grumbled their apologies and admitted to Mary that her pen-pal idea sounded like a good summer adventure.

But it was with the mention of their childhood hero, Eisenhower, the boy's pluck and daring had flashbacks to memories of Saturday morning picture show newsreels showing D-Day and the Normandy invasion.

"I wonder if anybody ever caught those guys," Tall Jerry said.

"What guys?" Mayor asked.

"The Nazi POW guys," Jerry said.

"Not that again," Holbrook said.

"The two POWs that escaped from Pine Camp," Tall Jerry said.

"I never heard about that," Mayor said.

"That was during the war. Wouldn't they just be free now with the war being over?" Holbrook asked.

"They never caught them, I don't think," Barber said. "They probably crossed over into Canada."

"Nobody knows," Tall Jerry said.

"How could anybody escape from an army base, anyway?" Mayor asked. "Pine Camp is an army base. A big one."

"They didn't escape from there," Barber said.

"That's not true, they did so," Tall Jerry said. "During the war they kept prisoners of war. Every day they took the POWs and had them work on farms down to Cortland."

"They had POW patches sewn on their backs. People knew to stay clear of them," Holbrook said. "My dad told me army troop carrier trucks hauled them back and forth every day."

"I heard they stole a horse or mule from a farm one day and just took off," Barber said.

"Well, they were POWs, and they escaped," Jerry said.

"From a farm, though," Barber added, getting the last word in.

"I'll ask my mom. She's reads the newspaper," Mary said.

"That's what we could do this summer. Let's figure out how we can catch the Nazi escapees," Tall Jerry said.

The meeting broke up with Mary's mind made up. Holbrook and Jerry climbed Farmer Parker's hill and cut through the farm to get back to their cave for a relaxing smoke. They waded the creek and climbed the cliff, making their way back up to their campsite. The first thing they would do was to build a fire, but not today.

"Let's go to the cave," Holbrook said.

"I wonder if that Eisenhower kid will write Mary back," Tall Jerry said.

"Think anybody down below will see our smoke coming out of the cave after we light up?" Holbrook wondered.

"You worry too much."

The lads sat in the cave, stooped forward, cross-legged, and facing each other, like Indian chiefs admiring their store-bought Meerschaums.

"Maybe the Nazi guys are hiding in a cave like this," Tall Jerry said.

Holbrook didn't answer.

The boys rubbed their fingers, gently admiring the honey-colored, varnished corncob bowls, sanded smoother than a piano key. They had achieved stature. They had just about anything a body could ever hope to ask for, ever need or want. They had a cave, they had pipes.

"We forgot tobacco!" Tall Jerry grunted.

They had everything but tobacco.

Holbrook wrinkled his brow.

"What're we going to do for tobacco?" Jerry asked.

Holbrook pulled his pipe from the side of his jaw, held the pipe bowl firmly with his thumb and forefinger and pointed the stem at the tip of Jerry's nose.

"Tobacco is a leaf, son," he said. "What we need are leaves. I'm thinking maple might offer the right aroma and piquancy."

Holbrook had seen the *piquant* word in a *Reader's Digest* word page.

"Elm leaves may be a tad coarse, son," he added.

"Holbrook, you call me *son* one more time and I'll bean you sure, glasses or not!" Jerry retorted.

Holbrook scowled, as if he was offended.

"And get that pipe out of my face."

It was true. It seemed the pipes were beginning to unsettle the lads' usual modest nature. They even started using long words.

"Let's venture out and fill our coffers with an ample supply of vintage maple leaves. We'll rendezvous back here."

Ole Charlie here followed them while they explored the campsite ground covered with fallen leaves. The top layer was the driest. The layer underneath was wet and less likely to burn. Pockets filled with leaves, the boys headed back to their new hideout.

The boys sat in the cave, respecting the silence as if it were a cathedral.

Holbrook took Jerry's pipe and packed dry and crunched maple leaf chips, taking extra care in tucking them into the imported pipe bowl with his thumb as tightly as he could. He handed the filled pipe bowl-first to Jerry to enjoy.

Tall Jerry took the pipe in his grip and picked up a kitchen stick match from the box on the cave floor. He placed the stem in his teeth, sampled a few different positions for comfort—for the best lock in his jaw. He scratched a kitchen match on a piece of shale on the wall of the cave and raised the exploding burst of flame over to his pipe bowl, sucking his cheeks, making them look like they were glued together on the inside.

Ain't nothin' that'll explode spark bigger than a wooden kitchen match.

Not wanting to lose the fire, the boy sucked in like he was working a lump of ice cream up a straw.

The dry leaf chips busted into sparks and then into leaping yellow-red flames, singeing Tall Jerry's eyebrow about the time a long torch of fire, like the tongue of a rattlesnake, sprung out the mouthpiece past his tonsils, maybe to his larynx. The lad started honking like a Canadian goose. He coughed ashes and snorted smoke out his nostrils. As Jerry gargled, swallowed, spit and honked, Holbrook grabbed Jerry's pipe and tossed it, along with his own forty-nine-cent prize, over the cliff.

Smoking, the two decided they would leave for the older guys.

Back down at the house, with no one at home, Holbrook took a scissors and did the best he could to even up Jerry's eyebrows, trying to match the scorched one. While he was at it, he pushed his own face to the mirror and snipped the four whiskers.

As the lads had pointed out, Big Mike pretty much knew all things. In this instance he didn't so much as make mention of Jerry's missing eyebrow. He pretended not to notice it, refraining as best he could from snorting a laugh or staring at the supper table, but you can bet it was a topic of conversation between Big Mike and Missus that evening behind closed doors.

Next morning Big Mike loaded Jerry in his car and drove him to the Hotel Syracuse and got that boy's idle hands busy.

He got him a summer job working for a friend of his, Mr. Bloom. Thirty-eight dollars a week; the boy finally had a full-time job, at least for the summer of 1953. More money every week than he had seen in a lifetime, not counting the reward money the club got for figuring out who burned down the gasoline station in Manlius back when ole Charlie here was still alive.

Tall Jerry's first summer job—Hotel Syracuse—1953

CHAPTER 5

TALL JERRY GETS A SUMMER JOB

If it weren't for the cellar under Hotel Syracuse smelling like wooden racks of fresh-cut flowers, vegetables and fruit crates, Jerry could have sworn his first day was down in a dungeon he'd seen in a Saturday morning motion picture show. The concrete catacombs of the most famous hotel in Syracuse were a varnished brown-black. At the end of one hall were two wooden, gate-staked freight elevators. There was a pastry chef, waitress, housemaid locker, and dressing room for ladies. Next to that was a chef's and waiter's locker room for the men. At the opposite end of the long hall was a furnace room big enough to hold a dozen garbage and trash cans. There was a floor-mounted steamer in the corner of the room where cans would be turned over, the pedal stepped down on and steam would clean them. On the floor by the other wall was a flat sheet of metal that looked like a large weighing scale. It was an elevator that went up to the sidewalk above. It took garbage cans filled with the empty and crushed tin cans and blown-out light bulbs up for hauling away to the city dump; or the other cans of garbage filled only with food waste from the hotel's kitchens, scraped from dishes for hauling off to pig farms.

Rusty was Jerry's boss, a short old man with brassy, red hair who'd been in the bowels of the hotel since he was a teen; he was in his late fifties now, not a gray hair on his head or from out his nose. He made it a point to never bother learnin' the names of his part-timers; he'd name them first thought that came into his head instead.

"Okay, Stretch, your working days are—" Rusty started.

"Why're you calling me Stretch?"

"You're joking, right, kid?"

"I can't help I'm tall," Jerry said.

"Huh?" Rusty snorted.

"I hate Stretch. I hate String Bean. I hate Bean Pole. My friends call me Tall Jerry. That's okay, but I don't like Stretch or String Bean or Bean Pole."

Rusty stared up at the boy, almost as if he were growing like a weed before his very eyes while he pondered. It was Jerry's first real summer job, so he decided to nickname him Summer.

"Summer, you work Mondays, Tuesdays, Wednesdays, and Thursdays. Be here at six in the morning. You're off Fridays and Saturdays. On Sundays, you come in same time, you hot wet-mop the floors and then go home."

"Do I work all day on Sundays?"

"Do the mopping and go home. Could be you're out of here by eight or nine on Sunday mornings."

"Okay."

"Clock yourself in and out. You don't clock in or out, you can't get paid."

"Okay."

"I won't see you on Sundays after the first time; I go to Utica on Sunday to see my momma. Sunday is when you hot wet-mop the floor; get her done good like I teach you, and then go home."

"Okay."

"Life here ain't hard if you listen to me and do what you're told," Rusty said.

It was thoughtful the man spared the lad detail about Utica's horse racetrack being open on Sundays and its racier section of town tempting track-goers to other, rowdier pursuits. Could have been Rusty's own conscience made him keep it to himself, or could be his belief in spirits and guardian angels for younger folks. It was all the same to ole Charlie here.

"Summer, you ride the elevator to the sidewalk with two cans at a time, but seeing you're the tallest twelve-year-old kid I ever seen, make dang sure to duck your head going up and don't be bumping it."

In the center of the basement, almost like an island, there was a glassed-in office where Mr. Blume and a clerk sat with two desks. There was a long hall with storage rooms with shelves filled with canned goods, and fruits and vegetables of every kind. Locked rooms had whiskey bottles and wine cases stacked on the shelves. As Tall Jerry walked the dark halls, bright lightbulbs, hanging maybe ten feet apart, would shine in his eyes. A few more feet and he'd be near blind again in the dark, trying not to bump his head and to make his way before his eyes dilated under the next lightbulb.

"We have a system and it's simple, Summer. Only gets complicated when we don't follow the system. Catch my meaning?"

"Yes sir," Jerry said, just as Missus and Big Mike taught him.

Rusty stopped under a lightbulb and looked up at the lad.

"Tips you'll be getting from me won't be in cash money, like the waiters and girls get upstairs, Summer, they'll be tips on hot wet floor mopping, on how to proper lift a garbage can without getting a sore back. My name is Rusty and on no account do you be calling me *sir*. Are we clear about that?"

"Yes, si….err…Rusty," Jerry stuttered.

Rusty turned on his heel and led Jerry to a waist-high, foot square, metal box with a thick glass lid flap on top of it, framed in steel. It was just outside the windowed office, so the machine had plenty of light on it.

"First job you do in the morning is break bottles. Why you do it in the morning is the hotel's heaviest drink serving and cooking is done at night. You wear those goggles on that hook. Go on, put them on and then hang them back up when you finish."

Jerry stretched the goggle band over his head and pulled them down over his eyes. He looked around, hoping nobody saw how goofy he looked in the reflection of the office window.

"There are all sorts of glass bottles that'll come down; wine bottles, beer bottles, and whiskey bottles. Mayonnaise bottles; all sorts and kinds, pickle bottles—and they're all glass."

Rusty lifted the handle of the thick, protective glass door on top of the box.

"Down in here there's a cylinder wheel with steel pegs, each bigger than your thumb. You drop in the bottles and close the lid. Then you push that red button on the wall, the pegs will spin, and they'll bust up," Rusty said.

"Where do they go?" Jerry asked.

"We'll get there," Rusty said. "There's a grinder down below the cylinder which grinds them down more; then there's another—acts kind of like a clothes washer ringer—to smash them up. By the time they hit the bottom, the paper labels are pretty much shredded and the glass is like sand. But don't touch it or get it on your skin or clothes. It's still glass. Shovel it using the flat coal shovel hanging on the wall in the furnace room. Dump it in a can and use the street elevator for taking it up. Put the lid on it tight, so glass doesn't blow around in the air. Wear gloves."

"I don't have gloves, Rusty. Can I use yours?"

Rusty handed him his gloves.

Jerry lined up trash cans filled with glass empties, put the gloves on and began dropping in one bottle at a time, slamming the lid down quickly and pushing the red button. It took maybe a dozen or so to properly entertain the lad's curiosity—then the bottles became work, a daily chore. It wasn't long before he was a speed demon of efficiency in glass-bottle breaking. Jerry went into the furnace room, grabbed the coal shovel and cleaned out the crusher, filling his first empty container. He pulled empty trash cans to the furnace room for steam cleaning and filled one onto the sidewalk elevator. Tempted as he was to ride up to the sidewalk above, he decided to wait for another can before going up. He hung the goggles on the hook and found Rusty for more instruction, handing him back his gloves.

"Keep them. You did good on that; keep them while you're here this summer, then give them back to me."

This was good. Jerry was earning Rusty's confidence. The boy learned quick and got tasks done without a lot of overseeing.

They next pushed open the door to the men's locker room. Chefs and cooks were sitting on benches and standing about, putting on uniforms, tall chef hats, black and white checked trousers. Two men were standing at sinks, shaving. They glanced in the mirror as Rusty and Jerry walked in with a bucket, sponges, and cloths. Both men realized they were shaving in the thirty-minute morning time slot needed to scrub down the ten sinks and mirrors.

"We're out of here, Rusty. Come on in. We're gone."

Rusty didn't say a word. He walked Jerry to the end sink by the far wall. The chefs splashed their faces, grabbed towels and stepped over to their lockers.

"This is about sloshing and washing," Rusty started, turning on the first hot water faucet. "It ain't about neat and tidy dry."

He began using a spotless white cloth, dipping it in the sink and slopping hot steaming water over the basin top and sides, scrubbing whiskers, soap scum and hair cream tonics from the porcelain white sink bowls and from around the faucets.

"You find a bar of soap, toss it. You find a razor, comb or brush on the sink; keep moving it to the next sink. Nobody comes and gets it by the time you're at the last sink, you toss it."

Rusty scrubbed the first sink. Jerry did the second, under his watchful eye, then the third. By the fourth, Rusty nodded approval and left the room, satisfied Summer could be counted on to get the job done.

The lad had two of his daily tasks down pat. The rest of the day would be looking out for filled cans coming down on the wooden freight elevator, replacing them with empty steamed ones and sending the elevator back up—then getting the filled ones hefted to the furnace room for sorting, furnace burning, and bottle breaking.

He'd listen to the maids, waitresses and cooks talking, flirting and carrying on, coming and going throughout the day. Jerry was feeling good about his routine—how he knew when to do things without having to be told. And the more he did them the less he saw Rusty.

His first Sunday was to learn how to wet-mop and then he could go home.

"First you walk the halls and the men's locker rooms and pick up anything that might be lying around on the floor. Toss it."

Jerry ran the halls and through the locker rooms, picked up and tossed out things he found on the floor. He hurried back to Rusty, near the hot water faucet. He was a twelve-year-old being paid a full $38 a week when a used car could be bought for $40. Learning what Rusty could teach him was important to the lad.

As Rusty talked, he was filling a large bucket with steaming hot water. He dumped in a cup of detergent powder.

"Follow me, Summer."

He used the mop handle to push and roll the steaming bucket to the end of one hall. He bounced the mop up and down, getting her sopping wet, lifting her out a steaming, dripping and plopping her on the floor at the end wall.

"Hot wet-mopping is like painting," Rusty said. "You never start where you want to end up. Start working backward and you work that-a-way. Mopping is about hot, wet and slopping. It ain't about neat and tidy dry. Quicker you learn that, quicker you learn hot mopping. Rats don't like no hot clean floors, cockroaches don't like no hot clean floors. There's never going to be no rats or no cockroaches at the Hotel Syracuse—not while I'm here, anyway!"

Rusty slopped the hot mop back and forth, slapping the walls on either side of the hall. The floor steamed like a morning frog pond. After backing down the hall, plopping and mopping, he stopped, stuck the mop in the squeegee the first time and squeezed the water out. He walked back over the wet mopped floor and plopped the dry mop down, repeating his motion, this time drying the surface. A couple of swipes and he'd squeegee again, leaving her clean as a garden pickle.

"Do it like me, Summer, like you do bottles and sinks, and next Sunday you're on your own."

When Jerry would stay over with Holbrook, he'd hitch a ride to work with Mr. Holbrook. He'd bunk with Holbrook and his brothers, Dickie and Ronnie. Double beds in the house of seventeen kids had multiple sleepers in them—smaller kids could fit four bunched up, maybe five with one across the foot of the mattress. Most rooms had a couple double beds, others had bunks.

Sometimes his brother Gourmet Mike, who went to Lemoyne College in Syracuse, would pick him up from work and drive him the eighteen miles back to Delphi Falls.

On nights he stayed at home, Jerry would take his pay envelopes and stack them, unopened, on his closet shelf. When he stayed at Holbrook's—knowing Holbrook used most of his own earned money to help his momma—Jerry would let Holbrook hold his pay, with permission to use any part of it for important growing up personal necessities, like the Remington electric razor he wanted for his whiskers, .22 caliber shells they'd use for plinking cans and light bulbs in the woods at the tree line behind Holbrook's house.

These two were friends who could be counted on but who never counted. They shared like brothers. Jerry would bring cardboard boxes filled with blown-out light bulbs from the hotel and they'd use them for target practice. They drilled holes down an eight-foot two-by-four and screwed in a bulb every six or eight inches.

"You working tomorrow?" Holbrook asked.

"Not at the hotel," Jerry said.

"Don't you work the barn dance in Cincinnatus?"

"I haven't worked there all summer. Mom said one job is enough."

"Dick works the square dances and has a job washing dishes up at the Lincklaen House, too. How come him and not you?"

"Dick scrubs pots and pans because he's in trouble. Mom makes him do it—for punishment."

"What sort of trouble?"

"Somebody telephoned and told her they saw them drag racing down Oran Delphi. Mom said he had to wash the supper dishes for punishment. Dick, being a smart ass, sassed back, 'Four plates—big deal!'"

"Uh-oh," Holbrook said.

"She put him in the car and drove to Cazenovia and got him the job washing dishes and pots and pans, six to six—twelve hours straight every Saturday until he learns his lesson on how not to talk back."

"It's going to be a full moon. You want to walk to Syracuse later and see the new Scenic Cruisers at the Greyhound bus depot?" Holbrook asked.

"Did you find out where?"

"The bus depot is on Erie Boulevard. Eighteen miles. If we left now, we could be there by morning."

"Can't your dad drive us? We could go in the morning."

"Dad won't be back from his train trip for two days," Holbrook said. "I don't have to work at Tully Bakery tomorrow."

"So we walk?" Jerry asked.

"We get a look at the new buses and be back by supper. Earlier, if we hitch a ride."

"Can we go to the Manlius Post Office on the way back?" Jerry asked.

"Why?"

"I want to look at the Wanted posters."

"I figured."

"Let's just see if they have mug pictures of the Nazi escapees."

"S'okay with me," Holbrook said.

"I got a feeling in my gut they're still on the loose."

"We'll go there on our way back."

"There's got to be a reward for catching them."

"I wonder how much," Holbrook said.

"So, we walk to Manlius after the Greyhound terminal?" Jerry asked.

"Sure," Holbrook said.

There was an air of independence about Holbrook. He was able to go about as he pleased. He earned it from the examples he set helping his family financially since he was ten. He and Jerry have been best friends since Jerry was eight. It was on the first day of school back in 1949, Jerry could tell how poor the Holbrook's were with Holbrook having to eat a ketchup sandwich at lunchtime. It was on that first day Jerry poked his lunch quarter into Holbrook's ribs making him take it to buy a hot lunch with in trade for his ketchup sandwich. Jerry had breakfast—he was certain Holbrook had not. To this day, Jerry still insists on the trade, every day. Tall Jerry's friends could pretty much leave the house without asking. Unlike any other generation, these youngsters had lived through years of a war that killed eighty million people. Now teens, they aren't that much younger than boys as young as 17 who won the war. They knew right from wrong—and they were encouraged to right a wrong—without having to ask permission—if they were careful. Not only were the young in the day trusted, most every adult in the crown watched over them. Being scolded by a neighbor, if called for, and your momma telephoned, was pretty much the way times were.

The boys began their journey just after sunset, walking up Berry Road under a bright full moon. They talked of how life this summer had been good for them; if hair growing in their armpits meant they should use a deodorant, which brands they might consider and whether any girls gave them a second look at the Fourth of July parade. Under the moonlight Holbrook could look at a tree's silhouette as they walked by and tell its species.

"Let's become forest rangers," Holbrook said.

"What do they do? Forest rangers?" Jerry asked.

"We take turns living up high in a tower in the Adirondack mountains, watching out for forest fires."

"All day long?" Jerry asked.

"There's a bounty on mountain lions. We could earn extra money hunting them."

"Maybe," Jerry said, not wantin' to give ideas of mountain lions much thinking time, walkin' in the moonlight.

Jerry learned the highways outside the crown riding with Big Mike on bakery business as far back as he could remember. The lads explored like Lewis and Clark, admiring nature, discussing topography, like exactly when does a hill become a mountain. They retold stories of glaciers that cut them and how to identify Indian burial grounds while walking that summer night, all the way to Syracuse.

The last mile or two were pretty much silent, respectful, not wanting to interrupt each other's thoughts or reflections. They found the bus depot at the crack of dawn. Holbrook stood and stared in awe of the enormous buses' beauty and quiet majesty. He counted ten shiny, brand new Scenic Cruisers lined up side-by-side like dealt playing cards and looking like Queen Mary ocean liners he'd seen on a wall calendar at the barbershop. The lads stood and took them into their imaginations, listening to the roars and the rumbles of the enormous diesel engines whining, air brakes tweeting. Tall Jerry reached his hand up the side of one and ran his fingers across the newly painted drawing of the Greyhound dog racing the side of the bus.

"I wonder if there's a real dog that looks like this," Jerry asked.

"You look like a midget standing there, Tall Jerry. That bus is bigger than my house," Holbrook said.

Tall Jerry stood back to look.

"Greyhounds are real dogs," Holbrook said. "They race them on tracks down in Florida, I think."

"Let's see if they'll let us go inside and see what the bathroom looks like," Jerry said.

Later that morning in the Manlius post office with a bulletin board filled with Wanted posters the boys were disappointed to find there were no posters of the two Nazi POW escapees. The postal clerk assured Tall Jerry they were still on the loose but probably an Army matter what with the war being over.

"I know they found the mule they'd stolen," the clerk said. "It was running loose up near Fulton. Everyone figured they got that far on the mule and got away from there on foot or hotwired a car or stole some bikes. Folks think maybe they rowed a boat across Lake Ontario to Canada."

The summer of '53 was one new experience after another in their growing up; a warm summer of work and fun running smooth and easy for Tall Jerry, Holbrook and their friends. Mary saved her popsicle cart sales money to buy clothes to fit the body she was blossoming into, and a phonograph record player to play her mail-order square dance records on. Barber's Mohawk-sheered head wasn't sun burning that much anymore, as the hair was growing in. Mayor and his brother built a tree house on top of the sledding hill behind their barn. They could see down the valley ten miles. Bases kept busy stacking dimes he earned from chasing foul balls. Randy Vaas rode with his pap every morning, helping on their milk can route, lifting and hauling cans from small farms to the dairy before the sun came up. On days off from the hotel, Jerry would sometimes hitch an early morning ride with them and just catch up with Randy.

"Holbrook and I walked to Syracuse," Jerry said.

"For real? Syracuse?"

"It took us all night."

"From where?"

"From his place."

"You walked to Syracuse from Berry Road?"

"Yep."

"Did you catch a ride?"

"We had too much to talk about. Time just went by."

"No rides?"

"We walked all the way."

"Wow."

"We went to the Greyhound depot to see the Scenic Cruisers."

"I heard about them."

"They have a lot of them, brand spanking new."

"I saw pictures in LIFE magazine."

"They're famous."

"Are they as big as they look in the picture?" Randy asked.

"Bigger."

"Wow."

"Randy, when you climb up into them and you get in the seats behind the driver you have to take two, maybe it's more, steps up just to get to where the passenger seats are."

"You sit over the driver?"

"Easy couple steps over him."

"That must be something," Randy said.

"In the back of the bus there's a door with a whole bathroom in it."

"For real?"

"I swear."

"You mean there's a toilet on a bus?"

"It has a door and everything."

"Dad, did you hear that?"

"If I'm lying, I'm dying," Jerry said.

"I'll be..."

"Well, there's no bathtub, but there's a toilet you flush and a sink with running water."

"Dad, it's got a toilet."

"Honest to God...and it even has a mirror."

"Why a mirror?"

"I guess in case you have to shave."

"Or a lady wants to powder her nose," Mr. Vaas said.

"Easy couple steps over the driver."

Jerry leaned an elbow out the window that predawn morning riding with his friend Randy, looking up at the starry sky and dreaming the memory of his adventure of following the moon and seeing the modernistic Greyhound Scenic Cruiser buses.

"A guy let Holbrook sit behind the steering wheel," he said.

Randy stared through the front windshield in a daze. How good life was becomin' that summer.

It was on a Wednesday in August when Tall Jerry's summer took a turn. Finished with his bottle breaking and sink sloshing, he was on the sidewalk elevator going up with two cans when he first saw the boy sitting alone in the hotel alcove. The boy needed a tub. He was in short pants and wrinkled shirt. His legs were dirt scuffed, knees scratched up, one scraped and scabbed over. He sat there looking away when Jerry took notice of him.

"Hi," Jerry said.

The boy turned his head sharp, facing the brick wall.

Jerry dragged the cans to their spot on the sidewalk and stepped back slowly.

"What's your name?"

Silence.

"Are you lost?"

No answer.

Jerry pulled his gloves off and decided to leave well enough alone, got on the elevator and rode down to the basement. He went back to work, thinking about the kid up on the street in the hotel alcove. Then an idea came to him. He went to the bench in front of his locker, opened the door and grabbed his paper lunch sack. Sanitary engineers and maids had to bring their own lunch; kitchen help got fed in the kitchen. He inventoried a peanut butter and jelly sandwich and a banana. He twisted the top of the sack, walked to the hall and put a nickel in the Coke machine, buying a bottle and wrench-snaffling the cap off. He went to the furnace room and placed his lunch sack and soda plunk in the middle of the sidewalk elevator. The lad didn't step on it himself but stood back and pushed the button, lifting her up to street level. When it landed up on the sidewalk he stood off to a side in the basement where he could see the light cracking through the edge of the elevator up near the alley. He waited. Good two minutes, it was. Then the shadow of the boy stepping onto the elevator and jumping off as quick, most likely with a good lunch and a Coca Cola to wash it down. Jerry waited a few minutes then pushed the button, bringing the elevator down clean as a whistle.

My, but ole Charlie here was proud of that young man. Mighty proud. He did that on his own steam—didn't think twice about giving up his lunch or spending the nickel to help a hungry kid he didn't even know.

That afternoon when he got home and with a silent little nudge from ole Charlie here, Jerry went to his folks' bedroom and picked up the telephone. He didn't need no more help than my nudge.

"Operator."

"Myrtie, can you get me Barber, please?"

"Why hello, young man. Have you had a busy summer?" Myrtie asked.

"I got a summer job."

"So I heard."

"I've been working at Hotel Syracuse. I'm a sanctitary…a sanitizer…a kind of engineer," Jerry said.

"Oh my, that sounds important."

"Well, it's…"

"Here you go, honey. You're connected," Myrtie said.

"Hello?"

"Mrs. Barber, this is Jerry. Can I talk to Dale?"

"He's right here, Tall Jerry. Come see us before the summer is over."

"I will."

"Hold on dear, here he is."

"Hello?" Barber asked.

"I can't explain, but I may need your help," Jerry said.

"Want me to call a meeting?" Barber asked.

"Not yet. It's about a kid. I think he's a runaway."

"Where?"

"In the alley."

"Tell me that word again?"

"What word?"

"I can't…I'll be right with you, Ma," Barber said.

"Oh, you can't talk, I get it. He's a runaway."

"That's what I thought you said."

"Can I come over Sunday after I get off work, maybe bring somebody?" Jerry asked.

"Are you bringing the…you know?"

"Not sure I could get him to come. Don't know about him, but could I, if I wanted to?"

"I guess."

"Something tells me the kid needs help."

"Who are you bringing beside him?"

"Just him, if I do. It'll be easier to explain on Sunday—not even sure why I called—but it would be after I get off from work."

"I don't know."

"Why not?"

"George Jay never showed this week."

"Who's George Jay?"

"Town drunk, he comes here for a meal, sleeps somewhere by a tree and works for his supper."

"What does he…?" Jerry started.

"I got chores Sunday after church."

"Chores he was supposed to do?"

"Yes."

"Like what?"

"I have to stack bales in the hay barn Sunday," Barber said.

"What time? I can help," Jerry said.

"It's up to me," Barber said. "I just have to get it done Sunday.

"Then wait for me to get there. All I have to do on Sunday is wet mop. I'll be done after that, and then church. I'll ride right over after. If I have the kid, I'll bring him with me," Jerry said.

Click.

Jerry figured the boy in the alley needed protein. He scribbled a note asking his mother if she might pack a meat sandwich, maybe liverwurst or salami in his lunch sack; maybe an apple and a banana, mentioning how this work helped him work up an appetite. He left the note on the counter, found a candy bar in a cupboard, and put it in his room to drop in the lunch sack for tomorrow.

Chapter 6

WHAT TO DO WITH A RUNAWAY

Morning chores flew by. Bottles broken, sinks washed and scrubbed, and trash burned in the furnace. Jerry kept walking by the clock, figuring when the best time might be to ride the elevator up. He wanted his work done so he might take time on the sidewalk alcove without getting missed down below. Four cans needed going up. His plan was to take the first two up, along with the lunch sack for the boy. He figured he'd save the soda for the second trip. Then he'd ride up with another load and see if the boy would talk.

As the elevator rose into the light of day, sure enough the boy was there. Shorts and shirt—sleeve torn, shoes and socks but dirty as all get-out. When Jerry caught his eye, he'd turn sharp toward the brick wall again.

Walking toward him, Jerry said, "You don't have to talk if you don't want to, kid. But you've got to eat. Here."

Standing over the boy, Jerry could tell he wasn't older than nine or ten. He set the lunch sack down by the boy's foot, turned and went about his business pulling cans off the elevator busy-like, not looking up or glancing back at the boy. He stepped on the platform and pushed the red button, starting it down.

"You want a Coke to go with that? I can bring it up next load, if you want one. I already got it."

This time the boy looked over at Jerry as the elevator started to lower. He didn't say a word but looked Jerry in the eye and nodded his head yes. Jerry was back up in no time, with two more cans to haul to the sidewalk. He stepped around to the boy sitting there with a sandwich in his hand and mouth full, looking up at him. Jerry held the bottle out. The boy reached up and took it, turning his eyes back down.

"There's no law a guy has to talk," Jerry said, "but when someone tries to be a friend and gives a squirt his lunch and goes without, you'd think a guy at least says thanks. That's the way my friends were raised anyway."

The boy looked up. "How old are you?" his full mouth muffled his words.

"Twelve," Jerry said.

"You're twelve?!"

"I'm Tall Jerry to my friends. My dad is six foot six. I'm still growing.

The boy stared up, chewing in amazement at young Tall Jerry's height…a boy not much older than he was.

"Thank you for the sandwich and stuff," he said.

"You're welcome. There's a candy bar in there, too."

"Thank you."

"Don't eat too fast. If you haven't eaten in a while, you'll bloat your stomach."

Cheeks puffed out, the boy stopped chewing, looked down at his stomach and then up at Tall Jerry.

"What do you mean?"

"I know that after my horse runs, it's bad to let him drink a lot of water or he'll bloat."

"Oh."

"I told you my name, kid. What's yours?"

The boy didn't answer.

"You don't have to worry, I won't give your secrets away. You have my scout's honor."

Now Jerry was a tenderfoot scout, years back, sure enough was. But his scouting didn't last long. It was after the weekend campout in the back yard of the scoutmaster's house on the corner of Oran Delphi and Route 20. There were eight boys and four army pup tents pitched in the back yard next to a broken lawnmower.

About three in the morning two loud, diesel tractor short-haul trailer rigs carrying logs to the mill high-rolled down that big Cherry Valley hill backfiring, a-popping and belching right down past that back yard, shaking the boys awake, scaring dander out of 'em, they did. That's when Jerry decided his eighty-four acres of woods back home at the Delphi Falls, the cold, dark walk up the hill to my place for eggs, the cliffs topped with woods and two sixty—or seventy—foot waterfalls would do him for all the fright he'd ever need at night. That's when the boy quit scouting and took his tenderfoot badge home.

"What are you? Eight—nine—ten?"

"Nine."

"You got a name?"

"Bobby."

"Bobby?"

"Yes."

"Bobby!?"

"Yeah?"

"Well doesn't that just beat everything? Still another guy named Bobby. What happened, did the whole world go and run out of boy's names back during the war and they had to name most of them Bobby?"

Ole Charlie here lifted and sat on a barrel lid, under a beam of a morning sun. I was enjoying watching Tall Jerry rising to this occasion. The lad didn't need a scrap of help from me; he was a natural-born storyteller, picked up from Big Mike.

Trying to warm the boy up, Jerry would pause and tweak his chin as if he was an ole man thinkin'. He'd turn with big steps in an exaggerated circle, pretending he was talking to himself, thinkin' out loud.

"Let's see now, I have one friend, he's Bobby Pidgeon—we call him Mayor; oh yeah, that's right— and there's Bobby Holbrook, can't forget him—we call him Holbrook. And wouldn't you know, there's even Bases—his name is Bobby—Bobby Mawson, so we call him Bases. That's a handful, and there's probably a half dozen more. Why there's a Bobby everywhere, like rabbits. Kid, what are we going to call you?"

The boy looked up, stopped chewing, raised his eyebrows timidly. "Bobby?"

Jerry looked down at the boy. His heart sank, watching the kid sitting there by himself—a little boy, looked eight, crouching in the alley, cold, dirty—alone in the world with nothing of his own to hang on to solid but maybe his name. The idea of being alone, having no one, crossed Jerry's mind.

"You know, you're right," Tall Jerry decided, stomping his foot down. "Only makes sense to have at least one Bobby to be called Bobby, doesn't it? Only makes sense. Okay kid, you're it. You're our Bobby!"

The puff-cheeked boy cracked a smile and started chewing again, this time like he was eatin' chocolate ice cream. His eyes looked settled for the first time. Not taking them off Tall Jerry, he reached around in the bag for the apple.

"Now it's none of my business," Jerry said. "I only mean to help you if you want, and none of what you tell me will go anywhere, I swear. Did you run away or get runaway from—you know, get unloaded...dumped? Don't answer if you don't want to. None of my business why you're here in an alley."

"My dad's in Auburn," Bobby said.

"Auburn?"

"He won't get out until October."

"Auburn—that's down near Cortland, near Skaneateles Lake, I think."

"Yes."

"What's he doing down there with you up here? And when you say Auburn, does he live there?"

"Prison."

"Prison? You mean, like he works there, or he's in prison?"

"Yes."

"Which is it?"

"In."

"Damn."

"I know."

Tall Jerry stood back, took a pause, looked into the kid's empty stare.

"Where's your mother?"

Bobby didn't answer.

"She'll be worried sick about you."

"He gets out in October."

"What did he do to get in there?"

"They said he doesn't have to be there in November, so that means the last day in October he'll get out, I guess."

"You okay?"

"I'll keep hiding till he gets out."

"I won't tell. You have my word, Bobby, but just so you know, your mom is probably worried sick about you."

"My mom is dead."

Jerry bent over. His stomach cramped up on him like he'd been slugged by heavyweight champ, Joe Louis.

"Kid, I'm sorry," he offered, gasping for breath and wiping a tear forming in his eye with a knuckle.

"Wasn't your fault," Bobby said. "German bombers bombed her Red Cross hospital in the war. They killed everybody. They buried my mom there. In Africa someplace."

Jerry stood, trying to imagine people dying like that all the way around the world—mothers of young boys dying violently, leaving families and kids back at home.

"My dad was in a submarine."

"Navy."

"In the Pacific Ocean."

"Pearl Harbor."

"When they told him my mom was dead, he went crazy."

"I would, too," Tall Jerry said.

"He beat somebody up pretty bad, got in trouble for doing it."

"When they put him in Auburn, did they forget about you and leave you on your own?"

"At first he was at Pine Camp."

"That's an army base."

"When the war was over, they moved him to Auburn."

"Prison," Tall Jerry said.

"They put me in the orphanage, but I won't stay there, and if you tell on me, I'll run away again, I swear."

"Are the orphanage people mean to you?"

"They aren't nothing to me. Oh, kids pretend to be friends, all right, but looking at them only reminds me I got nobody, like they got nobody."

"I told you I wouldn't tell on you, and I won't. But I need time to think how to help you. Stay here today."

"I won't go nowhere."

"If I come up with something, I'll bring up a trash can later and tell you my idea. I can't come up without a can. I'm good sometimes about having ideas."

And that he was. Jerry's eyes sparkled and it must have been contagious, because the little boy smiled back at him, first time ever showing his teeth.

"Thank you for the sandwich," Bobby said as the elevator lowered Tall Jerry down.

At the end of his shift Jerry started up the employee stairwell two steps at a time to the sidewalk, thinking about his telephone call to Barber when the idea hit him like a bolt of lightning. He walked around the corner and stepped in the darkened alcove where the boy was lying behind two cans, sleeping.

"I don't have long, Bobby. Do you trust me?" Jerry asked.

Hearing Jerry's voice, he sat up.

"Huh?"

"Can you trust me?"

"Why?"

"I have an idea on how to get you out of here."

Bobby considered his options. It wasn't going to be long before the police found him, or someone reported him as a vagrant. Jerry had been friendly and fed him without pressuring him. He figured that if Tall Jerry double-crossed him and squealed, and they took him back, he would only run away again. He looked down at the uneaten banana in his hand and looked back up at Tall Jerry, checking him over one more time.

Ole Charlie here could tell, Jerry had his doubts, too.

"I think I can get you taken care of at a place you like until your dad gets out, but I'll have to hide you out first before I'll know for sure."

Bobby looked him in the eye.

"I promise I won't rat on you."

Bobby didn't answer.

"Besides, there's escaped Nazis on the loose, nobody knows where."

"For real?"

"Can you trust me?"

"I guess."

"Then come on. No time to waste."

"Where you taking me?"

"My ride will be here any minute—around this corner."

The boy stood and stretched. Jerry offered his hand to help steady him with his leg still asleep. Bobby managed on his own, following Tall Jerry, never taking an eye off him, hoping he was doing the right thing and could trust his new friend. They stepped around the corner of the hotel to Jerry's brother's Chevrolet, parked and waiting.

"There he is—it's my brother, Gourmet Mike. Let me do the talking. Understand?"

"Yes."

They hurried to the car and opened the door. Jerry lifted the seatback forward and nudged the boy into the back seat. He got in the front without saying a word.

"Who's your friend?" Gourmet Mike asked, pulling away from the curb.

Jerry didn't say anything.

Gourmet Mike looked over at him for answers.

Knowing there was more Holbrooks in the county than there was wild strawberries, Jerry thought he'd test that surname.

"He's a Holbrook," Jerry said.

Mike leaned to the rearview mirror.

"Hey, kid, which Holbrook are you?" Mike asked.

This was about the time when the glue pot holding Tall Jerry's plan together might have splashed over a bit.

"What's your name, kid?"

"Bobby," came a weak voice from the back seat.

Jerry cringed and let out a gulp, as silent as he might while trying not to look like he was about to have a heart attack. He knew Gourmet Mike had already met his best friend Bobby Holbrook and things could go sour fast if he didn't distract his brother right then and there. He thought as fast as he could for a dodge to the "Bobby" name. He sat up tall in his disguise as a grownup.

"You ever eaten frog's legs, Mike?"

"Hmmmm," Gourmet Mike observed, paying no attention to Jerry and taking a closer look through the rearview mirror. "I could have sworn I thought you were a lot bigger, Bobby."

Thanks to Jerry's lucky stars Gourmet Mike was observant but not that engaged, and with a short attention span. Mike was distracted, twisting the knob on the car radio, trying to catch a baseball game. The Chiefs were playing. Jerry was convinced medical schools used up the brain cells necessary for a normal body to function more than one sentence or thought at a time. That and the fact his brother had what Jerry called the gourmet fever, eating snails, capers, and God knows what else for sport ever since he went off to college. He cooked on a hot plate, no less.

Soon they were driving through the hamlet, heading down the hill from the Gaines's farm, then up the corner on Cardner Road from the old Maxwell mill and home to Delphi Falls.

"Let us out at the alfalfa field."

"I'll take you to the house," Gourmet Mike said.

"Nah, the alfalfa field is better. Mr. Holbrook's going to meet us there."

Jerry lied again, knowing full well he'd have to confess the entire day to Father Lynch. Why, they were bald-face lies he told, they were. Near every word out of his mouth in that car ride was a lie.

The Chevy pulled to a stop. Both boys jumped out, stood and watched it drive up the road, over the bridge, and turn into the driveway.

"C'mon!" Jerry blurted.

"Where we going?"

"Follow me!"

Off they darted, high-tailing it, running through the alfalfa field to the base of the back hill. The climb was steep, and the boy's legs weak. Jerry would grab him by the hand and help pull him up from tree to tree. Safe on top, the boy caught his wind. They followed the horse path back to the campsite. Jerry gathered kindling. He knew there were dry kitchen matches in the cave.

"If you're afraid in the woods, I'll figure a way to sneak you down to the house after dark," Jerry said.

"I'm not afraid. Where do you live?"

"Down below. Come, I'll show you."

They walked to the top edge of the cliff. Hanging on to a trunk of a small pine tree Bobby looked down more than eighty feet at Tall

58

Jerry's house. He looked in the other direction, to the thundering lower waterfalls.

"Those are magic falls," Jerry said.

"I'm not afraid of them. It's scarier in the city."

"That's easy to say now—it's daylight," Jerry offered. "Help me stack enough wood to last the night; you get sticks smaller than your arm we use as kindling. I'll go down and get food and eat with you. We can come up with a plan. If you're scared then, I'll figure something out."

Jerry stoked the fire and put logs on to last until he got back.

"You okay here until I bring food?"

"I'm okay."

Jerry walked to the edge of the cliff over the white rock, Bobby following him.

"This is where I go down, and I'll climb up when I come back," Jerry said.

Bobby sat on the ground hanging his feet over the edge.

"Can I wait here?"

"Sit still, though. Keep down and don't be walking around near the cliff. I don't want you falling over."

Jerry slid down to where the white rock poked out from the cliff below. He turned and looked up, waved and continued down the rest of the cliff to the creek. Bobby never took his eyes off him. It wasn't more than fifteen minutes when Jerry come out the front door with a stuffed knapsack on his back and the lantern ole Charlie here gave him. He crossed the creek and climbed, balancing best he could with one hand, while the other held the unlit lantern. At the top Bobby offered him a hand up by taking the lantern to carry. They walked back to the camp and unloaded the knapsack, the blanket, a pillow and cans of food and started setting up a camp kitchen. A screech owl waited for Jerry to walk under his limb and fussed a call that ripped the dusk like nails clawing a chalk board.

"I think I'm going to be scared," Bobby said.

"Of the dark or being alone?"

The boy didn't answer.

"That's just a screech owl," Jerry said. "They're nothing to worry about."

"I want my daddy," Bobby sobbed.

Jerry stood there, thinking of the kid losing his mother the way he did, remembering she was bombed in a hospital. He thought of missing his own dad when Big Mike went to the TB sanitarium. He thought of the boy's dad, a nice dad who only went crazy when he heard how his wife and the boy's mother died in the war. He pointed at a log and told Bobby to sit and give him time to think. He needed to work through this. He feared that if he took the boy down to the house, his mom or dad might only do what they thought was right and call the orphanage. He wouldn't betray the boy like that. He had to hide him until after he wet-mopped Sunday and could ride him over to Barber's and talk about ideas.

A night owl hooted this time, a gentler welcoming to a setting sun.

"I have to hide you out until Sunday when I get off work. Are you afraid of the dark or being alone in the woods in the dark?" Jerry asked.

"Alone in the woods."

"What if you were up in a tree house?"

"A tree house?"

"It's off the ground, and it would only be for two days—until I get home from work Sunday morning?"

"I could do that."

"I'll see you have plenty of food."

"That could be all right. I'm not afraid of the dark, maybe just the woods and animal noises—being on the ground, I think."

"I know you miss your dad, Bobby, and your mom a lot."

Bobby looked up.

"Try not to cry. I think I can have a plan that will work until your dad comes back. I'll know for sure Sunday," Jerry said.

Sometimes, if a heart is pure, ole Charlie here can get through with a thought or two, especially if the moon is having a good night. This was those times.

"Just remember your mom is with you, wherever you go."

"She is?"

"She's your guardian angel forever," Jerry said.

"Is that true?" the boy smiled with his eyes.

"I can guarantee it. If you ever want to talk to your mom, all you have to do is look up at the stars for her. She's up there watching over you."

Bobby looked up into the dark sky.

"And when you talk to her, anything you imagine she says back is what she's saying," Jerry said.

Bobby's eyes grew in wonderment. He smiled with the promise.

As dusk settled in for the night, Jerry heated a can of beans over the fire. He got the skillet from the cave and stir-scrambled eggs with a fork. He diced up chunks of Spam and mixed them in with the eggs; he skillet-toasted two slices of bread in the drippings.

"Eat slow," he said.

Bobby was near starved for a hot meal. He sat on the log, knees together, balancing his pie tin plate of food like he was at a fancy city diner.

While he watched his friend eat the first decent meal he had had in weeks, Jerry dipped the skillet in the spring water, cooling it, scooped mud up in it and scrubbed it clean. He set it next to the fire to dry. He'd put the utensils in it for storage later in the cave.

"What does your dad do when he works?" Jerry asked.

"I don't know. He joined the navy. I think he wants to be a farmer."

"Was your mom his school girlfriend?"

61

"He met my mom after high school is what my nanna told me. Mom was a nurse. They got married, and I was born during the war. I lived with my nanna in Syracuse at first, but she died."

"Was she old, your nanna?"

"She got tuberculosis and died," Bobby said. "After my mom got killed, they took me to the orphanage, because Dad was in trouble."

My dad had tuberculosis," Tall Jerry said.

"Did he die?"

"No, they cured him."

"You're lucky."

"How long has your dad been in prison? Did he kill the guy?"

"He didn't kill nobody, but he got court-martialed and sent to prison."

"For what, if it wasn't murder?"

"At first he was at Pine Camp and now he's in Auburn. He'll be in until after October."

"Why did they move him?"

"The war stopped, I think."

"Slugging an officer could be bad," Jerry said.

"It got him court-martialed."

"Was it during the war?"

"I think so. I can't remember, anyway."

"I wonder if he was in the navy why they sent him to Pine Camp, an army base," Jerry said.

"It was a kind of mission they were on when it happened. I know they were friends and my dad said he was sorry, and the officer he hit told the judge my dad didn't mean it, but they found him guilty anyway," Bobby said.

Tall Jerry handed Bobby an empty bean can and pointed at the trickling spring.

"Help me douse the fire."

"Okay."

"I'll take you over to the tree house," Jerry said. "It's on the cliff on the other side of the house."

Jerry lit the lantern, held it up and looked the boy over. He was filthy, and he could use a soaking, but Jerry didn't want him getting wet and catching a cold crossing the creek below.

"C'mon, follow me," Jerry said.

They walked along the cliff edge and down the back hill the way they came up, through the alfalfa field and around the long way home. Dick's tree house was up the hill close to the house, but no one could see in it from the ground below. Jerry gave Bobby a leg up. Then he climbed into it.

"This is good," Bobby said.

It was dry and warmed by the lack of night air breezes blowing the chill through it and it was restful. Bobby made a pallet with the blanket and held the pillow in his lap like it was a luxury he had forgotten while sleeping in alleys.

"I better blow the lantern out, so nobody sees it and gets wise."

"That's okay."

"I'll come every day and bring food. If you're scared of climbing down in the woods in the dark and you have to go bad, try holding it until morning or just pee out of the tree house."

"I'll be okay."

"In daytime go up in the woods behind a tree and go there."

"I'm okay."

"On Sunday we'll ride Jack to Barber's. He'll help us."

"Who's Jack?"

"My horse."

The boy was distracted by the northern star he could see through the opening of the tree house. His dad, a sailor, had taught him how to find it. He lay back on his pillow, comforted with a new confidence he hadn't known since his mother had passed. Maybe it was a bad dream. Maybe he was getting close to a home, again. He

63

had never been on a horse, but he was beginning to trust Tall Jerry. Jerry climbed from the tree and went down to the house.

Ole Charlie here looked in on the boy; weren't that far up the hill from Jerry's room.

"Night, Mom," Bobby whispered to himself. "I love you."

A star shot through the heavens and twinkled. It was her winking back. He was certain of it.

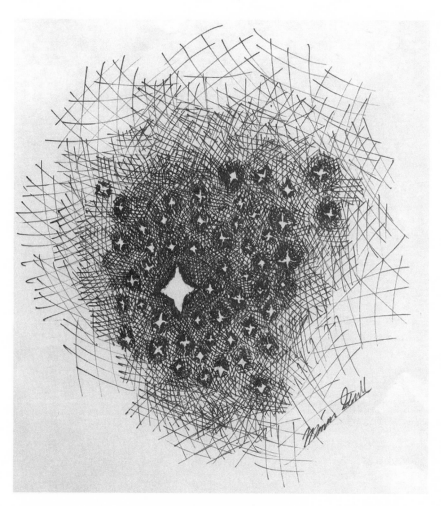

Bobby was certain of it.

CHAPTER 7

A PRAYERFUL SUNDAY

"Rise and shine. It's that time again, Jerry me boy, are you awake?" Big Mike said in a loud whisper from outside Jerry's bedroom door.

This was a still-dark Sunday morning, but they had to leave by five thirty in order to get Jerry to work at the hotel by six.

"I'm up, Dad."

"How late do you work today?"

"This is my wet-mop day. It takes maybe a couple hours."

Big Mike leaned in through the bedroom door. He was already in his suit and tie.

"Want to ride with me up to Carthage after you finish your work? I have to meet a customer up there. We could get good fishing in, maybe at Sandy Pond, on the way back."

Carthage was near the Canadian border. Jerry had to think on this one. Right next to lemon meringue pie and playing in my barn when he was young, Jerry's favorite thing was riding all over central New York State with his dad, visiting grocery stores to see if the bread loaves were neatly stacked on the shelves while listening to his stories and catching a fish or two along the way. It wounded the boy not being able to go this time.

"I'll be right out," Jerry said, stalling his answer.

In the dark, Big Mike drove around the swings, lights off, so as not to wake anyone inside the house with the glare. He edged around the front of the barn garage, the stable shed, and down toward the gate before pulling the car lights on.

"Dad, there's something I have to do today."

"Is the book club still going, Jerry? Are you up to another adventure?"

"I'd rather go fishing with you, but I have to do something important and I can't talk about it yet."

Big Mike grinned. He was an ardent supporter of the club. 'You have to write your own book in this life. No one will write it for you,' he would say. Big Mike was all for adventures and stories, the taller the better. He had hoped they hadn't outgrown the club.

"The club's still going," Jerry said. "I'll tell you about it when I can, okay?"

Big Mike didn't say another word. He knew he could trust the boy and his friends.

Now the lad didn't exactly lie about involving the club. Maybe the notion was a bit premature. He was, after all, taking the problem of the runaway orphan boy to Barber's to discuss it. That would be considered an executive meeting of the book club, was his thinking.

"I'll call your brother to pick you up and take you to church," Big Mike said.

No matter where they were on a Sunday, they went to Mass. Big Mike believed in it, even made the boys shine their shoes for it each week. Jerry's mom would have blistered her boys if they got caught missing Mass.

"Is Dick coming for me?" Jerry asked.

"Mike has a baseball game at the quarry today. He'll pick you up, take you to church, then home before his game."

"I'll head up to Carthage after I drop you at the hotel. I'll go to Mass up there."

"It's Sunday, Dad, why do you have to go to work—and all the way to Carthage?" Jerry asked.

"A customer called the bakery, said she'd found a cockroach in a slice of bread."

Jerry cringed.

"I have to go see her about it."

Jerry knew that couldn't be good. The first he'd heard of cockroaches was from Rusty, and the reason he hot wet-mopped the floors every Sunday was so cockroaches would stay away. The boy had a suspicion they must be evil, ugly, and dastardly, so he decided not to open more conversation about the subject. The car pulled up to the employee entrance of the hotel.

"Dad, where can I find out if those Nazi POW guys who escaped from Pine Camp during the War ever got caught?"

"Why that's almost ten years ago, son…"

"Pine Camp was a prison, too—for soldiers, right dad?"

"It's a big base, son. Yes, there was a section for prisoners of war and another for military prisoners."

"Did the Nazi guys who escaped ever get caught?"

"I haven't seen anything in the news, son."

"Where could I find out?"

"I'll ask around."

"How old was I?"

"You would have been three when they escaped."

"Wow."

"Remember, son, if your club needs help—tell the older boys—make sure you let Dick know."

"We will."

Jerry started to close the car door.

"Dad, if you want, I can show the bakery guys how to hot wet-mop the floors so there won't be any cockroaches."

Big Mike smiled and drove off.

Jerry completed his Sunday tasks—picking papers up from the floor of the hotel basement and hot wet-mopping the floors and halls to a steamy sparkle. Gourmet Mike was on time and took him to St. Ann's for church and then dropped him home before heading to the quarry to play baseball. Jerry ran to the small barn stable and gathered the blanket, bridle, and saddle. He was becoming a good rider, but he hadn't had a lot of experience in the saddle off the property, riding on slick summer asphalt. Big Mike would warn Jerry about a horse's nature to want to dead-run home to its barn.

"Show the horse who's boss, son. Stay in control," Big Mike would preach.

Jerry walked to Jack and threw the blanket on his back, then the saddle. He put the bridle bit in Jack's mouth, pulling it up over his ears after the horse lowered his head almost to the ground to help him. Jack knew they were going for a ride and he liked that.

"Show him who's boss," he would repeat to himself.

That seemed to be enough. Once saddled up, he tied the reins to a post and ran into the woods to Dick's tree house. Young Bobby was sitting in its doorway.

"Hungry?" Jerry asked.

"A little."

"We'll eat soon."

"Okay."

"Leave the blanket and pillow here. I'll get them later. Follow me."

They walked the hill through the woods above the house rooftop not to be seen, then down to where Jack was tied. Jerry climbed on first, and then gave a hand down to Bobby and helped lift him up behind the saddle.

It was a sight, it surely was, trotting down the asphalt road, tall in the saddle with little Bobby bouncing up and down while holding on to Tall Jerry's belt for dear life. The two were off on an adventure. Jack strutted along in the late summer air, his nostrils smelling the fresh-cut hay and roadside clover. Coming over the hilltop curve and cutting through the Gaines's Falls View Farm, they saw the Gaines's horse in the distant pasture. Jack whinnied a friendly hello; the horse whinnied back politely.

They headed into the hamlet and turned north to the Barber farm. Trotting through the hamlet Tall Jerry gave a salute to Bases, who had his bicycle upside down on the sidewalk, fixing a flat tire. When they got to Barber's dirt driveway, a hired hand shouted that Barber was out back in the hay barn and he was expecting them. They rode Jack to the side pasture where he and Bobby dismounted. Jerry took the saddle off and put Jack out to graze with Barber's short white horse. He carried the saddle while Bobby carried the bridle and blanket to the barn to put up.

Barber finished backing a tractor into the barn and shut her off. He took a gander at the kid, jumped off and walked over, wondering who he might be.

"Barber meet Bobby. Bobby, meet my friend Barber."

Barber shook the boy's hand.

"Call me Bub or Barber. Either will do. New to the area, are you, Bobby? Need a tour of the place?"

"Why don't you give us jobs?" Jerry asked. "Tell us what to do. I'll fill you in while we're working."

"Okay, you get on top of the hay wagon, Tall Jerry, throw the bales down."

"I can do that," Jerry said.

"Go easy on them. Try not to split or bust them open when they hit the ground."

"I'll get the hang of it."

"Drop them as flat as you can. I'll take them from here back into the barn for stacking."

Barber looked at the boy.

"Bobby, why don't you go get that pitchfork over there on the barn wall and pitch loose hay from broken bales here to that main bay area. It's the floor behind the tractor over there. Separate the bailing twine from the hay, so cows don't swallow the twine."

"Okay."

"On the wall behind the tractor you'll see the hay chute door that looks down to the milking stalls. Pile the hay on the floor in front of that opening."

70

"I can do that," Bobby said.

After the first couple, Jerry could throw bales down without busting them. Dale would drag and stack them like stair steps inside the hay barn. Stacking them that way made it easier to get to the top of the pile. Bobby was having a good time, being useful.

"The kid's a runaway," Jerry said.

"He is?"

"From an orphanage in Syracuse, said he had no friends there," Jerry said.

Having an orphaned cousin, knowing kids around the area who lost their parents and have been taken in, Dale paused and listened.

"I could be in big trouble if they find out I'm hiding him."

"His folks gone, are they?"

"His dad's in Auburn for starting a fight in the navy."

"Auburn?"

"The prison."

"Just for a fight?"

"He punched a guy who told him about the boy's mom getting killed," Tall Jerry said.

"Just a punch? No club or knife?"

"That's what he says."

"Where's his ma?"

"She died in a bomb attack, somewhere in Africa during the war. A nurse."

Barber lowered his head, not to look obvious. He lifted his eyes and stared over at the young boy walking and balancing a pitchfork filled with hay.

"Why's he in Auburn just for a punch?"

"The guy he slugged was a sergeant or an ensign or something high up like that, I think. It was the guy who told him about his wife dying."

"That'd do it," Barber said.

I think it was something about wartime on a submarine, and the guy he slugged being an officer."

"That for sure would do it," Barber said.

"The guy he slugged was his best friend on the sub. He didn't mind getting slugged, even said he'd have done the same thing if his wife got killed that way, but someone turned them both in, and the kid's dad got court-martialed anyway," Tall Jerry said. "His dad gets out in October."

"That's not far off," Barber said.

"He wants to be a farmer. I thought…"

Barber stopped, smiled. "I know that look, Tall Jerry," he said.

Jerry smiled back.

"You're thinking about the empty Toby place, the shack we have up the road and maybe they could sharecrop or help work the farm or something, aren't you?" Barber asked.

Jerry didn't say a word. He knew the Barbers had big hearts.

Barber lifted another bale into position, walked through the barn and over to Bobby. He motioned the boy to follow him to where Tall Jerry was standing.

"You want to be a farmer?" he asked.

"I don't know about farming, but my dad does. I'll bet we'd be good ones. This is fun," Bobby said.

"You say your dad wants to be a farmer?" Barber asked.

"Yes, he told me."

"Well, all right."

"What?" Bobby asked.

"Look me in the eye."

"Huh?" Bobby asked.

"Go on, look me in the eye," Barber said.

Young Bobby stood there and looked Barber straight in the eye.

"Here's the way it is, kid, and listen good, because I'm not going to be chewin' my cabbage twice."

"Okay."

"After we get done stacking bales and go in to eat, best you let me and Tall Jerry here do the talking, you hear me?"

"Okay," Bobby said.

"And if my mom asks you a question—any question—best you come right out and answer the truth, the whole truth, so help you God."

"I will."

"The truth will serve you good here, and I'll warn you now, my mom surely can see right through a stammering in answers. Any stalling like there is in a liar's eyes while he's thinking to make something up to say."

"I understand."

"Won't be nuthin' she ain't already heard before."

"Okay."

"Just be honest, tell it like it is and don't be making anything up."

"I will, I promise."

"And I'll tell you this, whatever my mom says she will do, she'll do—and you do the same back."

"I promise."

"Other than that, I ain't making any promises," Barber growled.

"Okay."

About the time they got the hay bales dropped, dragged and stacked, Mrs. Barber was on the side porch reaching for the iron rod from the hook on the porch to ring the triangle dinner bell, letting those within earshot of it know it was going on noontime—time to eat with the family and their farmhands.

Farmhands were people who worked the farm during the day and went to their own houses at night. Tall Jerry and Bobby were right proud hearing the dinner bell calling them, imagining that made them farmhands on Barber's farm too.

"Farmhands at noon Supper"

The eating table, covered with crockery bowls and platters of food almost as big around as the room, filled up with farmhands gathered about it.

"My, you sure have grown, Tall Jerry. Why Lord all mighty, just look at you. How's Missus?" Mrs. Barber asked.

"Mom is fine, Mrs. Barber. She and Dad say hello."

"Did you and your friend here have fun this morning? Grab cornbread, dear, while it's hot and a pork chop or two. There's plenty of butter."

"Yes ma'am. This is Bobby. He helped us with the hay."

74

Mrs. Barber reached and handed a full plate of food to the boy, knowing he was younger and maybe needed help. All the while she was looking him over. Ole Charlie specked she knew something was up or the boy's introduction to her would have been more proper. But the big tell was the boy was way too dirty for a Sunday going-to-meeting church morning.

"Fence in the east pasture needs a looking at," Mr. Barber said with cornbread in his hand. "The posts are rotted underground and the barbed wire's coming loose. Art, tend to that sometime, will you, son?"

The farm hands ate and listened. Art answered Mr. Barber with a twist of the pork chop bone in his hand and a nod of his head.

"I wonder should we put electric fencing up for the bull-run back by that hill, or keep the pen here by the barn?" Mr. Barber asked.

"Back by the hill is best for when heifers are in season," a voice said.

Mrs. Barber sipped her coffee. She couldn't take her eyes off the young boy sitting across from her.

"Young Bobby, I don't recall seeing you about anywhere. Whose boy are you?" Mrs. Barber asked.

Bobby looked up, his eyes widening and then peeking over at Tall Jerry, signaling with a raised eyebrow for help.

"You're not blond enough to be a Cook; you're too dark for the Dwyers—they're mostly lighter or with red locks. Are you Pidgeon kin, maybe?" she riddled. "Eat your snap peas, dear. They're fresh-picked, and grab you another deviled egg."

The noises of utensils on the plates, spoons clanking on serving bowls, and platters being slid around the table pretty much drowned out the ability to converse. Tall Jerry and Barber ate and stared at Mrs. Barber, knowing she was intuitive; hoping and praying she was as gentle and in a good mood this morning as she most generally was. The woman with a full table and a heart of gold was becoming suspicious about the lack of responses from the boy. She could understand and tolerate it from hungry workers who'd been up since five and could grunt back and forth with each other in a code of their own, but not from a child. She stood, pushed her chair back and announced:

"Boys, and you know who you are, I need to see you in the pantry. Now, please."

She had a firm look in her eyes as she walked toward the kitchen. Bobby looked up at her walking out of the room, and a cold fear came over his face. Mrs. Barber suspected as much, lifted her left arm and shook her index finger in the air in his direction.

"You, too, young man. Tall Jerry, bring your friend and come join us in the pantry. Your food won't be touched. It'll be here when you get back to it."

Noise at the lunch table came to a stop momentarily, eyes gazing up. The boys stood and followed Mrs. Barber through the kitchen into the pantry, faces looking like they'd been sent to the principal's office.

Jerry took the lead. "Mrs. Barber, this is all my doing."

"Talk to me, son," Mrs. Barber said.

"I've been hiding him out for two days."

Mrs. Barber started, looked down at Bobby.

"I knew you would know what to do. That's why I brought him here, Mrs. Barber."

"Who is he?"

"He's all alone. He's got nobody."

Mrs. Barber looked into Bobby's eyes.

"This true, son?" she asked.

Bobby nodded his head.

"I found him sleeping in an alley up in Syracuse behind where I work at the hotel."

"Sleeping in an alley?"

76

"He's supposed to be at an orphanage until his dad comes back to get him, but he ran away, and if I double-crossed or ratted on him and told anyone he would only run away again, Mrs. Barber. That's the honest truth," Jerry said.

Mrs. Barber took it in with a deep breath. She reached and picked a stalk of hay from the top of young Bobby's head and ran her fingers through his hair a few times, straightening it, looking for a part that wasn't there.

"Just where's the boy's mother and father?" Mrs. Barber asked.

"That's just it," Jerry said.

"What do you know about him?" she asked.

"His mother's dead and his dad is in Auburn for hitting a guy, but he'll be out in October. The kid's got nobody," Barber said.

"Missus and Big Mike don't know, I'm thinking?"

"No, ma'am."

"Not a word to them all this time, sure enough?"

"No, ma'am."

"Oh, lad, you're in such big trouble when they find out, I reckon," Mrs. Barber said.

"I know," Jerry said.

"Now why would the man be in Auburn just for hitting a man? Did he hurt him bad?" she asked.

"They were on a submarine in the war and he slugged the officer who told him about the boy's mom being killed with a bomb in a hospital in Africa," Jerry said.

Mrs. Barber flinched at the thought of the boy losing his momma like that. She stood back with both hands covering her mouth, pondering. Then she placed the soft palm of her hand under the boy's chin and lifted his face up.

"You miss your daddy, don't you, son?" she asked, looking into his eyes."

"Yes'm."

"I just know you do."

Bobby didn't say a word. A tear rolled from his eye.

"When does he get out, son?" she asked.

"The last day in October. He'll be able to come home before November," Bobby said.

"October? The last day, you say?" Mrs. Barber asked.

She looked up on her wall calendar.

"That will be Halloween. We'll have to bake him a pumpkin pie. Would you like to help me make one for him, young man?"

"Yes 'm, I surely would."

"I'll bet you have your momma's hazel eyes, Bobby."

"I can't remember," Bobby whispered.

"I'm sorry about your momma, son. She's with God now, looking after you."

"I know, ma'am."

"She surely is looking after you right this minute."

"My dad's going to be a farmer. I know how to pitch hay good." Bobby's voice cracked as he pointed to Barber. "He taught me."

Mrs. Barber sighed, and took the boys in her arms like a big ole momma bear; she glanced up at the picture of Jesus.

"Lord knows we have plenty of room. I'll find the orphanage and make it right with them. When your father comes to get you, we'll see what more we can do then. But for sure there will be a fresh warm Halloween pumpkin pie, maybe two, waiting for him."

Bobby broke into happy tears, rubbing his eyes with his knuckles and a warm trust.

Mrs. Barber stood back, gathered her thoughts. She lifted the front of her apron and wiped the boy's tears.

"This is an honest house, young man," she said, "It's a house where even Jesus can feel at home."

No one spoke.

"Tall Jerry, you must tell your folks what you did—bringing the boy here without them knowing."

"Yes ma'am."

"Tell them the truth, now."

"I will, I promise."

"Take whatever you have coming."

"Yes ma'am."

"Dale, you explain it to your father later. At the supper table might be best if he doesn't already know. We want it all in the open. Kindness is best served that-a-way, in the open. A good life is living by and giving examples of kindness. Now go eat, put some meat on your ribs. You're growing boys. Go on."

Mrs. Barber held Jerry's and Barber's shoulders for another word for their ears.

"After mealtime, you two go for a horseback ride. Bobby is going to need a good soaking in a hot tub, clean clothes and to help making up his own bed."

She beamed a broad smile.

"Now git! Go eat."

The lemon meringue pie was the best Jerry ever had, and while he savored the sweet bite of its tart lemon he thought of the boiled eggs and can of beans and the tree house the night before and of Bobby's having no breakfast this morning because Big Mike was in a hurry to see that lady in Carthage about the cockroach in her bread.

Feeling good about themselves, Barber and Jerry grabbed toothpicks from a box on the windowsill, stuck them in their mouths like ranch hands might, stepped off the side porch and ambled out to the pasture to fetch the horses for a ride. Last they saw, Bobby got busy being useful while feeling wanted by somebody for a change. He stayed back, helping Mrs. Barber stack and carry dishes from the table to the kitchen with a smile on his face and meringue on his chin.

"It's going to be a happy Halloween for Bobby, sounds like," Jerry said.

"Sounds like," Barber said.

"A good kid," Jerry said.

"Tough times it's been for him."

"Yup."

"Seems like the war won't never leave us alone," Barber said.

"This has me thinking we've gotta come up with a plan to find and catch those Nazi escapees," Jerry said.

"The crown's got plenty of empty milk cans being delivered to farmers over two counties," Barber said. "What if we attach secret messages and tape them on the cans?"

"I like that," Jerry said.

"We maybe could use your dad's bakery trucks like we did to catch those burglars down in Groton."

"My mom says she hopes people don't forget the war. Thanks for letting me bring the kid over."

"What if the two escaped Nazis were the same ones who bombed his mother's hospital?" Barber asked.

"I don't know about that, but no telling what could have happened to him in that alley in Syracuse," Jerry said.

"We have time before the silage wagon comes to be unloaded," Barber said. "Let's ride through the big cornfield. It was fresh plowed a week ago. It's a shortcut across and up to Pompey Hollow Road behind it for your ride back."

Silage was made up of chopped corn stalks, mixed with chopped alfalfa sometimes. It smelled like molasses. Silage work was more dangerous than dragging and throwing bales of hay, and it took a grownup. It traveled on conveyor belts like elevator straps up into the tall, round silo behind the barn. Silage and hay fed cows through winter months when they couldn't graze because of the snow in the pastures. At silage time Mr. Barber needed Barber to sit on the tractor that ran the conveyor belt and pull the choke from time to time and keep her running.

"I'll ride as far as the creek," Barber said.

They took hold of the halters and walked the horses, Jerry's big gray, Jack, and Barber's short mare, Tink, from pasture to the hay-barn for saddling. Mr. Barber stepped in, walked over and handed Jerry two dollars.

"Thank you, son. Appreciate your help," Mr. Barber said. He looked around the barn at the stacked bales and the small mound of hay neatly piled in front of the tractor by the milking stall chute.

"You boys did a right nice job of stacking. It's a fine-looking hay barn. Good job," Mr. Barber said.

"You don't have to pay me, Mr. Barber. I had lunch and you're helping Bobby. Dale's my friend."

"One's got nothing to do with the other, son. You earned the money. Put it in your pocket."

"Thanks, Mr. Barber, I'll work anytime you need me when I'm not at the hotel, and for free. Tell Dale or call my mom and tell her."

"Give this to the boy," Mr. Barber said, handing Barber two dollars. "If he lives here like I think he's about to, after this he works for his keep like the rest of us, and he's your responsibility, Bub."

Mr. Barber checked the saddle cinches, pulling the straps on both Jack and Tink to be certain they were secure.

"Have a good ride, boys," he said. "Careful with the mud in the back field."

They mounted and walked the horses over to the house's side porch door.

"Mom, we're riding to the creek," Barber yelled. "Tall Jerry's going home."

Mrs. Barber pushed the screen door open, came out on the porch, flipping a freshly wrung-out pair of Bobby's shorts and shirt, hanging them next to his underwear and socks, already on the clothesline strung on the porch for drying wash.

"It's a blessed day. That boy fits most of your old things, Dale. It's a blessed day. You have a nice time riding, boys."

Mrs. Barber turned, pulled the screen door and looked up at the sky before going back in the house.

"Will you just look at that pretty August sun," Mrs. Barber said.

Tall Jerry glanced down the road and saw his dad's Oldsmobile coming up Oran Delphi toward the hamlet. Passin' by, he reached his arm out the window of the car and gave a big wave. The boys turned their horses and slow-walked the dusty drive between the barns, gabbing among themselves like they'd been on a long trail and doggie drive.

"A lady in Carthage thinks there's a cockroach in her bread," Jerry said. "Dad had to go see about it."

"A cockroach ain't nuthin'," Barber said. He leaned over and spit. "Mice love wheat, that I know," he offered. "A mouse can chew a string off a feedbag and get to it like they were in a grocery market."

"They can?" Tall Jerry asked.

"Lucky she didn't find a dead mouse in her sandwich."

He leaned and spit again.

This was too soon after a wedge of lemon meringue pie to be talking about cockroaches and dead mice. Tall Jerry chose to change the subject.

"Let's just ride," he said.

The boys sat tall, listening to the leather of their saddles stretch and creak, just as they did as young boys listening to the Lone Ranger on the radio ever' week. When a lad grows up listening to radio, sounds are important. Television ain't caught on in the country yet. No time to watch it on a farm, and most can't afford one, anyway. They rode between the red barns and tool sheds as though they were in a Hollywood western riding into a cattle town looking for a saloon. Making it through the back gates without getting bushwhacked, they each tugged on the reins and moaned a gentle "Whoa."

They sat up, resting their mounts at the front of the longest, widest plowed field in the hollow, taking it all in. It stretched as far as the eye could see. The corn had been cut a week before, and beans were about to be planted. All that was there were mounds of dirt furrows about four inches tall rolling out of the ground in straight rows. Big ole muddy patches throughout the field reflected in the sun.

"Big rain Wednesday," Barber said.

"The field looks a mess," Tall Jerry said.

"Watch out for mud."

Barber pointed to wet puddle patches here and there, but it was just after that warning when he gave Tall Jerry a start. The lad raised his voice a notch, offering a new challenge.

"Race you across the field."

"Huh?" Jerry asked.

"Race to Limestone Creek!" Barber shouted.

With that, he made a sound with his mouth that was the *giddy up* mouth signal every horse on the face of the earth knew by heart.

"KTCH, KTCH…"

Hearing it, Barber's horse, young Tink, sprung off on all fours like a kangaroo. She'd been waiting for that sound from the minute she got bridled. She took off like a race pony on a merry-go-round, galloping across that muddy field, kicking up divots of mud every which way, as fast as her short legs could carry her and as far as the mud would fly.

Jack knew the signal good as any horse alive. The big gray stirred, it surely did. With the commotion and the mud flying, Jack's instincts had no choice but to rise to the challenge. He pranced, four hooves in place, his eleven-hundred-pound body trembling, his ears twitching like roof-mounted weathervanes.

Jerry's heart sank somewhere down around the lemon meringue pie. The boy hadn't ridden much more than a bareback trot ever around the waterfalls.

Jack's eyes were glued to Tink's butt, crossing the field like a pig to trough. He opened his mouth, twisted his neck, stretching out and shaking his head, pulling the reins from Jerry's hands. He let out a whinny that could be heard down in Cortland.

It was too late to jump off. Tall Jerry's eyes danced about, looking for things he could grab hold of.

Off Jack sprung, nearly losing the lad from the saddle. That horse galloped like it was the lead horse of a runaway stagecoach! Tall Jerry hung on to the pommel in front as best he could, and the back of the saddle with his other hand. It was a blur of images to the boy—the back of a horse's head heaving in a full-out gallop, his mane slapping up and stinging Jerry's face, the plowed corn rows rolling under, like cracks in a broken sidewalk.

"Horses like to get home in a hurry, Jerry me boy. A dead run, they call it."

Big Mike had warned Jerry about that horse trait, but he forgot to give the lad a bit more instruction on the "Show him who's boss, son" part of his lecture.

By this time Barber was across the field and had stopped and turned with a big grin on his face, like he'd grabbed the brass ring on the merry-go-round at Suburban Park in Manlius and won another free ride. He showed no signs of being aware of the trouble his friend might be in.

Tall Jerry was more vocal. The boy was howling prayers at the top of his lungs, promising God about anything it would take to stop his horse.

At that moment of personal reflection and prayer offerings, best I figure is God must have been distracted, back in the hay barn admiring the neatly stacked hay bales and taking a break from His prayer listening, because that's when Tall Jerry took flight. Jack's head wasn't bouncing up and down anymore mainly because Jack wasn't there anymore. Jerry's arms flopped in circles like a rooster flapping its wings, his hands clawing the air, fingernails digging into the palms of his hands. His feet, out of stirrups, were levitating on their own above the saddle. Jack wasn't under Jerry. The boy was airborne and upside down.

It was a wet, muddy, plow furrow he was diving head first for.

Sploooot!

"Are you okay?" Barber shouted.

He was alive, this I knew. He was holding his breath but alive, lying with his face buried to his shoulders in soggy wet mud and cow manure.

He pulled himself to his knees, face still buried in mud, like an ostrich. He put both hands on the ground by either side of his head and pulled out of the mud.

Rolling onto his back, he picked the mud off his face. After a spell he opened his eyes. Inches from his nose was Jack's muzzle, sniffing to see if the boy was breathing. Barber helped him up. Jerry put his foot in the stirrup and mounted Jack again and the boys slow-walked the horses to the creek, where Jerry splashed mud off his head, face, arms, hands, and the saddle.

Tall Jerry waved a thanks for taking in Bobby and headed home. Jack's mane, the saddle, his rump and legs still had mud hanging on. When he turned in the driveway Big Mike was sitting on the swings in front of the house talking to Missus, on the swing next to him. He tied the reins to the small barn door and walked over to ask about the cockroach. He'd already decided he would tell them about Mrs. Barber taking Bobby in later, maybe at supper.

"Did you go to Carthage?"

"I was just telling your mother."

"What happened?" Jerry asked.

"What happened to you, son?" Big Mike asked.

"Jack tripped in Barber's cornfield. I'm all right."

"The lady was nice. She has four young boys. Her husband works at the X-ray laboratory at Camp Drum. They're studying new ways X-ray machines can be used to find diseases for hospitals."

"Where's Camp Drum, Dad?"

"It was Pine Camp. You've been there a few times with me. The bakery sells them bread and pastries. They changed the name to Camp Drum after the war," Big Mike said.

"That's where the German POWs escaped?"

"I asked about them and word is they're still on the loose."

"What happened with the cockroach, Dad?"

"The lady poured coffee and we talked. She handed me the slice of bread she thought had a cockroach in it. I looked at it closely. I reminded her we make a fine loaf of raisin bread, and I suggested it could be a raisin. She thought, maybe, but still wondered if it was a cockroach."

"Was it?"

"I put the bread in my mouth and swallowed it. 'Yep...it was a raisin,' I told her. Then I gave her loaves of warm bread fresh out of the Carthage bakery. I gave each of her boys a chipboard Indian head bonnet I had in the trunk of my car. She's a happy customer again."

Big Mike stood and started to walk toward Jack and the stable shed because he could tell something more serious happened than a simple tripping, by the looks of the mud splotches.

"Was it a raisin, Dad?"

He didn't answer.

"Was it?"

Big Mike lifted the saddle and blanket off Jack and put them on the ground for Jerry to put away. He looked Jerry over, making sure he was okay and not bruised. He turned to walk toward the house.

"I'm not sure," he said, walking away.

Jerry stood there bug-eyed, his imagination going a hundred miles a minute, wondering if his dad had swallowed a cockroach. Big Mike turned and caught the boy's eye.

"Close your mouth, son. You'll catch flies in it," he said. "And clean that saddle. Soap it down good."

CHAPTER 8

CONFESSION AND PENANCE

Dick wasn't at supper—only Jerry, Big Mike, and Missus. Just as well. It was time to confess about hiding Bobby out and taking him over to the Barbers' without telling his parents.

I was there, sitting up on the buffet side table next to Missus's china cabinet for best vantage, admiring its contents.

Big Mike lifted a bowl of meatballs and passed it to Jerry to take a couple and pass over to Missus.

"Mr. Vance is going to be logging in the area," Big Mike said. "I told him he could leave his work horse in the alfalfa field as long as he needs to."

"What do you mean, logging, Dad?" Jerry asked.

"Logging. You know, cutting timber."

"Like a lumberjack?"

"That's right. He's what you call an independent lumberjack."

"Is he cutting our trees?"

"A lot of the trees in the hills around here need thinning out. Pine and valuable hardwoods."

"Why can't his horse stay with Jack and Major out front here?"

This was the family supper table, and Big Mike didn't want to go into a lot of detail about Mr. Vance's horse being a fresh mare work horse needed for his livelihood all season, and their Jack, a stallion and Major and the birds and bees and why they needed to be separated during a cutting season. Big Mike handed Jerry the plate of sliced bread.

"Hard to explain," Big Mike stammered. "She's a workhorse. Lots of work to do pulling logs through the fall and winter, I imagine, hard to explain."

"Won't alfalfa bloat a horse if it eats too much?" Jerry asked.

"Son, we've been calling that old field the alfalfa field for years. Why, there hasn't been alfalfa in it since before the war."

"When's he coming?"

"He didn't give me an exact date. Sometime this month, I suppose."

The lad stalled as long as he could. He inhaled a deep, thought-refreshing breath. He wanted to take care in parsing his words about his deception in handling the orphan boy and taking him to the Barbers. But his mom was more guarded about endorsing the club's activities she was aware of. She was less permissive than Big Mike was. She would never tolerate their disobeying an adult, cheating anyone or breaking the law. These notions, of course, could pretty much tie his friends' hands from catching grown-up crooks, which most crooks traveling through the crown were.

It was time.

Mrs. Barber made him promise he would confess and take whatever medicine was spooned out for him in terms of punishment. Jerry decided to put a toe in the water by first trying to put it all on his mother's shoulders by telling her how she raised him to be a good lad and to help others in need whenever he could. He spoke slowly and deliberately, leading up to telling how he found the boy in an alley in Syracuse and how he hid him up in the tree house for a couple days before he took him to the Barber's.

Missus paused and rested her salad fork on her salad plate. Big Mike sat back and listened.

"Young man, I can't believe my ears. Are you telling us you found a runaway boy you didn't know, and you helped him runaway further by hiding him in our woods?"

"Well…"

"Explain yourself."

"Mom, he was in trouble."

"Not half the trouble—"

"He had no place to go and nobody to turn to. That's why I did it."

"If he had no place to go, just how did the boy happen to go to the Barber's? Explain yourself."

"Well, ah…"

"My own son would leave a neighbor with the impression that his mother wouldn't care for a child's welfare right here at home."

"But Mom…"

"I'm disappointed, young man. No, I'm hurt."

Big Mike wouldn't touch this one with a long fishin' pole. The Missus was a wonderful mom. Anyone who knew her thought she ranked among the best. Like any good mom, and the president of the PTA, she was hurt by being overlooked.

"How'd I do that, Mom?"

Jerry sat up in his chair, as tall as he could; reminding Missus he was almost a teenager, Tall Jerry now and near full adult.

"I promised the kid I wouldn't tell anyone until I figured out what I could do to help him. I hid him up in the woods, is all. A promise is a promise, Mom, even you told me that. I cooked for him, I gave him a blanket and pillow. It was only a day or two that he was up there. I fed him good."

"Fed him well, dear; you fed him well."

"I fed him well."

"You couldn't come and tell your mother about the boy? The mother who brought you into the world, nursed you, kept you from harm's way; but you could go tell someone miles away—a complete stranger? I'm disappointed."

Everyone knew Missus and Mrs. Barber were good friends; they met and talked at Hasting's store on a regular basis.

"Barber's the first guy I met when we moved here, Mom. I was scared that first day of school, but Barber never asked me who my mom or dad was before he could be my friend. It didn't matter to him. I knew the Barbers take care of orphans sometimes like other families around here do. I just thought—"

"The Barbers are good people. I know them both. Walter and Gertrude; they're fine folks." Missus finally admitted knowing them. "Wonderful caring parents. I know they are warm, kind, hardworking, God-fearing."

But she still didn't pick up her salad fork.

Jerry looked over to his dad for help.

"Son, why don't you begin at the beginning? Tell it in your own way. We'll listen and then we can talk about it after you're through. How's that, Mommy? How'll that be?" Big Mike asked.

Big Mike nodded down to Missus for affirmation to his suggestion. She offered it, with pursed lips.

Now ole Charlie here is only a guardian angel. I can't be putting words in the boy's head. Can only sit up here and pray he puts them in.

Jerry took a deep breath.

For color he thought he'd start with how to smash glass bottles, the varieties of bottles and how he shoveled the remains into the barrels. He told of cans he was in charge of that went off to pig farms and how others went to the dump, and his knowing the difference, and how he knew when to ride them up the special elevator, and where to put them on the street where he met the boy.

Missus loosened her pursed lips and offered a proud motherly smile. She liked his sentence structure and the patience Jerry was taking in telling the story—the specific detail he proffered. She picked up her salad fork and began puncturing a wedge of tomato on her salad plate.

This was a good sign.

Frustrating thing about being a guardian angel is I can't be helping a lad say the right thing or keeping one from saying the wrong thing either, or telling him when to shut up.

"Mom, I knew you would do the right thing. It never entered my brain you wouldn't. You'd probably know what to do better than anybody, but you've trusted me in the past in letting the club work through things liked this on our own."

Now this is when Jerry ought not to have said that—bringing up the Pompey Hollow Book Club like he did. The mention of it got Missus thinking, and when a body is in what could be called a hot seat like Jerry was, sparking thoughts into an adversary's brain could work against a person. Missus looked over with a smile, lifted a serving bowl of boiled canned corn kernels in one hand, the plate of butter in the other and handed them to him. Warm corn kernels and a melting stick of butter were her bait.

"Go on," she said softly, inviting him to spill his guts.

Her invite to "go on" was a dodge, a stall, giving her time to think.

The lad saw her smiling at him, took the corn and butter from her hands and developed the thing he didn't need at that moment—confidence.

"I can see how it might have looked like I was avoiding bringing him to you, Mom, by taking him over to Barber's. I was only taking him to Barber—you know, Dale—to talk about what the book club could do to help the kid. You know—to sort things out before we brought him here. Honest, Mom."

His knee began to bounce up and down all nervous, like a spring under the table. He was feeling low, but he did nothing wrong. He kept a promise to a boy.

She placed her salad fork down.

"There are many reasons your mother is proud of you, Jerome," Missus began. "Your values and those of your friends are to be admired. You're a young man with fine character qualities. Isn't he, Mike?"

"And he's tall," Big Mike said.

"On Wednesday I'll drive over and pay a visit with Gertrude, after my PTA meeting. I'll see if there is anything we can do as a family to help the boy. In the meantime, young man, there'll be no movies for you in Cazenovia, Manlius, for the rest of August."

"How about apple pie?" Big Mike smiled. "Keep your seat, Mommy. I'll get it."

Pleased with himself for only being banned from movies, the near-grown Jerry stuffed a heaping fork filled with sugar cinnamon fresh warm apple pie and flakey crust in his mouth.

"Don't forget Saturday, dear," Missus said.

"Saturday?"

"You have an appointment with Dr. Webb."

Would the boy's penance never end? He swallowed his mouthful of pie without chewing or choking.

"Mom, do I have to?"

"Of course."

"It's still summer vacation, for Pete's sake," Jerry's voice cracked. "I don't have any baby teeth left. I'm too old to go to the dentist. I brush."

Missus rested her salad fork on the plate but kept her grip on it. She smiled, understanding for the first time tonight that the lad's voice and his emotions were in rehearsal for adulthood.

The lad decided not to push it, to enjoy the pie. He had the inkling this wasn't a moment to test her fire further than he already had.

Tall Jerry's work week flew by. He felt good every time he rode the elevator up to the street not seeing young Bobby cowering in the alley.

CHAPTER 9

PAIN AND THE ROAD PIRATES

By Saturday Jerry had forgotten the dentist appointment. He was going to stay over at Holbrook's and spent the morning throwing things as he could remember them into his knapsack to take. If he got there early enough, they were going to trek through Holbrook's backwoods, see their small waterfalls, maybe slide down them. Mr. Holbrook would be driving into Syracuse at 5:00 a.m. on Sunday for his work as railroad brakeman and would give Jerry a ride to the hotel.

The lad was in the kitchen, pouring his second glass of lemonade from a gallon jug, trying not to spill any more than he already had. Missus was standing in the book den, staring out the picture window down the hundred yards or so toward the front gate and Cardner Road.

"Wipe your spills," Missus shouted as if she had eyes in the back of her head.

"I am," Jerry said.

"I don't want ants," Missus offered.

"I'm wiping," Jerry said.

"What on earth are those men up to?" she asked herself. "They surely can't be thieves. Only lunatics would try to steal an eight-foot piece of iron fence in broad daylight."

She walked back and forth the length of the four-by-eight front picture window, lifted a small pot of African violets from the sill, poking a finger in it, testing the soil.

"Oh, well."

"Who you talking to, Mom?"

"No one, dear."

"I heard you talking."

"Well, myself."

"I wiped up the lemonade."

"There're two men, out by the fence—parked there."

"Where, Mom?"

"It seems, for no other reason, looking at that piece of iron fencing your father left leaning there."

Jerry hurried to the window to look out.

"That looks like either a '40 or '41 Chevy truck. It's missing a door," Jerry said. "Maybe they have a flat tire."

"I was looking at the lovely late summer colors on the side hill when I first saw them…oh, there they go. They're leaving."

"What would anyone want with a hunk of rusted fence?" Jerry asked.

"Your father asked Dick more than a week ago if he and friends could put that fencing in the barn garage. I think it's too heavy for them to carry, and they gave their pickup to Mrs. Holbrook."

"Maybe he's waiting for Conway or Dwyer to bring a tractor by to help lift it," Jerry said.

Missus turned and walked to the kitchen to water her African violet. "Finish the lemonade and brush your teeth."

"Huh? I brushed this morning."

"Do it again."

"I'll lose the taste of the lemonade."

"You're walking to Dr. Webb's for your checkup."

Jerry's day was officially off on the wrong foot. He had forgotten about the dentist.

"With all the lemonade you drink, it'll be a miracle if you don't have cavities. Dick went Saturday, had two cavities. Go brush and get ready."

"I'll take my bike."

"Walk."

"I can ride Jack."

"Walking is good for you. Let the bike and horse rest. You need the exercise. Young people today are spoiled by cars and bicycles chauffeuring them about. The walk will do you good. What did you do with the glass? Find it and put it in the kitchen. Rinse it. I don't want ants."

Like many mothers of the day, Missus thought having a boy walk everywhere in the country was good for the blood, somehow, like they were Buicks. Parents could ramble on about the mile they had to walk to school when they were kids.

Jerry liked the doc. He had a regular dentist office in Syracuse, but on the weekends he would see neighbors at his house up past Farmer Parker's and down a piece.

For dentistry he had a room with a chair in it. A person could sit there looking out the window at his ducks or fish and frog pond while he looked at their teeth.

Jerry walked to the front gate, turned left up the road past Farmer Parker's, on his way to the doc's. Just halfway up the hill he looked over Farmer Parker's cinder drive as he usually did, but this time he saw the old man slouching over, leaning against the back side of the barn.

"He's having a heart attack," Jerry said to himself.

On closer look he could see Farmer Parker's hand over the visor of his train engineer cap. He was looking around the corner of the barn. He caught Jerry's eye, stepped back behind the barn and waved at the lad to come running, motioning with a hammering arm wave for Jerry to keep low. In no time Jerry was standing beside Farmer Parker.

"Whatcha need?" Jerry asked.

Farmer Parker turned, leaned his back against the wall.

"Peek around the corner, Tall Jerry. Slow, real slow."

Jerry was getting spooked, but he looked.

"Tell me what you see under the bridge."

"Two old guys sitting under it, Farmer Parker."

"Thought so. Don't have my specks."

"They're on the cement ledge. One's writing on a scrap of paper, one's smoking a cigarette. No, wait, they're both smoking. There's an old, beat-up truck; looks like it's a '40, maybe a '41 Chevy sitting near the bridge, down just a way."

"That's their truck all right."

"Why's it parked down past our alfalfa field so far from the bridge?"

"Can't park on the bridge," Farmer Parker said.

"Wait a minute, that's the same truck my mom and I saw this morning by our front fence."

"It's the same truck, all right," Farmer Parker growled.

"If it's the same truck, it won't have a door on the other side," Jerry said. "The truck bed's filled with junk, tires and stuff."

"Stolen scraps—metal and tires, I reckon," Farmer Parker said.

"What would anyone want with a lot of old junk?" Jerry asked.

"Rubber and iron. They sell it."

"Somebody buys that junk?"

"They get good money for rubber and iron these days, selling it for scrap."

"You think they're stealing?"

"My eyes aren't as good as yours. Take another gander. See if you can see any milk cans on their truck," Farmer Parker said.

Jerry peered around the corner of the barn.

"I can see milk cans."

"Thought so. Take a good look. See if there's writing on them."

"Looks like four cans, but there may be cans buried under the junk. I can see two toward the back good. I think there's a capital C, and a capital F—maybe it's a P on both of them looks like, in black paint."

"Conway Farms, sure enough. The Conways are up on Route 80."

"Conway helped us catch the store burglars, remember?"

"Sure enough do," Farmer Parker said, kind of talking to Jerry, mumbling to himself, at the same time.

"They're not afraid of anything, the older guys," Jerry said.

"Is it clear to look?" Farmer Parker asked.

"Not yet."

Jerry slowly peered around again.

"They're driving off. Coast is clear now," Jerry reported.

Farmer Parker didn't look.

"They'll be back, those two, to get my cans, and to get your dad's iron fence, sure enough."

"Mom was watching them for the longest time. She wondered what they were up to. I got to get to the doc's. I'll come here after. We'll think up something, in case they come back."

"Oh, they'll be back, and I'll have my double barrel to welcome them," Farmer Parker said.

"Don't worry," Jerry said. "We can roust kids in the crown. Once we get the word out, there's no way those two crooks are going to get so much as an empty tin can out of any place around here anymore." Jerry snap-clicked his finger. "They'll come running, just like that. Meantime, don't do a thing, Farmer Parker."

Jerry headed out to the road, gave a wave and climbed up and over the hill, and down to the doc's.

Dr. Webb was a short, pleasant man with smiley teeth, a slight paunch and silver hair. He wore his glasses like his hero Teddy Roosevelt wore his—pinched on the bridge of his nose. He was outside on a stepladder in his starched and pressed khaki slacks and flannel lumberjack shirt, standing six rungs up. He was putting seed in the bird feeder near his pond. A blue jay was snapping loud, mean chirps from a branch nearby. The doc was interrupting his mealtime.

"Hi, Doc."

"Hello young fella! Is it that time already?"

"Yes sir."

"I need two more minutes. Go on in the kitchen, get yourself a fudge brownie or two from the missus while I finish here. I won't be long."

"Doc, how's it going to look with my mouth full of brownies with you trying to check my teeth for cavities?"

"You got a point, son."

"I brushed two times today."

The doc began to ramble like he hadn't had company in a while.

"We'll wrap a few for you to take home. How'd that be?"

"Thanks, Doc."

"Some maple sugar, too. I boiled a nice batch best spring freeze in years. A freeze after a thaw makes the syrup flow, you know."

"I know, Doc."

"Want to help hanging the sap buckets when it's nearing spring next year?"

"I'll help you, Doc."

"Goes faster with two. The trees are marked. We just look for the sugar maples with the shingle nail stuck in and the small piece of red ribbon tied on them."

"I'll help gather kindling for the sugar cabin fire, Doc. A lumberjack, Mr. Lance, will be leaving a lot of branches, I'm betting. Good firewood for your sugar cabin."

Folks in the hollow had a dentist who had a sweet tooth and didn't mind his patients having one, too.

Jerry liked sitting in his fancy dentist chair. It made him feel like Captain Video, the television character who told stories and showed old movies in the afternoon. He liked leaning back and watching the ducks swimming about, quacking and wobbling around in the pond.

"This won't hurt a bit," the doc promised.

The lad clenched the arms of the chair best he could.

The doc, as usual, was more or less right, because he'd say it after he pulled the needle back out of their gums. He'd never say it before he stuck the needle in. Doc Webb hated pain, and he didn't want to alarm a body. No sense thinking about something in advance of when you had to; you'd just fret, was his theory. He started ripping cotton from the roll and stuffing it around Jerry's gums, making his cheeks, which the lad couldn't feel now, puff out.

"Will you be wanting gold?" the doc asked with a snicker. He knew none of Jerry's family or most country patients ever got gold. But with the mention of gold, Jerry's brain sparked, and the lad tweaked his eyes about, thought of the thieves he saw under the bridge, and turned his head toward the doc.

His face was swollen with cotton and his mouth was numb, so there was no way anybody alive could tell what Tall Jerry was about to say next.

"Ewewww rot a dot uh guuuuld her noc?" he asked.

Danged if the doc didn't understand.

"I keep just enough to set a tooth or two," he said.

Jerry looked around at the doc and tried again.

"Yers rooks chrithin awont," he said.

This time the doc paused, looked over his specks at the lad, trying to decipher if he heard it right. He laid his tool down and handed a pad and pencil to Jerry.

Jerry wrote:

"Crooks—2 old men, old Chevy truck. Stealing!"

He handed the scribble, pencil and pad back to the doc. From there on out, Jerry didn't have to say a word. Doc Webb did all the talking.

"An old man with a beard, and a young buck whippersnapper— well, old to you maybe—why I saw that rattletrap heap of junk truck pass by here, slow, not only this morning, but last Saturday, too."

Jerry scribbled another note and handed it to the doc.

"Farmer Parker and I saw them under the bridge up by us."

"Sneaking about like a patrol truck, were they?" the doc asked.

Jerry nodded his head.

"Why, I bet they're looking slow and steady at everything they pass by, yessiree-bob. I thought their load looked like it didn't belong to them last week. They appeared too quick for me to see closeup this morning."

Jerry sat back, lost in thought.

"Can your boys club catch them, sure enough?"

Tall Jerry thought he'd save telling the doc about the club's girl president, Mary, and the club's coeducational status for another time.

"Unn-hunh," Jerry answered through the cotton.

"Bully!" Doc shouted.

The doc had a picture of Teddy Roosevelt on his wall right under a big American flag. Most knew he liked to shout "Bully" like Teddy, as if he was charging horseback with a bugle horn. The panes in the window shook with the bellow of his voice. Ducks outside could hear it and would straighten their necks and turn heads toward the window.

"You catch them scallywags, Tall Jerry. Give them a showing of what being on the wrong side of the law is about."

The doc paced back and forth, working himself into a lather.

"When your club comes up with a plan, come tell me and the missus, and we will do anything you need to help."

"Ehnn Ewe," Jerry said.

"Don't mention it," the doc answered.

The lad would have said more than a *thank you* but decided it best to come back another time when he could form words without dribbling water on his T-shirt or nibbling his lip trying to pronounce his consonants.

On the walk home, the numbness began to wear off when he started up over the hill by Farmer Parker's. He came down the other side. He walked in the cinder drive down behind the barn to find the old man hitching his horses, Sarge and Sally, to a buckboard wagon with a roll of barbed wire in the back. They were getting ready to fix fence up top of the hayfield.

"Don't worry, Farmer Parker. We'll come up with a plan to catch those crooks," Jerry said. "Even the doc wants to help. If you see those two again, call my mom, but don't tell her you saw them. Make something up. Tell her you need me to help milking or for pitching hay or something."

Jerry stepped around front of the horses and gave them each a brownie. They loved them, almost wanted to follow the lad home.

"What are you again?" Farmer Parker asked.

The old man didn't know Jerry's number. He had a telephone, probably never used it. But the lad knew what he meant.

"New Woodstock 78," Jerry said.

"Thankee, son."

Jerry walked up the cinder drive. Farmer Parker waved and slapped the reins.

"Let's go, Sarge."

The harness leather stretched along with the tinkle of harness chains as the horses started to pull the wagon away. Jerry bolted home, running as fast as he could.

"Finish packing your knapsack, Jerry. Mr. Holbrook will be here in twenty minutes."

"It's packed."

"Don't forget your toothbrush," Missus said. "It's on the sink."

"I'll get it."

"How are your teeth?"

"One. He filled it."

"Too much lemonade. Drink more milk."

Jerry went into his mom and dad's room and picked up the receiver.

"Operator."

"Myrtie, can you get me Barber, please?"

"Hello, young man. How do you like your summer job at that fancy Hotel Syracuse?" Myrtie asked.

"I like it a lot."

"How is everybody?"

"Everybody's fine."

"Is young Mike still in college coming this fall?"

"Yes, ma'am, he's still at Lemoyne in pre-med. Sometimes he brings me home from work."

"Hi to your mom. Here you go, honey," Myrtie said.

Jerry could hear the other end pick up with a barking dog in the background.

"Touser! Touser!" Mrs. Barber shouted into the telephone. "Will somebody come let this dog out? Hello?"

"Mrs. Barber, is Dale there?"

"Is this Tall Jerry?"

"Yes, ma'am."

"Honey, Dale is in the back pasture helping his dad and Art fix the electric wire fence for the bull pen they're putting up."

Jerry remembered Mr. Barber mentioning at the lunch table the farm had need of electric fencing. If an animal touched the electric fence wire, they'd get a shock to warn them to stay away. Barber touched one at Dwyer's one time and jumped a foot in the air. When Jerry asked how it felt, he said, "It won't kill you, but it'll make you wish it had."

"Can you tell him I called, Mrs. Barber?"

"Young Bobby is with them. He's such a sweet boy, that boy. God bless you for bringing him. Your momma and I had a good talk. What wonderful sons we have."

"Are they building a bull pen, Mrs. Barber?"

"We're trying to keep the bull from breaking through the back fence up along the Pompey Hollow. That old bull crosses the creek and leans into the fence, busting it and climbs the hill for the taller grass."

"Dale told me."

102

"They'll be home by supper."

"Mrs. Barber, can you tell him I called to set up a meeting? He'll know what that means."

"I will tell him."

"Tell him to make it after I get off work tomorrow. I'm going to Holbrook's and stay over tonight."

"You say hey to the Holbrook's for us, honey."

"I catch a ride to the hotel with Mr. Holbrook in the morning."

"I'll tell him, honey. Come see us and plan on pumpkin carving, for sure. Don't forget our full moon hayride with friends from all over is coming. It's harvest time."

"Yes ma'am. I'll be there. Thank you, Mrs. Barber. Bobby loves the farm. Is he getting used to things?"

"He's such a nice boy. He has a nightmare from time to time. I bring him warm bread, milk and sugar to settle him. He follows Dale around like a twin. I read to him and help him with his spelling for letters he writes to his father. Two of the boys from the orphanage write him postcards. He carries them in his back pocket, reads them over and over and writes them back. I give him postage to send to them. He's a good boy with a good heart. We've been blessed."

Jerry said his goodbye and walked down to the gate to wait for Mr. Holbrook.

CHAPTER 10

SCARED TO DEATH

Turning onto Berry Road with Tall Jerry, Mr. Holbrook looked up at the visor and snatched a slip of paper from it that caught his eye.

"Blast! The wife gave me a grocery list, knowing I had to go past Shea's Corner. I've got to run back for things I forgot."

He pulled up and braked by a tree next to the house.

"Go on in, Tall Jerry. The kids are either inside, up playing with Judy, or will be along soon. The wife went to Tully to pick Bob up from work. They'll be back."

"Thanks for the lift," Jerry said.

He got out and walked around back of the house, throwing his knapsack on the stoop. Most of the seventeen— Holbrooks and half brothers and sisters— were killing time before walking to friend's houses for a stay-over or waiting for a ride into Manlius's Suburban Park to walk around enjoying the lights, sights, sounds and the smell of cotton candy.

It weren't long before Mrs. Holbrook and the '38 Dodge pickup came pulling in. Holbrook jumped out, ducking back by the tree for good reason. It wasn't seconds when near half a dozen or more jumped by him like squirrels up a tree, climbing into the bed of the pickup or stuffing into the cab, to be hauled to where they were headed.

Mrs. Holbrook looked around, made a head count, studied the list on a piece of paper, and accounted for the kids absent and where they were. As the pickup backed out, Holbrook started and shouted for his mom to stop. He walked around, pulling something from his back pocket. It was his crumpled and folded up pay envelope from the Tully Bakery.

"Here," Holbrook said. "Pass it around so the kids can have pocket money. Maybe take Dad to a movie if he can stay awake. Get yourself something, Mom."

The woman clutched the crumpled envelope in her fist, wrinkled a happy eye trying to hold back a tear as she watched her son turn and walk away, slapping at his T-shirt, puffing the bakery flour off before going into the house. She knew there wasn't much in that envelope, but she knew it was all the boy had. The gesture alone meant more to her than having everything in the world ever could.

Now I'm just ole Charlie, ya know, dead and buried long before this ever happened—long before I became a guardian angel. You might take a lesson from this, the way it was with young people in those days—days when young ones thought more about people around them than they did about their own selves.

Holbrook walked to the stoop and sat down.

"Want to plink bulbs?" Holbrook asked.

"Sure," Tall Jerry said.

"I've got a new box of .22s and the board has fifteen light bulbs screwed in ready back at the tree line," Holbrook said.

"Maybe Wednesday I'll have another carton of bulbs to bring from the hotel. I'm only working there another two weeks."

"Why only two weeks?"

"Mom wants me to have time off before school starts. I'll bring as many as I can load up."

"We can use them," Holbrook said.

"Go get the rifle, and let's shoot bulbs," Jerry said.

"Want to slide the falls after?" Holbrook asked.

Now the Delphi Falls behind Tall Jerry's house was near seventy feet tall, and near straight up. The four waterfalls in the woods be-

105

hind Holbrook's place were lower, slanted and smooth—good for sliding down.

"Sure."

Holbrook looked up at the horizon.

"It'll be getting dark."

"So?"

"There won't be sun to dry us after we slide. I'm getting a towel. You want one?"

"Get me one," Jerry said.

Holbrook grabbed Tall Jerry's knapsack to take upstairs. Jerry walked around under the tree, staring at the cemetery across Berry Road. The lad could imagine Revolutionary War soldiers and their families resting there. Holbrook pulled the upstairs bedroom window open to let in the near dusk breeze. He threw two towels for Jerry to catch. They swirled about and landed on the ground. Wasn't long before he came down and handed Jerry a box of bullets.

"Open this and give me one at a time; I'll load the rifle. I need eight."

Holbrook was sporting his new .22 semiautomatic rifle. No cocking the bolt needed. Just pull the trigger, one shot at a time. A rifle to folks around the crown was not a luxury. It was food, plain as day. A rifle that reloaded automatically could mean more food from a hunt, and Holbrook was good with it. Squirrels and rabbits mostly. His food-hunting secrets were simple: don't waste bullets unless you're target practicing; never shoot into a horizon lest you want to kill a cow or a farmer on the other side of the hill without knowing it; make sure squirrels weren't on the nest early spring with young ones, and let a rabbit run (it'll run full circle around you every time and stop). When a rabbit starts running turn around, take aim and wait. You're sure to have rabbit stew.

Holbrook handed Jerry the loaded rifle to hold and took the box of bullets and was stuffing it in his back pocket when Tommy Kellish puttered onto the side lawn driving his daddy's Ford tractor.

He pulled to a stop, pushed the clutch, set the brake, shut her down and jumped off.

"Where is everybody?" Kellish asked.

Kellish was speakin' of the Holbrook and Bradshaw girls. He had a fancy for a pretty face and there were a lot of pretty faces at this particular rural route number on Berry Road.

"It's Saturday," Holbrook said. "No telling."

"I came to tell you Barber called a club meeting tomorrow—noon at the cemetery," Kellish said, "Mary's dad said he will be by here at eleven thirty to get you but you're on your own for a ride back home. That's all I know."

Unspoken rule was nobody talked about anything outside of the meetings, so Jerry kept still. Oh, he'd spill about the crooks to Holbrook, his best friend, when they were alone. For now, he was passing time admiring the workmanship of the rabbit and squirrel rifle his friend had asked him to hold. It was a mighty good thing he was admiring the black plastic butt pad on the gun stock and that the rifle barrel was pointing down, for somehow the gun went off with a loud *BANG!*

"What in the hell!?" Holbrook yelled.

It startled the boys out of a few years and up off the ground in a jump, each a wondering if they'd been shot and where. The spent brass bullet casing sprung out, twirling from the chamber ejector and ricocheting off Kellish's belt buckle before dropping to the ground. A smoky puff of gunpowder drifted up into their nostrils.

Tall Jerry dang near fainted and immediately went on the defensive.

"I didn't think the gun was loaded," Jerry pleaded.

Kellish bent over, looking down to see if he was hit anywhere important and checking to see if his pants were dry at the same time.

"You handed me the stupid bullets to load it," Holbrook reminded him.

"Yeah, but I didn't cock the bolt," Jerry said, his argument crumbling.

"It's semiautomatic. It cocks itself."

Holbrook grabbed the rifle, pointed its barrel down and flipped the safety lock.

The boys, hearts pounding like bass drums, looked around the ground between them to see where the bullet hit and how close their feet were at the time and who could have lost a toe. They were still shaking, feeling mighty lucky, and learning the lesson never ever to put a bullet in the gun until they were ready to fire it.

Kellish mounted the tractor and headed back to his farm.

"I'll be ready for Mr. Crane tomorrow," Holbrook repeated.

He picked up and handed Jerry the towels to carry and they headed toward the tree line near the sliding falls for target practice.

"I don't feel like shooting anymore," Tall Jerry said.

"You scared?" Holbrook asked.

"Let's just slide the falls."

Holbrook stopped walking, turned the gun on its side and emptied the magazine and chamber by clicking each bullet out, sending them flying to the ground.

"Scared the crap out of me," Jerry said. "Go put it away."

He picked the bullets up and handed them to Holbrook. The rifle was returned to the house, and this time the boys went out front and up Berry Road to the small bridge over the swimming hole called Berwyn bathtub. It was by the Revolutionary War cemetery. From there they waded downstream to where the four falls were behind the property. It was shallow from this side of the bridge to the top of the falls. Jerry liked finding fossils underfoot from prehistoric times. They were what was left from the great ice glaciers that formed the hills, falls and streams of the area. He'd pick one up, examine it and pitch it to the creek bank to come back and get later, 'cept he'd usually forget.

At the longest falls, the boys stripped to their skivvies and slid down and climbed up a passel of times. Holbrook was good enough to slide standing up and balancing barefoot. Tall Jerry sat for the ride down, leaning back with his legs up. They spent time returning to the innocence of their childhood, putting the edginess of growing up and talk of whiskers behind them for the moment. Here's when they knew times were changing, and they promised to be there for each other for life no matter where life took them.

With the fun, the sunset had come and gone unnoticed and the glow of the moon was all that lighted the way for the boys to climb the creek bank onto the field and pull their jeans on close to the back tree line and to ring out their wet underwear, towel their hair off, and pull their sneaks on.

Holbrook was toweling his head, looking off the hundred yards to the left to see if there were lights on at the house. Then he looked down the tree line about the same distance.

He stopped rubbing his head, looked down the tree line again, turned, grabbed Jerry's shoulder and yelled in a loud whisper,

"Get down!"

"Huh?" Jerry asked.

"Quick! Get down!"

Holbrook yanked Tall Jerry's T-shirt by the shoulder and pulled. They both dropped to the ground.

"What's wrong?" Jerry asked.

"Wait! Be quiet! Don't move!" Holbrook grunted.

Fear came over them like a low-flying fog creeping into a musty cemetery.

"The boulder behind us," Holbrook whispered.

"What about it?"

"Back by the bank; the rock near the middle falls," Holbrook whispered.

"I know it," Jerry said.

"Keep down and slide back to it."

"Now?"

"Get behind it, but for creep's sake stay down and be quiet," Holbrook said.

The boys edged on their elbows and stomachs, rolling backward like caterpillars toward the boulder twenty feet behind them.

"Leave the underwear, towels and sneakers," Holbrook said. "They'll be like flags in the dark. Leave them."

Now Tall Jerry was scared, ain't no two ways about it, and he weren't sure why. But because of the boys' time in the woods, stalking crows for hours on end, watching beavers build dams without being seen or heard, they trusted each other. They were of one mind in the woods. They'd never question one another's instincts for survival. Once behind the boulder, Holbrook sat up and rested his back against the stone.

"I think I saw a dead body," Holbrook said.

"Holy crap."

"No crap, holy crap," Holbrook said.

"I was afraid it was something like that," Jerry groaned.

"Not in a million years…" Holbrook started.

"Wait, do you mean a dead body like a dead animal body or—"

"A dead person body."

"Holy crap," Jerry said.

"I saw legs—naked, dead legs."

"We've gotta run," Tall Jerry said.

"It's lying over there in the corner right where the tree line and the other end of the field meet up."

"Holy crap!" Jerry repeated.

Holbrook turned slowly and lifted up to look over the boulder.

"Let's go tell your dad," Jerry said.

"Hold on, let's look."

"Please, let's go get your dad."

"I'm looking," Holbrook said. He shaded his glasses with his hands so a glare reflecting off them wouldn't give them away.

Together the boys edged their way up the back side of the boulder, leaning their heads at an angle so one eye and their jaw might be the only thing rising above the rock. Off in the distance there was no doubt. A partly naked body was lying at the edge of the woods behind the field.

"Maybe a hunter killed him by accident and didn't know," Jerry said. "Your gun went off on me and if it was pointing up it could have hit somebody a mile away, even killed them without our knowing."

"Maybe he was murdered in Syracuse and dumped out of somebody's trunk," Holbrook said.

"Cut it out," Jerry said.

"Left to rot or to get eaten by wolves or pigs, so there's no evidence," Holbrook said.

"I wonder why it's naked?" Jerry asked.

The two shivered with a cold fear, their faces growing pale. They turned and slid back down. This was a situation they couldn't dream happening. They searched their brains, trying not to waste time on worthless suggestions. They were both coming to the same conclusion that they should tell a parent.

"Let's look again," Holbrook said.

Tall Jerry agreed this time, his adrenalin pumping. They watched the lifeless body lying alone in the cold night air. A breeze was flapping the shirt tail.

"It's not naked. I think the dead guy is wearing shorts," Holbrook said.

"Maybe he drowned swimming," Jerry said.

"In the middle of a field!?"

The boys' hearts felt sorrow for the lifeless body's loneliness out there. It became a person—someone they didn't know—wondering who it was, where it came from. Then, just as they were about to turn and sit back down again, a figure of a man stepped out into the clearing at the far corner of the field and walked toward the body.

"Holy crap!" Jerry said.

"Keep it down," Holbrook said.

"We've got to tell somebody," Jerry said.

"It's the murderer," Holbrook said.

Praying they wouldn't be seen by a cold-blooded murderer, they studied the man walking over to the body, how he looked down at it, how he stepped around it in a full circle. He seemed to point to the woods.

"Duck down," Holbrook whispered.

Holbrook reached over and squeezed Jerry's arm.

"No sound. Don't move," he whispered.

They peered over the boulder again.

The man knelt, his back to the body. He grabbed the body's arms behind him and slung them over his shoulders, lifted himself up and the body on his back along with him. Long hair flowed from the head of the body. The boy's hearts dropped into their stomachs.

"It's a girl," Holbrook whispered.

"You sure?" Jerry asked.

"It's a dead girl. Look at her long hair."

The man stood with a forward lean, the body on his back as he staggered, trying to keep his balance; the bare legs and feet of the dead girl swaying back and forth, limp and lifeless, her ankles turning in and out like they were broken. Once he had his footing, the man carried the corpse into the darkness and shadows of the woods, and out of sight.

"Let's go!" Holbrook whispered, "Run like blazes!"

Tall Jerry jumped to his feet, not taking his eyes off the other end of the field.

"Stay low, grab the stuff. Don't leave any clues that we were here or that they've been seen," Holbrook said.

Hearts pumping like Ford pistons the two ran barefoot, holding their breaths to get away without making loud breathing sounds. They followed the creek's tree line, shaded from the moon back to the house. Jumping to the top step, they bolted in and upstairs to Holbrook and his brothers, Dickie's and Ronnie's, bedroom. They knelt on the floor with the room light off to catch their breath, leaning on the bed, holding their faces and panting like racehorses after a full gallop.

"We can't tell anyone about this," Holbrook panted.

"I think we have to," Jerry said.

"Not a soul."

"We could get into big trouble if we don't."

"We can't tell," Holbrook said.

"I got in trouble not telling about taking Bobby to Barber's—big trouble—even with my dad. This is a lot more serious."

"That body isn't going anywhere. It's dead," Holbrook said.

"Well no shit, Sherlock!" Jerry barked.

"We'll tell the club tomorrow and then decide what to do. Maybe then we tell somebody."

"I don't know," Jerry said.

"We can catch the murderer and get a reward," Holbrook said.

"Did you get a good look at him?" Jerry asked.

"We know it's a guy, and we know where he's burying the body. All we have to do is find a fresh-dug dirt pile or a stack of rocks over the grave or a bed of lye," Holbrook said.

"What do you mean a bed of lye?"

The boys shuffled on their butts in the dark over to the bedroom window and stared out across the back field to the tree line.

"Lye, it's white. You can't miss it. Lye will eat up a body, clothes and everything—all the evidence. Lye leaves nothing but bone dust," Holbrook said. "It would just look like old dried up deer bone dust."

"Don't turn the light on," Jerry said. "That guy could see up here and identify our faces and come after us."

"You're right," Holbrook said. "He won't want witnesses."

"What was he pointing at? He was pointing at something."

"Getting a fix, probably," Holbrook said.

"A fix?"

"Sun was down, moon was up. He knew where he was going to bury the body. He couldn't take a chance of being seen, so he had to do it without a flashlight. He had to get a fix on what direction to go in the dark to get to the place. He pointed to get a fix where he needed to go, and then he'd keep his eyes on the direction he pointed and try to carry the body in a straight line."

"I do that sometimes—you're right," Jerry said.

The boys sat in silence. They hadn't experienced anything violent like this other than in movie newsreels of the war.

"You ever been this scared?" Jerry asked.

Holbrook didn't answer. He peered out the window.

"I remember being scared of the woods when we first moved to Delphi Falls," Jerry said. "I used to have to walk to Charlie Pitts's place to get the eggs."

"I know," Holbrook said.

"Charlie talked me into not being afraid of the woods and noises and what to do. I sure wish he was here now, ole Charlie."

"How could he help?" Holbrook asked.

"He'd tell us what to do," Jerry said.

"Don't say anything until tomorrow," Holbrook said.

"I'm only saying Charlie could maybe have told us what we should do," Jerry said.

"But Charlie's not here," Holbrook snapped.

Ole Charlie was there all right. First rule for a guardian angel being no whispering in their ear, but ain't no rule says I can't tear up if others have a good word for me. It's nice to be remembered.

"Why are you so edgy?" Jerry asked.

"If the girl was alive and the murderer was hurting her, sure, we'd run in with clubs and help her, but she's dead."

"I still can't believe…" Jerry started.

"Worst thing we could do is scare him off before we can catch him," Holbrook said.

"You do the talking tomorrow," Tall Jerry said.

"We'll know when the time is right to tell them," Holbrook said.

"I'm not saying a word," Jerry said.

"It may not be until after Mary lets us know what the meeting is about. We have to handle this just right or we'll spook them into blabbing it to their folks."

"I know what it's about," Jerry said.

"You know what *what* is about?"

"The meeting tomorrow."

"How do you know?"

"I'm the one who asked Barber to call it."

"What's it about?"

"Crooks are stealing stuff all over the place."

"How do you know?"

"Farmer Parker and the doc saw them. They say the crooks are stealing and selling stuff for salvage; metal and rubber."

"So, we'll tell them about the murder after that," Holbrook said.

"We need to catch them, the crooks," Tall Jerry said.

"We need to catch this murderer, too," Holbrook said.

"Yes," Jerry said. "But I'm scared."

"Okay, but swear we don't say a word about the murder until we're in the cemetery tomorrow and then only after the other business. I have to think on how to bring it up."

"You do the talking," Jerry said.

"Swear?" Holbrook asked.

"I swear," Jerry said.

The lads shook on it, sitting in the dark, staring out under the moon, looking for signs of life at the back-tree line. They thought of the girl's body alone and cold.

"I wonder how old she was," Jerry said.

CHAPTER 11

PLANS OF PRESIDENTS

Mr. Holbrook was in the car, warming it up for the ride into Syracuse when Jerry climbed in. They pulled off the lawn and onto Berry Road.

"Mr. Holbrook, has there been murders on trains you ride?"

Mr. Holbrook was caught by surprise so early.

"Trains are like cities, son—cities that have no countries moving on their own steam. Only the rails hear the secrets. If there was a murder and say a body dropped out while we were crossing a high bridge climbing a mountain pass over a gorge, there'd be no way of knowing, I suppose."

"I read about a murder on a train in a Sherlock Holmes," Jerry said.

"There was a time back in the Great Depression," Mr. Holbrook said, "railroad owners hired thugs to beat up hobos and vagrants setting on the boxcars and riding the rails. Maybe shoot them for trespass, kill them dead. That's when the country was out of work."

"Did they really shoot them for riding the rails?"

"I never understood how they could call that depression great. It sure wasn't all that great, if you ask me. Not so much the killing anymore, but they will take a billy club to someone riding a boxcar with no money for a ticket, that's for sure."

The car pulled in front of the Hotel Syracuse employee entrance.

"How you getting home today?"

"It's Dick's turn to get me. Thanks for the ride, Mr. Holbrook."

Jerry watched the car drive off and jumped down the steps into the hotel's basement. He didn't go for the mop and bucket first as usual on this Sunday. He shuffled through trash barrels that were on the elevator for a newspaper—yesterday's, today's—it didn't matter. He grabbed one and unfolded it on the floor in the best light and knelt over it, scouring the headlines page after page, running his finger down the columns looking for a story about a murder or a missing person and a police hunt. No luck. He put the paper back in a trash container and spent more time than usual nervously walking the halls, turning on lights. He hadn't slept well, thinking of the dead girl and dreaming of corpses. He picked scraps from the floor, hot mopped them to a glistening shine and went up to the street to wait for Dick.

Dick was already sitting there in his car, the '38 Willys.

Jerry jumped in.

"I can't go to Mass today," Jerry blurted.

"What's up?" Dick asked.

"I have to get to the cemetery."

"What's going on?"

"Are you going to tell on me?"

"Why would I tell? I'm scrubbing pots at the Lincklaen House, starting at one. Only reason I was going to Mass was to take you."

"Take me to the cemetery."

Dick lit a cigarette, rested his elbow out the driver's window, and puffed away, looking at his image in the rearview mirror, trying to look older than sixteen.

"Who makes Willys?" Jerry asked.

"Best car sixty-five dollars could buy, this Willys," Dick said. "It's a '38, built when cars were cars. Every cylinder in this engine has two spark plugs. No other car like it. This car will run forever."

"Can I ask you something?" Jerry asked.

"You can try."

"What makes you and Duba not afraid of anything?"

118

"Huh?"

"How come you get away with murder, and we get caught?"

"Being sixteen is a lot different than being twelve," Dick said.

"That's not an answer. You've been in trouble ever since we moved to Delphi Falls. You get away with everything."

"If we got away with everything we'd never be in trouble, now would we?"

"That's not what I'm asking. How is it you guys aren't afraid to do stuff most of us are chicken to do?"

"The war," Dick said.

"That's not true. We remember the war, too. My friends remember it."

"You were too young to go to war," Dick said.

"What do you mean?"

"You never had to think about being drafted."

"They didn't draft kids," Jerry said.

"The Nazis were drafting twelve-year-olds in the war?"

"For real?"

"If it kept going, Duba, Dwyer, Conway, and I could have been drafted to fight."

"There's no way."

"What do you mean, no way?"

"This is America."

"So?"

"Ain't no way they would have drafted a thirteen-year-old here in America. Only eighteen-year-olds."

"It's a fact! The army drafted seventeen-year-old guys in 1944 and '45, made them go."

"They did?"

"We were running out of soldiers, so they dropped the draft age from eighteen to seventeen. That age could have gone down more."

"Is that the truth?"

"Truth."

"So, you guys take chances because you were afraid you could be drafted in the war or because you weren't drafted?"

"We got cheated."

"Cheated from dying?"

"Cheated from seeing the world. There'll never be another war like that, ever. We're stuck here."

"Why won't there be another war?"

"A world war, there won't. Jet planes and the hydrogen bomb changed everything," Dick said.

"What?!"

"There are jets and hydrogen bombs today."

Dick took a drag on his cigarette and exhaled, staring blankly out the front window. Jerry let it be. He understood for the first time the older guys playing chicken with their cars. They felt rooked out of a chance to become heroes.

"Dick, what if I told you we have the biggest SOS you guys could ever dream about? Could you get off work to hear about it?" Jerry asked.

"How big?"

"Bigger than you could imagine."

"Big enough for me, Duba, Conway and Dwyer—all of us?"

"Way bigger."

"I'll need more than that to go on—if I take time off from work. I need the money."

"It'll be worth taking off."

"Give me a hint—a clue or something."

"Promise you won't say anything?"

"Nuts to you," Dick blurted.

Dick was offended. His friends had a code of honor and they lived by it. He pitched a spent cigarette out the window and lit another one.

"Murder," Jerry said.

120

Dick started, jerked his head around, and looked Jerry in the eye. "Yeah, sure."

"Murder."

"For real?"

"For real."

"Who?"

"We don't know."

"Tell me where you want us and when," Dick said.

"Well, there's two things, the murder and something else, too—not as big as the murder," Jerry said.

"Where and when?"

"We're meeting at noon. Let us do the talking first and then you guys come at twelve thirty. Pretend you don't know anything what I just said, and that's when we'll tell you about the murder and the other stuff we got. Maybe you can help keep everybody from wanting to tell the police about it until we want them to know."

"Who else knows about the murder?"

"Only me and Holbrook."

Dick pulled into the ESSO gas station in Manlius and went in to get a pack of cigarettes from the vending machine while his gas was being pumped and his window squeegeed by the attendant.

As Dick pulled into the cemetery, he backed out to turn around. Jerry started to step out of the car and paused.

"Dick, any of you guys have a gun?"

"Only dad's old foldup four-ten."

"Where is it?"

"I sold it to Duba."

"You sold Dad's shotgun?"

"Sold it."

"I wanted that gun. Does Dad know you sold it?"

"He'd better never find out."

"Why'd you sell it?"

"I wanted a carton of cigarettes and Duba needed a shotgun to shoot a dog."

"What dog?"

"He gave me a buck eighty-five for it."

"What dog?"

"It was a good swap and Dad better not find out it's gone if you know what's good for you– besides, he never used it, anyway. He left it under the seat of his Oldsmobile."

"What did Duba do with it?"

"Duba shot the dog; walked in on it with blood and feathers over its face after it had killed eighteen of their good laying hens. It would have killed hundreds if Duba hadn't walked in on him."

"Whose dog was it?"

"A neighbor's—across the road. Duba had warned him plenty to keep his dog home and that he would shoot it if he kept getting into the chicken barn. The neighbor didn't listen, so—boom!"

"You guys will need the gun, better tell Duba to bring it," Jerry said. "I'm thinking the murderer may have a gun."

"We'll have it," Dick said.

"Don't forget to wait until twelve thirty or after before you come in. We'll be meeting back near Charlie Pitts's stone."

Jerry walked up the cemetery drive listening to voices in the foreground. Holbrook and Mayor were throwing pine cones over a branch. Barber was flipping mumblety-peg with his jackknife. Mary was reading. As Jerry neared, they stood, settled, and gathered around.

Mary started.

"I know you have something, Tall Jerry. I got a letter from my pen pal. Who goes first?"

The lads were impressed and told their president to go ahead.

"Let's hear the letter," Mayor said.

"Okay, here goes," Mary said. She pulled a folded sheet of paper from an envelope.

"Dear Pen Pal Mary,

Thank you for writing me. How are you? I am fine. I live on a farm. My grandfather is famous, but I am not supposed to brag so I can't tell you about him. Maybe someday my father will be a general, too. Do you have any brothers or sisters? Please write soon. Yours truly, your pen pal David Eisenhower"

"That's from the kid you told us about?" Holbrook asked.

"Well, yeah!" Mary said.

"He's like the grandson of the president," Mayor said.

"I'm confused," Tall Jerry said. "Wasn't the president a general? Wasn't he General Eisenhower at Normandy? What's he saying about his father being a general?"

"It didn't say that. Both his father and grandfather are soldiers," Mary said. "It's just that one is a general and he's the president now. I think his dad is like a major."

"Can I hold the letter?" Mayor asked. "The president of the United States may have touched it."

The boys were impressed. Each in turn held and admired the letter Mary received from her pen pal.

"Tall Jerry, you called the meeting," Mary said. "What's up?"

"There are these two guys, driving around. We think they're stealing metal and rubber. My mom saw them first. Farmer Parker has seen them. I saw them. They're old guys. Even Doc Webb saw them. They had milk cans from Conway's farm on their truck."

"Where did you see them?" Barber asked.

"Under the bridge by our alfalfa field. They were sitting under there, smoking cigarettes. Their truck was parked down the road maybe fifty feet," Jerry said.

"Sounds like an SOS. Who wants to vote *yay*?" Mary asked.

Every hand went up.

"Tall Jerry, tell Dick about it and see if the older guys will take it on as an SOS," Mary said.

Two cars drove into the cemetery. It was Dick with Dwyer and Duba and Conway in his new Chevy. Jerry looked at Holbrook, signaled him to get ready to do the talking.

"I told Dick we had something to talk about. That's why they're here," Jerry said.

The cars stopped a good thirty feet back. They got out, walked the last thirty feet side-by-side in their headlights, strutting with the confidence of gunfighters walking into a gunfight.

"Listen up!" Duba barked.

"Let's hear it!" Dick said.

Holbrook stepped around Mary to the front. He stretched his neck to look down the cemetery drive making certain no one else was listening or coming in.

"We think we saw a murder," Holbrook said.

"What!?" Mary shrieked along with Barber and Mayor shouting in unison, completely blindsided.

"Well, we didn't actually see the murder, but we know we saw a dead body and we saw the murderer carrying it into the woods to bury it," Holbrook said.

"Who?"

"We don't know."

They stepped in closer.

"Where?" Dick asked.

"Berry Road," Holbrook said.

"That's a long road," Duba said.

"The big field behind our house."

"Your place is at the Berwyn bathtub, right?" Dick asked.

"On the west side of Berry Road, but yes," Holbrook said.

"The body was lying back of the field behind our house in a corner by the tree line."

"What makes you think it was a dead body?" Duba asked.

124

"Oh, it was dead all right," Tall Jerry said.

"The legs were like rubber and the ankles looked like they were both broken, just flopping around when the murderer carried the body," Holbrook said.

"It was dead all right," Jerry repeated.

"Why do you think it's buried in the woods?" Dick asked.

"It has to be—buried or under lye or rocks or something," Holbrook said.

"But you don't know that," Dick said.

"We know it's a girl," Holbrook said.

"A girl?" Mary exclaimed. "A dead girl?"

"We could see her long hair," Jerry said.

"Did you see any cars around?" Dick asked.

"We ran like all get-out. We weren't looking for cars," Holbrook said.

"We were too scared," Jerry said.

"She was dead," Holbrook said.

"It scared the crap out of us," Jerry said.

"We have to tell someone," Mary said.

"Hold on," Dick said.

"If this is murder, we need to tell the sheriff," Mary said.

"Not yet," Dick said.

"We could get in all sorts of trouble not telling this," Mary said.

"Isn't there a law that says we have to tell the police if we know something like this?" Barber asked.

"You want our help or not?" Dick asked. "I could be earning money at the Lincklaen House."

"What if the dead girl is somebody we know?" Mayor asked.

"She'll be from Syracuse or Cortland," Conway said. "Nobody around here's going to be murdering anyone. They maybe want to, but it just won't happen around here."

"People in the crown are different," Jerry said.

"The crown? What the heck is the crown?" Duba barked.

125

"I invented it when we moved here. I was trying to explain the crown to Charlie Pitts. I traced a line to where my new friends lived. It looked like a crown when I was a kid. I pretended I lived in a crown."

"Shut up everybody!" Holbrook shouted.

"You shut up," Duba barked.

"Just shut up and we want your guys help. Like it or not, this is an SOS, so none of us can turn it down."

"We've got to know more," Conway said.

"We don't know more. We only know what we saw. We think we saw a dead body and somebody carrying it off to bury it. How stupid will that sound telling it to the sheriff?"

"He's right," Mary said. She paused in thought. "We could make it an SOS, but only on one condition, or I'll have to tell my folks."

"What's the condition?" Dick asked.

"Today is Sunday. If we don't know any more than we do on Wednesday, we have to tell the sheriff," Mary said.

"By Wednesday?" Dick asked.

"We have to agree to that or it's no deal."

"Or we at least have to tell our parents by Wednesday and let them tell the sheriff," Mayor said.

"Wait here," Dick said.

Dick, Duba, Conway, and Dwyer stepped back by a nest of pine trees to talk in secret.

Ole Charlie here is a pleasant-spirited guardian angel, but in the middle of a murder, the ghostly part of my nature comes up from my grave and joins me, ready to howl. I followed the four of them back to the pine trees to have a listen.

Dick told his friends what Jerry and he had talked about in the car and that he thought it was for real and asked if he could borrow Duba's dad's black rain slicker, case he needed it. Duba said yes. It was hanging in their chicken barn, and they agreed the murder was worth looking into, and they had nothing else to do, anyway.

They walked back to the group.

"It's a deal," Dick said. "We have until Wednesday."

"Yes, Wednesday," Mary said.

"Now listen up!" Duba yelled.

"The full moon will be gone in two days," Dick said. "We need darkness. The quarter moon will do it. We meet up at midnight on Tuesday. Be on the bridge at the Berwyn bathtub next to the Holbrook's. Midnight on Tuesday. Get dropped off if you have to, but no cars park there. We don't want to raise suspicion."

"Good place," Mary said.

"Nobody else is to know about it—not a soul."

"Our regulars will be there," Mary said.

"Okay, those and just whoever is here is to know about any of this," Dick said.

"Right," Mary said.

"Don't anyone wear white or light," Dick said.

"Why no white? My T-shirt's white," Holbrook said.

"Wear dark colors. If you don't have dark colors borrow something dark or roll in the mud or stay home. We don't want to get caught," Dick said.

"Caught by who?" Mayor asked nervously.

"We don't want to be easy targets in the dark," Duba said.

"Are you sure we should be doing this?" Mayor asked.

Mary turned to the club members. "Who's in? Let me see a show of hands."

Everyone raised a hand.

"Spit!" she said.

"What?!" Barber asked.

"Spit!" Mary said.

The club had stopped spitting on pledges years back. This time Mary used it as a reminder of how important this mission was about to be.

Every member spat.

Mary turned back to the older guys. "We'll be there," she said. "Berwyn bathtub, midnight on Tuesday."

"On the bridge," Dick said.

"Yes, on the bridge," Mary said.

The older guys turned and walked away. Dick paused and stepped back.

"Jerry, what was the other thing you were going to tell us?" Dick asked.

"Two old guys in a stake-bed—I'm thinking it's a '41 Chevy—are stealing things, metal and rubber scraps from around here."

"How do you know they're stealing?" Dick asked.

"Mom saw them looking at the iron fence you and Duba were supposed to put in the barn garage."

"We needed four to lift it," Dick said. "I doubt they could have stolen it if there was only the two of them."

Conway stepped back and stood with Dick.

"Farmer Parker saw them looking at it like they wanted it."

"That's not proof they were stealing," Dick said.

"Doc Webb saw them looking at things. I saw them smoking under the bridge."

"Still no proof," Conway said.

"Yeah? They had milk cans from Conway Farms on the truck," Tall Jerry said.

"So that's where our cans have been going," Conway said. "I wondered what was happening—and they sure aren't scrap."

"Proof, right?" Jerry asked.

"Where did you see them?"

"They were sitting under Parker's and our bridge, smoking. And one was reading a folded-up piece of paper. They parked down past the alfalfa field. The truck is missing a door," Jerry said.

"We'll check it out, but keep this murder top secret from now through to midnight on Tuesday, do we understand?"

"We understand," Mary said.

128

"Don't even talk about this among yourselves," Duba said.

"Loose lips sink ships!" Barber said.

The meeting adjourned. The kids could sense the seriousness. Murder was not a laughing matter. Holbrook caught a ride to Tully with Duba to go to work at the bakery; Mayor caught a ride to Penoyer Road with Conway; Mary and Barber started walking toward the hamlet. Mary had popsicles to sell before summer ended, and Barber had farm chores to do. Jerry climbed the back hill and headed for home.

Coming down the other side, Jerry could see over Farmer Parker's barn and house. He could see his house at the Delphi Falls across the road. He could see the small bridge and the alfalfa field. There was an old pickup truck pulling what looked to him like a large horse trailer. It was stopped off the road, right by the alfalfa field gate.

Jerry had forgotten this was the day Mr. Lance was coming. The lumber man was dropping off his workhorse. Jerry could see him walking the fence lines in the alfalfa field, examining it, most likely being certain the fence posts were in good repair. Jerry high-tailed it down the hill in a pant and then up the small knoll, running through Farmer Parker's back and front yards. He waved at Mrs. Parker coming home from church, taking her bonnet off. He jumped onto Cardner Road and dashed down it to the alfalfa field. He caught the man's eye.

"Lock the gate behind you young man!" Mr. Lance shouted.

"Are you Mr. Lance?" Jerry asked.

"I am indeed," Mr. Lance said. "And who might you be, my good man?"

"I'm Jerry."

"Nice to make your acquaintance, young man, Jerry."

Jerry strapped the gate secure and walked over to a wagon so large it could have been a circus wagon.

"You must be Big Mike's older son, Jerry."

"I'm twelve."

"My goodness, you are a tall one."

"My friends call me Tall Jerry."

Mr. Lance shook Jerry's hand.

"Well, it's good to meet you, Tall Jerry."

On Mr. Lance's command, a horse slowly backed out of the trailer and down the ramp behind it onto the field. Jerry watched in amazement.

This animal was huge, twice the size of Farmer Parker's work horses. Taller and one or two feet wider, it seemed.

"Tall Jerry, meet Molly," Mr. Lance said.

Almost like a ringmaster at a circus, Mr. Lance lifted his cap, tilted it hello and went on to show off his horse, explaining that Molly was a genuine one-of-a-kind trained lumberjack's workhorse who liked to play, loved kids, and wouldn't hurt a flea. He mentioned that in weeks away his logging team would be going into woods around the area, cutting and hauling timber out for farmers.

"Big Mike was gracious enough to let us use the field for Molly in the meantime," Mr. Lance said. "We'll be cutting fifty to sixty trees throughout the area this fall, and Molly here will haul them out, dragging them behind her with a log chain."

Molly lowered her huge head, almost like she was taking a bow; then she stretched her neck out and down, letting Jerry scratch under her chin.

"I know Molly looks big and fearsome to most, Tall Jerry," Mr. Lance said, "but never you mind that, young man. Put the thought out of your mind. She's gentle as a lamb, loves to be ridden bareback, and can hold maybe five or six at a time."

"Can Molly drag a tree by herself?" Jerry asked in amazement.

The lad had taken notice that Molly's back stood taller than the pickup truck that pulled the trailer she rode in.

"Young man," Mr. Lance said. He paused with pride. "She can."

"Wow," Jerry said.

"I know it's hard to believe, but yes, she surely can. Why, this lady could go through a closed barn door if she had half a mind to, I reckon."

"Is Molly afraid of anything, like snakes or noises?"

"Nary a thing, son. Snakes are afraid of her. And the more noise the better. In fact, she likes it."

"Lightning?" Jerry inquired.

"A lightning storm has been known to lull her to sleep. She's used to trees crashing down and my yelling…"

Mr. Lance paused again and cautioned Jerry to step back a bit for a demonstration.

"Stand back, son, and let me demonstrate." Mr. Lance raised his voice and hollered long and loud:

"TIMMMMMMMMMMMMBERRRRRRRR!"

At the sound of this Molly bolted tall, turned a full circle with her head high in the air, her ears twisting in happy excitement, her eyes twitching and nostrils flaring. She was filling with an air of anticipation, as though she were looking out for a tree to crash down around her somewhere any second now, and couldn't wait to get hitched up to drag it out of the woods. While turning around—her feet stomping on the field—her big rump bumped against the rounded front fender of the old pickup truck, taking the tire off the ground and bouncing it back down, jiggling and shaking the truck so much that dust came off it in a cloud of poofs.

"God, that word makes her one happy lady!" Mr. Lance said, grinning.

Mr. Lance raised and fastened the back gate on the horse trailer and walked around to the side of the bed of his pickup.

"I have to drive to Hamilton to get supplies. Do you think your dad will mind if I take the stone boat out of my truck bed and lay it next to a fence until I come back for Molly? Nobody's going to take it. Do you think he'd mind?"

"What's a stone boat?" Jerry asked.

"Take a look, son. It's a heavy-duty, iron-strapped, wooden sled—like a toboggan for hauling rocks from farm fields so they can plow. Molly can pull it loaded with rocks. Some use a tractor, but it's a big wooden sled for stones called a stone boat."

"Dad won't mind, I'm sure."

"Good. I'll leave harness and rigging in the wood box and we'll tip the boat over to hide it."

Tall Jerry helped Mr. Lance pull the heavy wooden toboggan-like skiff out of the truck bed and set it onto the ground. They hauled it over to a side fence and let it rest there.

Closing the tailgate, Mr. Lance said goodbye to Molly, talking as if Molly understood. He waved to Jerry and drove across the field and onto Cardner Road. Jerry followed on foot and locked the gate behind him. He walked across the bridge and headed home in search of something dark he could wear on Tuesday night. He was trying to work up the nerve he was going to need to look in the nighttime woods to find a dead body.

Jack and Major, the horses on the house side of the creek, were whinnying and pacing about, wondering who the mare was.

It was near sunset when Dick came driving up the driveway, home from scrubbing pots and pans. He caught Jerry's eye walking and slowed so they could talk through the moving car window.

"Who closed the alfalfa field gate?" Dick asked.

The field was his usual parking spot when he and Duba had plans for sneaking out late in the night to drag race or go out with girls.

"Didn't you see the horse?" Jerry asked.

"No."

"How could you miss it?"

Dick pulled in front of the barn garage. "What horse?"

"There's a horse in the alfalfa field. Molly. Dad let Mr. Lance, the lumberjack man, leave her there for a while. She's a lumberjack

132

horse. She's enormous. He said she can pull logs out of the woods better than a tractor."

Dick backed his Willys into the barn garage and started walking to the front gate and the alfalfa field to look at Molly. Dick loved animals, and there was sun left in the day.

Missus stepped out on the front porch. "Did Dick come home?"

"He's walking over to see Mr. Lance's horse, Mom."

The lad had to be careful and talk only about Molly and not about the "other" situations. Missus would get the sheriff on the telephone at the first hint of trouble, sure enough, and a dead body was trouble. She would stop the book club from catching the scrap-iron thieves, too. Missus was a curious person, not a suspicious one. She enjoyed listening to her Tall Jerry go on about what she was thinking were exaggerated tales about a mythical giant, this Molly horse he spoke of. Jerry was telling a new story when Missus looked to the front gate and started by what she first thought was an elephant coming through the gate. The woman removed her glasses, wiped them with her handkerchief, and placed them back on.

"My Lord!" she said.

"That's Molly, Mom!" Tall Jerry said.

Dick was riding Molly bareback, with no bridle or saddle. He was holding on to a fistful of her mane as she trotted like a great dinosaur, swinging her head about in pride, not a care in the world.

Clip clop, clip clop, clip clop, clip.

The ground shook. Right up the middle of the drive she came, with large puffs of dust coming up as her hooves, the size of inverted milk pails, hit the ground with echoing clops. The dog, Ginger, was running full circles around the monster without yipping a sound, wondering if it was a moving building or a live horse and not a parade float. Jack and Major were galloping and bucking, biting at each other and whinnying.

Clip clop, clip clop, clip clop, clip.

133

Dick had a grin from ear to ear, so it weren't a secret he and Molly were best friends already. There was no doubt in anyone's mind, it was love at first sight between Dick and Molly.

Clip clop, clip clop, clip clop, clip.

Dick would tell her "right" or "left" or "whoa" or "giddy up," and Molly would do whatever he told her, and he would lean forward and pat the side of her neck with loud, friendly whacks.

"Whoa, Molly," Dick said.

Dust sprayed up from four hooves as she halted.

"Isn't she great?" Dick asked. "Can I keep her, Mom?"

It was like a miracle. The same boy who was mostly in trouble for walking on the edge by trying to act like he was a nineteen-year-old know-it-all when he was sixteen, was sitting on this gigantic horse, blubbering and blabbering away like a little schoolboy.

"Can I keep her? Huh, Mom?"

"She's not ours. She seems like a nice horse, but no, you can't keep her. She belongs to Mr. Lance. Go put her back and come in for supper."

Dick blurted: "Right, Molly."

Molly turned right, sharp as a West Point cadet.

"Right, Molly."

She turned right again.

"Giddy up, Molly," and she began trotting back toward the gate, tail flying like a wind sock.

Clip clop, clip clop, clip clop, clip.

Jerry didn't want to get in trouble with him for bringing up the murder. Dick ate fast, looked over the table and nodded for Jerry to meet him in his room.

Jerry stepped in and pulled the door closed.

"I looked under the bridge," Dick said. "I found crunched-up packs of Pall Mall cigarettes. Cigarette butts all over the place—snuffed out on the wall, on the ledge."

"I saw them smoking," Jerry said.

Dick stuck his hand into his jean pocket. "I found this paper under a pack of matches on the ledge. I left the matches so they wouldn't get wise to me taking anything."

Dick handed the folded paper to Jerry. It was a handwritten note either in code or in a foreign language. Jerry looked at it, trying to make sense out of it.

"What's it say?"

"I don't know," Dick said.

"It looks like some kind of a list," Jerry said.

"I think it's in German or Italian or something," Dick said.

Dick took the list from Jerry and slipped it in his desk drawer and pushed it closed.

"We'll get them," Dick said confidently.

"How do you know?"

"They leave too many clues."

"When do we start?"

"We'll talk about it after the other thing is done."

"The murder," Jerry whispered.

He went to his room to find something to wear Tuesday night. Hearing Dick sneaking out of the house to go drag race with Duba gave him an idea. He went into Dick's room and lifted the paper Dick had found under the bridge from the desk drawer, took a pencil and a sheet of paper and copied every word and symbol on it. He traced the drawings. He folded the copy he made and stuffed it into his pocket and returned the original to the desk drawer.

CHAPTER 12

SECRETS AND NOTES

Tuesday's quarter moon was hidden by rolling black patches of dark clouds. Lightning flashed and thunder rumbled overhead like bowling balls in the night's alley. The youngsters arrived one at a time on the bridge. Holbrook was already under the bridge, waiting like a troll to redirect them to the vacant chicken coop his father was building. Black tar paper tacked over the walls and its door blocked the light. They would be safe inside. The coop was behind the house down a slope near the creek. One by one they crossed the bridge, down a patch of lawn and stepped inside the coop. Once inside, someone lit a candle.

By eleven thirty the count was Holbrook, Tall Jerry, Barber, Mayor, and Mary. Huddling on the floor, they waited for the older guys. Randy and Bases couldn't be there. Dick and Duba were smart enough to drive up Berry Road with their headlights off and pull on the lawn in front of the house unseen. At midnight Holbrook would go out and tell them where they were hiding. Until then they sat in the coop, hearts pumping. Tall Jerry remembered having his copy of what Dick had found under the bridge. He leaned over to Mary, whispering in her ear.

"I have something. Can you mail it to the Eisenhower kid?"

"What is it?" Mary asked.

He handed her the folded piece of paper.

"Mail it right away," Tall Jerry said.

"What's it for?" Mary asked.

"I don't know, but it could be a clue. Just ask him if he can find out what it means."

Thunder grumbled outside like distant kettle drums, vibrating the walls. Mary leaned toward the candle.

"I need to know what it is, first," Mary said.

"Dick found stuff under our bridge—a note, for one."

"The bridge?"

"The crooks we talked about."

"You mean the men stealing things?"

"Yes. I copied it best I could."

"Why mail it to David Eisenhower?" Mary asked.

"Dick says it looks like Italian or German."

"Did Dick say to mail it?"

"He doesn't know I copied it. Mail it to your pen pal and ask him if anyone there knows what it says, what it means."

"I'll put it in the mailbox with a letter when I get home," Mary said.

"Don't say anything until I tell Dick I copied it."

"I won't."

"What's the fastest way?" Tall Jerry asked. "Is it air mail?"

"Special Delivery. That would get it there quickest. Costs thirty-five cents, though. They deliver it right to the door, even on Sunday," Mary said.

"I'll pay it," Jerry said. "Do it that way and ask him if he could mail you back—what did you call it?"

"Special Delivery."

"Ask him to send it back that way. Put stamps in with the letter he can use to write back? Tell him to mail it Special Delivery."

"I'll pay for those stamps," Mary said. "It's been a profitable summer selling popsicles."

Mary looked at the paper.

"If it's in a foreign language, don't you think David's a little young to know a foreign language?"

"Who knows?" Jerry asked.

"What do you mean, who knows?"

"His grandfather's the president, right?"

"Yes."

"So, he could have a secret cellar at their farm in Gettysburg."

"You've been reading too many comic books."

Barber, listening in, got into the conversation.

"In World War II Ike had underground bunkers in England."

"So?" Mary asked.

"He might have left-over secret decoder machines at their farm."

"Just send it Special Delivery," Jerry said. "Let's see if he comes up with anything."

A closed fist slapped several times against the chicken coop door, shaking the tar-paper walls, scaring every soul inside. The door yanked open. Hearts pounding, eyes as big as quarters, heads looking up at the doorway into the outside darkness. Standing there in silhouette of a quarter moon in long, black rain slickers were Dick, Duba, Conway, and Dwyer, their faces darkened with axle grease. Behind them, across Berry Road, a sudden long flash of white lightning struck down in the middle of the cemetery, lighting the night like a flashbulb, splitting a dead limb from a tree.

Craaaaaaaaaaaaaaaaaaaack!

A breeze snuffed the candle out.

"Who's made it here?" Dick asked.

"Tall Jerry, Holbrook, Barber, me, and the Mayor," Mary said.

"That's five. You were supposed to be six," Duba said.

"We're four, now they're five," Dick said. "Duba, do the math."

A heavy rain began pouring in sheets, and wind began to howl.

The older guys stepped inside the coop and pulled the door closed.

"The field is about three hundred feet," Duba said. "There are nine of us. I figure we walk thirty feet apart."

"We need signals," Conway said.

138

"He's right. There should be different signals depending on whether we're to pass it to the right or to the left," Dwyer said.

Lightning cracked from cloud to cloud across the sky.

"This will blow over," Duba said.

"It's too late to come up with signals," Dick said. "Holbrook, where do you think the body is buried?"

"I think it's in back of the far corner of the tree line," Holbrook said.

"We saw where he went in with the body," Tall Jerry said.

"There are woods maybe fifty feet deep. After that, it's a grassy hill down to a pasture," Holbrook said.

"You think it's in the woods or behind the woods?" Dick asked.

"The body has got to be buried in the woods," Holbrook said.

"What if the murderer's still in there?" Barber asked.

"So, what if he is?" Duba asked.

"Then we catch him," Dick said.

"It's been four days," Duba said. "If he buried the body deep and pitched camp over it, he could be pretending he's a camper."

"Meanwhile, he's waiting for leaves to cover the fresh dirt and the evidence," Dick said.

"Yeah, maybe he's just there keeping dogs or wolves from digging it up before the weeds grow over it and hide any scent," Dwyer said.

"Right," Conway said. "If he's pretending he's a camper he won't be shooting at anybody coming through innocently, like hikers or other campers."

"We have to go in looking like campers," Dick said.

"Right!" Duba said. "Lost campers who can't find their way back to camp."

"Not looking like you guys do, you won't. With grease on your faces, you can't go in," Mary said.

"She has a point," Duba said.

"Mary's right, we can't go in with this get-up on—and rain slickers. We look like the Jesse James gang," Dick said.

"So what's next?" Duba asked.

"New plan," Dick said. "I need new math."

"Shoot," Duba said.

"The club has to go in pretending they're campers. Not like they're looking for someone, but like they're lost," Dick said.

"We hang back on the outside of the tree line, ready to grab the murderer if he tries to make a run for it out in the open," Duba said.

"Give me the math on that," Dick said.

"Then we stand ten feet apart, down by the end of the field in front of where we think the body is. That way we can help each other if he's too strong for any us to bring down," Duba said.

"Ten feet apart—good," Conway said.

"If we stand and wait, he might see us and not come out into the open," Dick said.

"We should lie down so we can have the advantage of surprise when we jump up," Conway said.

Duba clicked on his flashlight and looked at his watch. "It's midnight," he said.

"The rain's stopped," Dick said.

"That's a break," Mary said.

"Holbrook, if you find him and can get close enough, jump quick, grab him, and hang on tight," Dick said.

"Try to surprise him," Duba said.

"Wait a minute, wait a minute," Mary blurted.

"What now?" Dick asked.

"What if he has a gun?"

"If you see he has a gun, don't make a move toward him," Duba said.

"Stand there looking friendly and quiet, and send somebody out for us," Dick said.

"He's not going to shoot anyone," Duba said. "He won't suspect anybody knows about the body."

"Okay, I'll go first and lead the way." Holbrook said. "Mary, would you rather wait here?"

"What is that supposed to mean?" Mary asked.

"It's dark, we're going in the woods. I thought in case..." Holbrook mumbled.

"It's because I'm a girl, isn't it?"

"I was just..." Holbrook stuttered.

"It's because I'm a girl."

"I, ahh," Holbrook rattled.

"Let me tell you something, buster! I'm older than you. I have my own business, you don't. I get up early in the morning and go out in the dark and deliver newspapers on country roads, even this one...And I wear a bra."

A young man's personal passage into adulthood was his whisker count. A young lady's was her need of a brassiere and the advent of an otherwise personal womanly body function. Mary spared the group that detail, but she made her point clear she was every bit as grown up and capable—and as daring—as any lad in the coop. And that included the older guys.

"You do? Wear those?" Mayor whimpered, feeling the loss of his childhood mate.

"I'm sorry," Holbrook said.

"Then why'd you say it?"

"I was wrong."

"So, I'm a girl. What difference does that make?"

"Nothing."

"Want to see who can do the most pushups?"

Holbrook wasn't getting out of that one.

"Okay, you tell us what to do," Holbrook said.

Mary took charge.

"You know the woods," she said to Holbrook. "You go in first. Behind you, paired up, will be Tall Jerry and me, and behind us will be Barber and Mayor."

"We'll walk together to the corner of the tree line," Dick said. "Then we'll get in our formations."

"Keep it quiet," Duba said.

Carefully they stepped out of the chicken coop and into the quarter moonlight, each knowing this was the moment of no turning back. People said a prayer to themselves. Most had a cold fear in their eyes. All felt melancholy over the dead girl in her lonely, cold grave.

Twenty feet from the far corner of the back tree line Dick signaled the older guys to spread out their ten-foot intervals and to lie down. He shrugged his shoulders to Holbrook as though he were signaling to him the question of where he planned to go in.

Holbrook raised his arm and pointed between trees to show his fix. He pointed just as the murderer had pointed the night he carried the body to its grave. They paused, staring at the woods, dark and heavy, still dripping from the earlier rain. The older guys lay down on the ground. Holbrook looked to see if his crew was ready. Each gave a thumb up. He turned forward, walked to the edge of the tree line and stepped into its dark shadows. He motioned the rest to be quiet and to follow. Holbrook and Tall Jerry, experienced campers, knew they were lucky because of the heavy rains that night. The ground would be damp, making fewer noises underfoot. Damp twigs would bend and give. Dry twigs were brittle and would snap when stepped on. They began to get their night vision, eyes dilating to the darkness. The quarter moon helped as they moved deeper into the woods. There were few sounds. No birds, no rustling of leaves in the trees. All was still.

Stepping around a large maple tree, Holbrook paused, stepped backward and motioned the others to get down. Everyone went to a squat and froze. Holbrook leaned forward again, looking around the tree.

"I can see the glow of a fire," he whispered. "There's a camp up ahead."

"How far?" Mary whispered.

"It must be in the opening behind the woods. I can only see the tip of a fire, where the grass hill goes down from the woods," Holbrook said.

"Should we go get Dick and the guys?" Tall Jerry whispered.

"I know these woods," Holbrook said.

"I wish we had a gun," Mayor said.

"Duba has a shotgun," Tall Jerry said.

"Let's go get Duba," Mayor said.

"Shut up, you guys. No guns," Mary said.

"I'll bet the murderer thought the hill would shield the fire and hide the glow from Berry Road," Holbrook said. "It almost does, but not from here."

"The grave could be anywhere around here," Barber said.

"Let's keep going," Mary said, "but if you see a gun anywhere, stop like the guys said."

The five moved forward, cautiously stepping between trees, carefully holding bush branches for each other and not letting them swing back. They moved closer toward the glowing flicker of a small campfire. Holbrook could now see the campsite. He stood and took it in, examining the smallest details, so he could give an accurate report, and they could come up with a strategy. He stepped back, motioning to get down quietly. He had them lean in, so they could hear his whispers.

"The body isn't buried," he whispered.

"What?!" Mayor mumbled.

"It's lying on top of the ground and covered with a tarpaulin."

"You sure?" Mary asked.

"I can see the body lump under the canvas. The grass hill where he is, is too steep to pitch a tent. The killer's out in the open."

"Is he alone," Jerry asked.

"Yes, he's rolled up in a blanket by the fire. He's asleep, I think. The fire's dying out."

"He'll be waking up for firewood," Jerry said.

"He hasn't buried the body?" Barber whispered.

"I told you, the body is on top of the ground with a tarpaulin over it," Holbrook said.

"Then he must have a gun and is desperate," Barber whispered.

"Did you see a gun?" Mary whispered.

"No gun."

"Look again, be sure."

Holbrook stood and turned, then sat back down.

"I don't see a gun anywhere."

"Think we can rush him?" Jerry whispered.

"Tall Jerry, you go straight," Holbrook said. "Run as fast as you can, but keep to his left. Barber, you and Mayor go to his right. Make sure you keep in between him and the firewood stack, so he can't grab a club from the woodpile. I'll run and dive on him and grab hold of him, you guys jump in and help me. Mary, you stay here and get ready to run back to signal Dick and Duba and the guys to come on in."

Each signaled they knew exactly what to do.

"Ready on three," Holbrook whispered. "Remember, pick your feet up, so you don't trip. Be careful to watch your footing. One. Two. Three!"

Like a herd of deer bolting in the night the boys lunged forward, overtaking and surrounding the murderer. Holbrook sprung through the air, landing squarely on top of him, grabbing both of his arms and pulling them behind his back in a tight grip.

"What the hell!?" the murderer muffled.

"Don't move and you won't get hurt!" Holbrook demanded.

"Who are you? What's going on?" the murderer screamed.

Barber, Mayor, and Tall Jerry pounced and grabbed the guy, holding him secure, letting Holbrook free to get back to his feet. Holbrook signaled Mary to get Dick and Duba and their crew.

"I don't have any money," the murderer said.

"We're not robbers, mister," Holbrook commanded.

"Take the food, whatever there is. Just take it."

"We don't want your food and we don't want your money. We're taking you in for murder."

"What!?" the murderer declared.

"Murder," Holbrook said. "You heard me."

He pointed to the tarp lying on the ground, "And over there is all the evidence they'll ever need."

Holbrook stepped around the fire to the tarpaulin covering the corpse.

"Murder? Murder?" the guy yelled, "Are you people insane? You're crazy, all of you! Let go of me!"

"You'll get the electric chair," Holbrook said.

He leaned down, and gripping the corner with his fist, he began lifting the damp tarp.

"If we're crazy and you're not a murderer then why are you hiding this body?" Holbrook shouted as he ripped the tarp up in the air and away from the body.

"Explain this!" Holbrook said, throwing it behind him like a bullfighter's cape. He looked down at the lifeless girl's body.

"This is her, all right," Holbrook said. "This is the girl we saw you carrying."

Holbrook looked at her sadly, looking for murder wounds and marks. He knelt beside her, reached his hand as a gesture of respect to straighten a strand of hair hiding her cold face, when her eyes opened wide and as big as silver dollars and she screamed at the top of her lungs…

"*EEEEEEEEEEEEEK!*"

145

The girl struggled, trying to lift up, making it up enough to rest on her elbows.

"What do you want!?"

"Yikes!!!" Holbrook screamed.

"Don't hurt us!"

Holbrook's eyes opened as big as breakfast biscuits, they surely did. The lad turned shades of white, then a pale green before springing easily a foot off the ground like a kangaroo in shock.

"The body moved!" Holbrook stammered. "She looked at me! The body talked!"

The lad stiffened like he was about to faint and plopped backward, first tripping over a fire log he stepped on, then landing on an old, rickety wooden wheelchair, hidden under bush branches. His legs and arms flailed, his eyes widened, and the chair cracked under his weight. A wheel popped off the axle and rolled down to the pasture fence below.

"She's not dead!" the guy screamed. "Let go of me. She's my sister…Let go of me…She's not dead, I tell you! All right, all right, she's got polio! Are you happy now? Are you satisfied?"

"She does?" Barber whimpered.

"Now will you leave us alone?"

"We thought…" Mayor started.

"Just go away and leave us alone!"

He broke into sobs.

Barber, Mayor, and Tall Jerry let go of their grip and got up from the ground and stood staring at the girl. They helped the guy get onto his feet.

Dick, Duba and the guys stepped into the clearing with Mary leading them.

"She's not dead…she's got polio," Tall Jerry said.

"She's crippled," Barber said.

No one said another word. Duba sheepishly emptied his shotgun, put the shell in his pocket, folded and hid the gun behind his back. Holbrook crawled about the ground, feeling for his glasses near where he first landed in the wheelchair. He stood up, hands shaking and frozen, looking at the girl as he side-stepped her to stand over next to Tall Jerry.

"We can't afford another wheelchair," the guy said. "I hope you're all happy. Now will you please leave?"

"Buddy, we didn't know," Dick said.

"Just get out and leave us alone."

Mary walked around the fire and stepped over by the girl who was leaning up, resting back on her elbows.

Mary knelt beside the girl.

"My name's Mary. What's yours?" Mary asked.

The girl lifted her elbows and lay back, resting her head.

"Please don't let them hurt us."

"Nobody's going to hurt anybody," Mary said.

The girl turned her head away from Mary and closed her eyes.

"What's your name?" Mary asked.

The girl shook her head no.

"Look, I know you're scared but we're not going to hurt you. Talk to me," Mary said.

The girl turned her head toward Mary.

"Alice, my name is Alice. He's Roy. He's my brother."

Alice turned her head away again.

Mary took the girl by the hand, felt how frail it was and looked up at the guys standing around.

"You guys go and get food," Mary said.

"Who?" Tall Jerry asked.

"All of you."

"Let's go," Dick said.

"Take Roy with you and come back with food. Roy, you can trust us. We're here to help you. Everybody go."

"Will you two be okay?" Dick asked.

"Hurry. We want to talk, alone," Mary said.

"We can hide in the chicken coop until the older guys come back with the food," Holbrook said to the club members, beginning to get his color back. "Don't make any noise. We don't want to wake the kids in the house."

"Wait for us in the chicken coop," Dick said. "Duba, can we raid your refrigerator for food?"

"If we're quiet about it," Duba said.

"Don't anyone go home yet," Mary said. "They're going to need our help. We need a plan."

Holbrook looked at Mary. He knew he was looking at a new Mary. The lad had felt she was changing in recent times, now he was certain of it. His childhood pal was coming into her own, becoming a woman.

Mary looked at Roy, still with tears in his eyes.

"Roy, don't worry. You and your sister are safe with us. Don't worry a bit. Go with the guys and come back with food. She's weak. She needs warm food. Hurry."

Dick put his arm around Roy's shoulder in a friendly gesture and they began walking back through the woods. He started explaining why they were there in the first place and how it was all a big misunderstanding.

"When you come back, pick up firewood on your way through the woods," Mary shouted.

Mary found a log to sit on and dragged it around next to Alice. She picked up the blanket that had covered Roy earlier, shook it in the air and put it over Alice, tucking in the sides.

"You must be freezing," Mary said.

Mary watched for the guys to be out of sight. She explained how Holbrook and Tall Jerry had seen her brother carrying her into the woods from a distance and how they jumped to conclusions like boys can do and thought the worst.

"Is he okay?" Alice asked.

"Holbrook?" Mary asked.

"The one who lifted the canvas," Alice said.

"That's Holbrook. He's okay, just embarrassed, jumping like he did and tripping into your wheelchair. It hurt his male pride, I think." Mary laughed.

Alice's eyes were tired, her lids heavy, but she managed a smile.

"Are you okay?" Mary asked.

"How can I be okay?" Alice said.

"You're safe now, is what I'm trying..." Mary started.

"Look at me," Alice said.

"I'm looking, "Mary said.

"I'm like a vegetable laying here, I can't move."

"Well you must have moved somehow, because you're here, aren't you?"

"Why don't you just leave us alone. We were fine until you came."

"Oh, I can just bet – you look fine here, freezing and hungry."

"You're pretending you care but you really don't care."

"How old are you?" Mary asked.

"Twenty-three. You?" Alice asked.

"I sometimes think I'm twenty-three," Mary said.

"How old are you?"

"Fourteen," Mary said.

Alice smiled.

"Are you camping?" Mary asked.

"We're hiding."

"Hiding?"

"How'd you find us?"

"We were looking for a dead body."

"Whose dead body?"

"Never mind. That's how we found you."

"When I heard you, I thought you were the sheriff," Alice said.

"Why would you think that?"

"I'm a teacher. I got polio and lost my job nearly two years ago."

"Just for having polio?"

"Yes."

"What grade do you teach?"

"Fourth."

"Why that stinks."

"They wouldn't even let me go home in a school bus, they made me get a ride."

"We had a president, Franklin D. Roosevelt who had polio for God's sake!" Mary said.

"I know."

"He was elected four times."

"He could hide it. I couldn't hide it."

"Shame on whoever fired you," Mary snapped. "It's not right."

"My children write letters. They miss my reading to them."

"I can imagine."

"I used to read stories."

"Explain why you have to hide."

"What do you mean?"

"Who are you hiding from?"

"They thought I tried to commit suicide."

"Who?"

"They said they were going to put me in an insane asylum."

"What?!"

"The judge ordered it."

"Did you, you know, try?"

"I would never commit suicide."

"Good."

"I could never do that. I had written something, though, expressing my thoughts, my depression, and someone read it and reported on me that I was suicidal. They told the judge I should go into an insane asylum for evaluation, maybe a year."

"So, your brother brought you here to hide out?"

"Yes."

"That was sweet of him."

Mary took Alice by the hand.

"He's a good brother," Alice said.

"Are you contagious?"

"Polio isn't contagious after its incubation—after somebody has had it five or six months. I'm not contagious."

"Why would you even think of suicide, a pretty girl like you?"

"I never thought of suicide, I tell you. I was just depressed."

Alice looked up with a hopeless smile, a tear rolled from the corner of her eye.

"Look at me."

"I see you," Mary said.

"All I ever wanted to be growing up was a fourth-grade teacher."

Mary took her hand and squeezed it.

"All I am is a cripple. I might as well have no legs."

Mary reached and gently touched Alice's cheek. Leaning in she looked Alice deep in her eyes.

"I hate being lectured to, but something tells me I need to lecture you. Can I lecture you, Alice?"

"If I say no, will that stop you?"

"No," Mary said.

"So, do what you have to do," Alice said.

"How long have you had polio?"

"Almost two years."

"Let me ask you something."

"What?"

"Sometimes I dream of falling. Do people with polio ever dream of falling?"

"Sometimes."

"When you sleep and dream, do you ever dream about walking?"

"Sometimes."

"Running?"

"Yes."

"Alice, I know a kindly old lady. She's a school teacher. She teaches French. Mrs. Young. One Christmas morning her husband of more than forty years was shoveling snow off their sidewalk and he dropped over dead with a heart attack."

"That's so sad."

"This summer the boy here tonight, Tall Jerry, he found an orphan boy sleeping in a back alley behind a hotel in Syracuse, nine years old. His mother was in the war and a bomb dropped on the hospital in Africa and she was killed with everyone in the hospital. He's only nine."

A tear rolled from Alice's eye.

"There's the little boy driving the tractor down Route 11 near Tully. He was delivering it to his daddy in a field. He pulled off the road too far onto an embankment and it tipped over on him, crushing him to death."

"I'm pretty selfish, aren't I?"

"Don't say that, Alice. Don't think it even. I didn't tell you those things to make you feel selfish. I told them so you would understand you weren't crippled."

"What do you mean?"

"I wanted you to know what being crippled is."

"I think I get it," Alice said.

"Mrs. Young, a sweet old lady has to go to bed alone, for the rest of her life. Her husband will never be there to hug her or kiss her good night…no more Christmas mornings with him. That's being crippled. But you can still walk and run just by closing your eyes and dreaming…"

"And Bobby, the boy Tall Jerry found in the alley, he's crippled. His mother is never going to come back from wherever they buried her in Africa, to tuck him in or sing a lullaby or read him a story… but you get to wake up in the morning with a beautiful mind…"

"And the mommy and daddy near Tully are both crippled. They won't get to look into their boy's eyes at the breakfast table ever again…but you can still read stories…and reading stories is all you ever wanted to do anyway, isn't it?"

"You're nice."

"Alice, you are much more than a pair of legs. Count what you have, not what you think you don't have. You have a brain that cares; you have pretty eyes that can see the beauty in others; you have a loyal brother who would do anything to help you. That's the end of my lecture, Alice."

"You are so nice, Mary."

"You're a teacher, Alice—a teacher, so good her children write her letters telling her how much they love and miss her. You're still a teacher. Nobody can ever take that away from you. You only have to find students to read to."

Alice dabbed her eyes with the satin corner of the blanket.

"I feel stupid," Alice said.

"Well, there you go. You see how normal you are, Alice? Only a normal person has the right to feel stupid from time to time."

"When did you get so smart, Mary?"

"I was a little girl during the war. One night I was looking out the window and crying at bedtime, feeling sorry for myself because my daddy had gone off in the war to fight. My grandma gave me a talk almost like this one."

153

"It helped, and you're right," Alice said.

"Come to think of it, FDR served four terms as the president of the United States of America in a wheelchair with polio," Mary said. "What are you intending to do with your life having the same advantages he had?"

"Anything I want?"

Mary smiled.

"Yes, that's it, anything I want," Alice said.

The girls grinned as Mary leaned in and they gave each other's neck a warm hug.

"Alice, I don't know much about polio. Is it your legs?"

"It's my leg muscles. The rest is normal. I can feel them. I can even get goosebumps, but the muscles won't move them."

"Does everything else work? Like is there anything you need, you know—girl stuff?" Mary asked.

"I could use a bath," Alice started. "And lady things if anyone has any they can spare."

"Aren't a lot of bathtubs on Berry Road. Plenty of girls, though. We'll come up with something," Mary said.

The guys came ambling through the woods, talking up a storm, carryin' food sacks, carryin' sticks of firewood, having a good time for themselves after staying up all night on a great adventure.

Mary stood up and took charge.

"It's almost dawn," Mary said. "I need to run through the important things. Anybody gets any ideas, speak up. Barber and Mayor, you two pass out the food. Tall Jerry, you and Holbrook stoke the fire. Make it big to warm the air, cut the dampness."

"We're listening," Dick said, wiping axle grease from his face.

Just watchin' them go about their business made ole Charlie's heart warm, the young ones coming together like this. Their parents would be proud.

"We need to get Alice's wheelchair fixed."

"No problem," Conway said. "I'll take it to Mr. Ossont at the school's mechanical shop. We'll make it like new."

"We need to hide them out for a couple days," Mary said.

"You're right," Dick said.

"At least until we can figure how to get them out of trouble with a judge in Syracuse," Mary said.

"Tall Jerry's and my camp on top of the cliff will be the safest," Holbrook said.

"Delphi Falls?" Mary asked.

"Yep!" Holbrook said. "There's even a cave."

"How're you going to get Alice up a cliff like that?" Mary asked.

"Four of us can carry her," Duba said. "We'll get her up there."

"How high up is it – that cliff?" Mary asked.

"Maybe seventy feet," Jerry said.

"We'd take her up the back hill," Holbrook said.

"Does anybody know what a stone boat is?" Jerry asked.

"Who doesn't know about stone boats?" Dwyer asked.

"I didn't," Jerry said.

"What's your point?" Dick asked.

"Anybody know how to hitch a workhorse to one?" Jerry asked.

Conway and Dwyer raised their arms.

"That's how we'll get her to the top of the hill," Jerry said.

"Does Farmer Parker have a stone boat we can borrow?" Conway asked.

"We have a stone boat laying in the alfalfa field, and we can have the lumberjack horse, Molly, pull her up the back hill into the woods," Jerry said.

"She could do it," Dick affirmed.

"It's settled," Mary said. "Whoever drives Alice to where that horse is, plan on leaving here at eleven o'clock; in the meantime, we need to find her clothes and a bath."

Alice looked over and caught Holbrook's eye.

"Are you okay?" she asked.

155

"I'm okay… sure glad you are," Holbrook said.

"Thank you, all of you, for caring," Alice said.

"Holbrook, would your mother and sisters help Alice when they wake up?" Mary asked. "Maybe lend her a couple of things, something warm to wear?"

"Sure."

"Can they take her for a dip in the Berwyn bathtub?"

"They'll be happy to," Holbrook said.

"Good. When they're up and ready, a couple of you carry Alice over by the bridge. Set her down gently, but then leave the girls alone with her."

The older guys flipped a coin to see who would come and drive Alice and Roy to the alfalfa field after her bath. Conway would pick Dwyer up and hitch Molly to the stone boat. They would get Alice secure in it and ride her up in tow, into the woods to the camp. Then they'd tow it back down.

Two guys lifted the wheelchair and broken wheel and put it in the bed of Duba's pickup.

The morning went beautifully, warmed by a late summer sun and tall fire. Roy and Alice could finally calm down with a hot breakfast and new friends, after their days of stress and tension. Tall Jerry and Holbrook had a big laugh about their "seeing the dead body" fiasco, but happy it was going to work out, or at least so far so good.

"Did she scare you, opening her eyes like that?" Tall Jerry asked.

"I think my hair is falling out," Holbrook said.

"You have two more whiskers," Tall Jerry said.

"I do?"

"They're gray," Tall Jerry said.

Mrs. Holbrook and the Holbrook and Bradshaw girls took Alice in the Berwyn bathtub for a dip and bath. Alice was able to swim with her strong arms and upper body, keeping her afloat. Those who had them shared girl's necessities with her; also, warm outfits

156

on loan. At eleven, Dick pulled onto the lawn in his Willys and backed it up to load Alice and Roy for the ride to the alfalfa field.

"Wait a second, guys," Mary said.

She stepped up on the Holbrook's back stoop, trying to get Mrs. Holbrook's attention.

"Mrs. Holbrook?" Mary said, tapping on the screen. "Thank you for helping this morning with Alice."

"It was a pleasure, Mary. Such a nice girl."

"Is little Judy still sick, Mrs. Holbrook?"

"Thank you, Mary, she's doing much better but still in quarantine, to be safe."

"Do you think Alice could visit a few minutes with Judy?"

Little Judy Bradshaw, the Holbrook siblings' half-sister was closed up in a bedroom with rheumatic heart, brought on by the fever. Until she got strong enough and well enough, they couldn't risk giving her a cold or flu or measles, so the kids could only talk to her through the door or play with her, sliding the cards back and forth under the door.

Mrs. Holbrook knew that matured polio was not contagious. The mother and caretaker of seventeen children read what she could get her hands on about childhood diseases.

"Judy would love a visitor," Mrs. Holbrook said.

The boys carried Alice into the house to just outside Judy's door and set her on the hall floor. Alice's arms and back enabled her to maneuver herself around into a position for sitting up, leaning on the wall.

Alice rapped a knuckle gently on Judy's bedroom door.

"Hi, Judy, it's nice to meet you," Alice said through the door.

"Hello. What's your name?" Judy asked.

"My name is Alice."

"Alice is a pretty name, are you Alice in Wonderland?" Judy asked.

"I'm not her. I love the name Judy."

"You do?"

"Do you like books, Judy?" Alice asked, "I like reading books to people."

"Will you read me a book, Alice?"

"I'm sorry. I didn't bring any books with me today. Someday I will though. I promise. I promise I'll come back and read a book to you," Alice said.

The corner of a book edged its way on the floor slowly, sliding under the door and out into the hall. It was Judy's book: *The Little Engine That Could.* Alice smiled, leaned over and picked it up and opened it.

"Chug, chug, chug; Puff, puff, puff. Ding-dong, ding-dong," she began. "The little train rumbled over the tracks. She was a happy little train…"

Alice read the story to Judy.

All ole Charlie here can say is, it was a nice day. It was the day a bunch of young folks and their older compatriots got to stay up all night and learn firsthand what it was like to be good citizens.

Everybody, including Mrs. Holbrook, promised not to talk about Alice and Roy until the coast was clear. They were safely hidden out at the campsite over the Delphi Falls.

Mary got home in plenty of time and dropped the letter in the mailbox to her pen pal, David Eisenhower, Special Delivery, before she had to head down to the hamlet to sell more popsicles and fudge sickles from her peddle cart before summer ended.

Molly pulls the stone boat with Alice and Roy

CHAPTER 13

TWO MIKES AND ONE JUDGE

Conway and Dwyer got Alice and Roy settled at Jerry's campsite and built a fire. They led Molly out of the woods, down the steep hill back to the alfalfa field. They unhitched her, put the harness in the wooden box, and tipped the stone boat to cover it. Dick led Molly by the halter to a fence post and climbed up to jump on her back for a ride around the field. Jerry came with a knapsack filled with food and provisions, two pillows, two blankets, and a lantern. He had a pup tent rolled and slung over his back with a rope.

"Dick, are you going to help me talk to Mom and Dad?"

"About what?"

"I have to tell them."

"Tell them what?"

"About Alice and Roy."

"Now?"

"At supper."

"Oh."

"Will you help me?"

"You lead it off. I'll cover you," Dick said.

"Thanks."

Jerry started crossing the field.

"Don't feel bad," Dick said.

"About what?"

"Thinking she was dead."

"It was pretty dumb."

"I'd have thought the same—seeing her legs like they are."

"You would?"

"Yup."

"Thanks."

"It could have happened to anybody."

"She sure looked like she was."

"Better think about what you're going to say to Mom."

"Okay."

"Try not to sound like a kid."

Ole Charlie here was proud of Dick right then. Showed he wasn't a selfish boy. He was seein' Jerry was growing up and challenged him. He reminded Jerry that when a lad thinks, he could use the young brain or the maturing brain, his choice.

Dick and Molly trotted around the alfalfa field for a first lap. They approached Jerry again at the edge of the back hill just as he was about to climb it.

"We've talked about it," Dick said.

"Who?" Jerry asked.

"Me, Duba, Conway and Dwyer."

"About what?" Jerry asked.

"About the iron and rubber scrap thieves."

"Yeah?" Jerry asked.

"They're scaring farmers and their women."

"I know. Myrtie said everybody sees them."

"Go ahead and call your SOS."

"You mean it?"

"We're going to take it on," Dick said.

"I copied the list you found under the bridge and we sent it to somebody we think maybe can translate it."

"Who?"

"Somebody in Pennsylvania. Don't worry, he won't say anything."

Dick turned Molly in full circle while thinking.

"Are you pissed?" Jerry asked.

161

"I will be if he blabs it," Dick said.

"He won't," Jerry said.

"Call the SOS."

"I'll tell Barber."

"Have everyone in front of Shea's store noon the Tuesday after Labor Day."

"That's two weeks away," Jerry said.

"We're going to need a lot of help," Dick said. "They could be part of a gang."

"But that's two weeks," Jerry said.

"We need to see what the note said. How soon will you know?" Dick asked.

"I'll ask Mary and tell you. It should be four days if Special Delivery works at the post office."

"It'll help if we know what it says so we can think up strategies."

"The guy may not be able to translate it," Jerry said.

"We need to know what it says," Dick said.

"What will it tell you we don't already know?" Jerry asked.

"How we have to map the area. How big an area they steal from."

"That's smart."

"It's better starting something like this when the most kids can be there to help—and that's after school starts."

"They'll keep stealing. They could leave the county by then," Jerry barked.

"It's a free country. Go catch 'em yourselves. You want our help and want to do it right, call the SOS—day after Labor Day."

Dick and Molly trotted off.

Jerry got home from making his deliveries to the top of the cliff. He put on a fresh shirt, washed his hands and scrubbed his face with a damp washcloth. Missus liked a clean face and a closed shirt collar at the supper table, and tonight Tall Jerry had to appear presentable when he started talking at supper. He stepped into his mom and dad's empty bedroom and picked up the telephone.

"Operator," Myrtie said.

"Myrtie, can you get me Barber, please?"

Myrtie must have been busy—lots of calls or something boiling on the stove—as she connected the call without her usual friendly chatter.

"Hello?"

"Who's this?"

"I'm Bobby."

"Hey Bobby, this is Tall Jerry."

"Guess what I get to do?"

"What?"

"I scoop oats and feed for the cows in front of them when they get in their stalls for milking."

"You're going to be a great farmer," Jerry said. "Is Barber there?"

"Hello?"

"Call a meeting for Saturday."

"For when?"

After two o'clock."

"Why so late?"

"It's my last day of work," Jerry said.

"Does Mary know?"

"Just do it."

"Okay," Barber said.

"Oh—and the older guys said to set up an SOS meeting," Jerry said.

"For when?"

"Tuesday after Labor Day. They're going to help us catch the two crooks."

"At the cemetery?"

"No. In front of Shea's store at noon the day after Labor Day."

"That's two meetings?"

"Yep."

"Can I talk about the harvest hayride," Barber said.

"Set up the meetings, talk all you want."

"Roger Wilko!" Barber said.

"Thanks."

"Are they hiding out?"

"Alice and Roy?"

"Yeah."

"They're good. I'm talking to my mom and dad tonight."

"Good luck on that."

"I'll need it."

Click.

Jerry went to his room and waited for supper to be called. Having spent a sleepless night the night before, he dozed off.

"Jerry?"

No answer.

"Jerry."

No answer.

"Jerry, supper's on the table," Missus barked.

"I'm up," Jerry muttered.

"Call your brother in, tell him to wash his hands and come to the table."

In time, the lads walked into the dining room. Waiting were Missus, Big Mike, and their Aunt Kate, who had come home with Big Mike from Homer for a short visit. Dick and Jerry sat and waited for grace.

"Neither of you used your beds last night. Would you care to explain why?" Missus declared, opening the supper conversation.

Jerry remembered Dick's advice about using the proper brain and had been thinking about it since. He would take his time when addressing adults—act more grown up. Missus wanted an answer and he could sound like a wimpy kid or he could sound like an adult. His choice. He gave the situation thought as his mother stared into the air, waiting for answers.

Jerry became Tall Jerry and sat up in his seat.

"We found someone who needed help and we let them camp in the woods until we can figure out how we can help," Jerry started.

"Oh?"

"They're okay," Jerry said.

"Well, here we go again," Missus said.

She looked across the table at Big Mike.

"Our boys spend nights looking for anyone in trouble and just drag them into our woods?"

She looked Jerry square in the eye.

"Is that it? Is that your excuse for staying out all night?"

"Actually, Mom, Molly dragged them up there," Jerry said.

"Don't be impudent, young man."

"I'm not, Mom, I—"

"You're hanging by a thread. You'll be doing dishes tonight."

"I wasn't trying—"

"What are you boys running over the falls, a hotel?"

"Why don't you listen to him, Mom?" Dick asked.

Aunt Kate leaned back, in case a wooden serving spoon flew past.

"He's right, Mom." Jerry said. "You got mad when I didn't tell you right away about Bobby, I'm telling you right away about these two, and you're still getting mad."

Big Mike saved the moment.

"Mommy, I ran into Mr. Blume in Loblaw's Grocery the other day. He came over and told me that our boy here was an outstanding summer employee and was welcome back to work at the Hotel Syracuse at any time, any summer he wishes," Big Mike said.

"He did?" Jerry asked.

"He did indeed, son. Now why don't you tell your story in your own words about why you were out all night?"

Big Mike saved that pot from boiling over. Now Jerry had time to think. With time to think, Ole Charlie here could tell the way Dick sat back, he had something on his mind, too—a look in his eye like if Tall Jerry began with the story about him and Holbrook thinking they saw a dead body, he'd be cooked. But if Jerry started a little higher up the ladder about helping a girl with polio he might have a chance of making it through supper alive.

Missus, the entire jury of one, rested her salad fork on the table. Others waited for the story as well. Me, the lad's guardian angel perched on the china buffet to listen to every word. This had the makings of a good evening.

"Holbrook and I found a school teacher and her brother over by Berry Road with a broken wheelchair. We had to help them. We couldn't leave her there without a wheelchair, could we, Mom?"

The lad was brilliant. Just as the kids had done with Mr. Hasting and the Thanksgiving chickens and geese in years past, the lad was about to completely implicate his own mother. Depending on her answer, from here on out, anything he did overnight would be on her shoulders, too. This was a classic ploy. Ole Charlie here was getting such an education from this.

"You did right. I'm proud of you." Missus smiled and picked up her salad fork.

"Do I still have to do the dishes?"

"Tell me. Why did you take them into the woods and not bring them here?" Missus added.

"Dad, I'm going to need you for this," Jerry said, turning to Big Mike.

"Go on, son," Big Mike said.

"The teacher's got polio and a judge in Syracuse is going to order her into an insane asylum, so she and her brother have to hide," Jerry blurted.

Missus's eyes rolled.

Now ole Charlie here was quite proud of the boy's finesse. He had managed to tell a compelling, brief story while leaving out about twelve important details. It worked like a charm. Missus straightened her salad fork next to her dinner fork and stood up at the end of the table.

"Why on earth doesn't the newspaper, radio or television do something about educating people about these things?"

She paused, stared down at the table top thinking.

"Boys, put your forks down," Missus said. "Go in the woods and get that poor girl and her brother and bring them down."

"Now?" Jerry asked.

"Right now, both of you. Move!"

Dick and Jerry pushed their chairs back and stood.

"Aunt Kate, get linens and help me make up two beds," Missus said. "Mike, you be thinking how you're going to clear this absolute nonsense with whoever that judge is."

"We've got to harness Molly before we can get her," Dick said.

"So, do it," Missus said.

"I have to go get Conway," Dick said. "He knows how to hitch her up."

"Don't dally, go," Missus said.

Dick and Jerry ran from the house jumped into the Willys and sped off.

"Aunt Kate, let's put two more settings at the table for our dinner guests," Missus said.

When the Missus and her family ate at night, it was supper. If they had guests, it was dinner. I am learning how to act in a house that has electricity, running water, and a telephone. In about an hour of Missus pacing about and Big Mike reading the *Post Standard,* Conway and Dick reappeared, hands clenched under and carrying Alice, sitting on their arms. Her brother Roy followed them in. They brought her to the table and set her on a dining room chair and lifted it into the table. Big Mike welcomed them. Roy took a seat next to Dick.

"Where's your wheelchair, dear?" Missus asked.

"We broke it. But we're having it fixed," Jerry said.

167

"You broke it?" Missus started.

Tall Jerry had left that small detail out of his story.

Big Mike gave Missus a look to not stir the pot and passed the bowls of vegetables and platter of pork chops just as though all was normal.

"Alice, we understand you're a school teacher?" Missus asked.

"Yes, well I was. Fourth grade."

"Was, dear?"

"I was let go when I got polio. It's coming on two years this fall."

"We live in the most loving nation on the face of the earth, but our ignorance and superstitions about things we don't want to understand amaze me," Missus said.

"They were afraid children would catch it from me."

"It wasn't that long ago they burned witches, Mom," Dick offered, completely off the subject.

"The audacity of preventing a person from teaching —from using God-given patience and caring in the most celebrated vocation on earth."

"They were afraid," Alice said.

"Tell me about the judge, dear. And Jerry, take your elbows off the table."

"I was depressed, and I wrote a note to myself, in a diary that I maybe shouldn't have, which may have implied I was considering giving up."

"Suicide?" Missus asked.

"Yes, well it may have sounded like that, Missus, but I would have never…I was just expressing…"

"I understand."

"Someone found it and showed it to someone else who convinced a judge that I had to be put in an insane asylum for evaluation, and that could take a year."

"Don't say another word, dear. Oh my, what you've been through. Roy, congratulations for standing up for your sister like a man. We are proud of you—very proud indeed. Jerry and Dick, thank you and your friends for helping."

The family and guests passed around pleasantries and talk of the shortcomings of a society ignorant of diseases and other social ailments, when there came a knock on the front door.

"Jerry, go see who that is," Big Mike said.

The lad came into the dining room pushing an empty wheel chair with a man and a woman following behind him.

"That's not my wheelchair," Alice said.

Big Mike stood, motioning for Dick and Roy to stand like gentlemen.

"Welcome folks, won't you join us?"

"Oh, no thank you, Mr. Mike. Hello Missus, everybody. I'm Harriet, and this is Mr. Cook, Wesley, my husband," Harriet said. "We're sorry to be interrupting your family meal time. We truly are. Maybe we should come back another time."

"Nonsense," Missus said. "Please join us."

"We just came by to deliver this." Mrs. Cook touched the wheelchair. "It's ours, and we thought Alice might be able to use it until hers gets fixed."

"Dick, Jerry, give your seats to our guests. Get two more chairs—find places." Big Mike said. "Jerry, get two plates, glasses and silverware for the Cooks. Sit down folks, join us."

Big Mike knew there was more to the story than two people stopping by with a wheelchair.

"How do we have the pleasure, Harriet and Wesley?" Big Mike asked, "Are you from the area?"

"We farm up in Berwyn. We're cousins to Conway, and when Jimmy's momma called and told us of Alice and her polio, we thought we'd come by to talk to her, if we might be able."

"Fill your plates. I'm sure Alice is all ears; I know we are. Let me introduce you around the table. I'm Mike. This is my wife, Mary.

Next to her, our Aunt Kate. And this is our son Dick, our son Jerry, and these are our new friends, young Roy and his sister, Alice."

"Thank you for inviting us to the table, interrupting your family hour. We heard from Jimmy about how they found Alice and her brother up on Berry Road and how most are wanting to help best way they can. We thought we'd stop by and offer, well…"

"Pompey, the Delphi hamlet, Tully, the whole area, Cazenovia— aren't we blessed living amid communities like these?" Missus asked.

"People are so nice," Alice said.

"People want to help, dear," Mrs. Cook said.

"Thank you for bringing the wheelchair, Mrs. Cook."

"Mrs. Cook…" Missus started.

"Please, call me Harriet," Harriet said.

"Harriet, how is it you came by a wheelchair, if you don't mind my asking? And call me Mary."

"Our baby girl, Marian, got the virus not long ago," Harriett said. "In her legs. It's our Marian's wheelchair."

"Did you lose the child?" Missus asked.

"Oh, heavens no! It was her idea we bring the wheelchair over for Alice to use. She can scoot around using her arms, leg braces and crutches. Why sometimes we forget she has polio. Jimmy told us your chair was broken, Alice. Marian insisted we bring this one over straight away for you to use until yours was fixed."

"Will you tell Marian thank you? That was thoughtful and kind of her," Alice said.

"If you'd like to use her leg braces or crutches, she said you're welcome to them," Mrs. Cook said.

"That's so sweet of her," Alice said.

"Marian would like you to come, Alice. Maybe read with her and show her things to study about the world," Mrs. Cook said.

"How old is Marian?" Alice asked.

170

"Just twenty-four, dear, but when you get to know her, you'll see there's nothing going to slow her down. She's promised herself a rich, full life."

"I understand," Alice said.

"God bless her," Missus said.

"Mrs. Cook, I would be honored. I absolutely will come by and read and talk with Marian. It would be my pleasure."

Missus looked across the table at Big Mike and caught his eye.

"Alice, what is the name of the judge?" Missus asked, not taking her eyes from Big Mike.

"Judge Munson," Alice said.

"Mike, it sounds like you and Mike Shea have your hands full straightening out the judge's misunderstanding," Missus said.

"Would you mind explaining?" Big Mike asked.

"Munson, Munson, hmmmm," Missus said. "We know every living soul in Munson's Corner. You even know the Munson fellow who runs the chicken farm. Surely there must be a relationship to someone there and this judge in Syracuse."

"There're a lot of Munsons," Big Mike said.

"Mike Shea is the most respected men in this area," Missus said.

"That he is," Big Mike said.

"Take him with you."

"Where?" Big Mike asked.

"I'm certain between you and Mike Shea you can convince a judge that this teacher is as sane as day and no threat to herself or anyone else."

Big Mike didn't respond but sat there, looking at Missus.

"Right, dear?" Missus added.

"You're right! We'll get on it first thing tomorrow," Big Mike said.

"Tonight, dear," Missus said, looking at her watch.

"Excuse me?"

"I'm sure Mike Shea would favor a visit from you about now. Explain to him we have a school teacher who would like to get on with her life."

"Yes, dear." Big Mike smiled.

It wasn't a few days 'afore the two Mikes were able to corner the judge. That's the way it was in 1953. Important people like a judge were accessible for talkin' to or being interrupted on their way into a building. Near everyone in the area knew both Big Mike and Mike Shea. They were prominent, respected businessmen.

Big Mike explained to the judge what happened and how Pompey Hollow was coming to their rescue. He made sense to Judge Munson and he shook the men's hands and promised he would get the case thrown out, and Alice could get on with her life. Big Mike asked him if he was a fisherman, and they talked about trying Oneida Lake sometime together. Mike Shea offered a free deli sandwich or hunting gloves at the store, if he was ever in the area.

Roy got to Syracuse in time to get back into school and get his diploma. Alice was able to rent a room on a farm on Ridge Road, and with Marian's help and the help of the PTA, children the countryside over would visit her for home tutoring. Miss Doxtator borrowed books from the library for Alice to read to the children.

On Saturday mornings throughout the balance of the summer, children would come, throw a nickel or dime in a can, but were never required to. They'd sit on the floor of the empty tool shed and listen to Alice read chapters and books to them while Marian poured and passed out paper cups of lemonade or cider and handed out sugar cookies.

It was a magical time for the Crown. People were learning tolerance. They were becoming one big extended family—and children were the beneficiaries.

CHAPTER 14

SECRET CODES AND MOONLIGHT HAYRIDES

It wasn't long after the Berwyn murder misunderstanding—as a matter of fact, it was the night before Jerry's last day at Hotel Syracuse—when the telephone rang, interrupting supper. Jerry jumped and ran into his folk's bedroom to answer it.

"Hello?"

"Tall Jerry?"

"Yes."

"Mary called an emergency meeting," Barber said.

"Okay."

"Midnight tonight, the cemetery," Barber said.

"What!? I work tomorrow."

"She wants it tonight."

"I have to be up at five, why tonight?" Jerry asked.

"Can you get Dick and Duba?" Barber asked.

"Do you know why?"

"Sounds important."

"Can it be all that important?" Jerry asked.

"Must be, or she wouldn't ask for Dick," Barber said.

It dawned on Jerry that Mary might have the translation of the secret note.

"Hold on," he said.

He set the telephone down and went to Dick, whispered in his ear about Mary calling a meeting and wanting him there at midnight. Dick nodded okay. Jerry went back and picked up the telephone.

"I'll be there," Jerry said. "Dick, too."

"Bring your lantern," Barber said. "My batteries are dying."

Eleven thirty came, and Tall Jerry grabbed the lantern, a handful of stick matches, and crawled out of his bedroom window to find Dick's car in the middle of the drive, him asleep in it. He got in, waking him. Dick sat up, rubbed his eyes, started the engine without thinking, rolled down to the edge of the front gate and pulled to a stop.

"Get out and walk from here," Dick said. "I've got to go get Conway and Dwyer. Duba's driving from Manlius. He's probably on his way now."

Jerry got out of the car in the darkness of a quarter moon. He walked up the hill and into Farmer Parker's cinder driveway. He opened the gate and went through the bull pasture and up the wagon trail, climbing to the top hayfield. Once across, he paused to light the lantern, crawled under the barbed-wire fence and led his way down through a deep fog that reflected the moonlight rays into the dark cemetery.

Most were there—Mary, Holbrook, Barber, Randy, Bases, Mayor, and Duba. They were waiting on Dick, Conway, and Dwyer. Jerry set the lantern on my gravestone. Sleepy-headed kids sat or stood staring into it, yawning, waiting for the meeting to start. Kids turned off their flashlights. In time, the Willys pulled up into the cemetery drive with Dick, Conway, and Dwyer stepping out of it.

Mary stood on my stone. I lifted myself from my grave to a pine tree branch high over Jerry's head. Mary looked Dick stern in the eye, then Duba, and then the other two older boys, one at a time, getting their attention.

"Don't laugh. I have a pen pal. His name is David Eisenhower. He's the grandson of the president of the United States of America."

"Ike?" Duba asked.

"Yes."

"You write to this kid?" Duba asked.

"Yes," Mary said.

"He's a pen pal?" Dick asked.

174

"He writes back, too."

"Why are we here?" Duba asked.

"I sent him a copy of what you found under the bridge, Dick."

"Jerry told me."

"Look what I got back."

"You're joking, right?" Dick asked.

Mary held up sealed envelopes addressed to her, each marked with a crayon: #1, #2, and #3.

"It's no joke," Mary said.

"What are they?" Dick asked.

"I was afraid to open them," Mary said.

"Who really sent them?" Duba asked.

"David Eisenhower, for real," Mary said.

"Isn't he just a kid?" Dick asked.

"What difference does it make?" Holbrook asked.

"He's right, what difference does it make how old anybody is?" Tall Jerry asked.

"At five we listened to the Normandy invasion on the radio," Mayor said.

"His grandfather is the president, for Pete's sake," Tall Jerry said. "Look at what Dad would do for us, and he only has a bakery."

"Can you imagine what the president can do for his own kid or his grandson?" Mary added.

"Open number one. Let's see what it says," Dick said.

Mary borrowed Barber's jackknife and slit the envelope open. She lifted the lantern for better light. Mayor and Vaas leaned in behind her. Randy took the lantern from her hand and held it up for her.

"It says:

'Dear Pen Pal Mary, Thank you for your letter. Does the Pompey Hollow Book Club have a decoder person? Give number two to your decoder person. Please write back. Yours truly, your Pen Pal, David Eisenhower.'"

175

Mary looked up.

"Duba, will you be our decoder?" she asked.

"Decoder person? He's got to be kidding," Duba said. "Decoder person?"

Mary handed Duba letter number two. He opened it, held it by the lantern and looked at the piece of paper inside.

"It's a code master, all right. It must be the code breaker for messages from him," Duba said. "Well, I'll be."

"Hide it," Mary said, "and don't lose it."

"I won't," Duba said, stuffing it in his pocket.

With that, Mary opened the envelope with number three written on it. She unfolded the piece of paper. It read:

*IDGRYT GDVO YPMDWYYP ATBX WOGY MDXW 0733
CTRYGN FBC PDF HZYTY NZYF DTY TYNCTG GBNE
IBGN DEDTX NZYX*

"This is in code for sure," she said. She handed it to Duba.

Dick and Duba turned and walked to the car and under the ceiling lamp. They carefully decoded the message using the secret code master. They read it, looked at each other and walked back to the group.

"Ready for this?" Dick asked.

They gathered around.

"This isn't a translation of the note we sent. What you sent him was a list of words. This is a warning from somebody. It says:

*'DANGER—NAZI ESCAPEES FROM PINE CAMP—1944—
URGENT YOU SAY WHERE THEY ARE—RETURN NOTE
DON'T ALARM THEM'"*

"Holy Cobako!" Tall Jerry said. "It's them!"

"Who?" Mayor asked.

176

"Wow," Holbrook said.

"Who?" Mayor asked.

"The Nazi POWs," Holbrook said.

"Right in our own back yard," Jerry said.

The group stood there with their mouths open.

"What does it mean, 'return note'? Does it mean to write him back?" Conway asked.

"They're the escapees from Pine Camp," Dick said.

"Dang!" Tall Jerry said.

"It must mean we're supposed to put the German's note back where we found it, so they don't get wise," Duba said.

"That's right—'return note, don't alarm them' must mean don't let them know we're on to them," Dwyer said.

"Mary, write this Eisenhower kid," Dick said. "Tell him we're putting it back and from now on we'll only copy others we find, and we'll keep sending them."

"Okay, I will."

"Be sure to tell him we want to catch them if we prove they're stealing."

"What!?"

"Ask him if he can tell us what that note we already sent said. Even ask him if we should tell somebody at Pine Camp about the two guys. Let's see what he says," Dick said.

"Now you're kidding, right?" Mary asked.

"Write him, say those things."

"Can't they arrest us if we don't do what they say?" Mary asked.

"*They* aren't saying anything!" Dick barked. "You've got a letter from a kid, probably your age, maybe younger. He could be making it all up."

"But—" Mary started.

"But he could be getting help, and it's for real," Dick said.

"Don't forget this kid gets to do something no other kid on earth can do," Tall Jerry said.

"What's that?" Duba asked.

"He can sit on the president's desk and play checkers with the president of the United States if he wants," Tall Jerry said. "If these notes are for real, they could be coming from the president…"

"He's right," Duba said.

"Write the letter," Dick said. "If he writes back, call a meeting. In the meantime, have everyone at Shea's, noon on Tuesday after Labor Day."

"Anybody have anything else to talk about?" Mary asked.

"We're having this year's hayride Saturday," Barber announced. "We could use one more tractor or a team of horses. Everybody come for sure. There'll be bobbing for apples, pies and cider, lots of corn on the cob."

"Can I bring my square dance records?" Mary asked.

"Sure. There may be a fiddler, but bring them, your phonograph player, too. We'll hook it up in the hay barn for dancing after the hayride."

Dick drove Conway and Dwyer home and then backed the Willys into the barn garage. He went to his room and got the original German note and, in the dark, followed the creek to the bridge to put it back under the pack of matches where he had found it. After, he stuck his head in Jerry's room.

"This all has to be top secret," he said. "Tell whoever was there tonight that it's top secret, and not to say a word to anyone."

"Do you really think they're the Nazi POW escape guys?" Jerry asked.

"I know they are," Dick said. "That code says it all."

"Dang!" Jerry said.

"Top secret—spread the word," Dick said.

"The club pretty much knows about why we called the SOS," Jerry said.

"All the others who weren't there tonight know is it's about thieves," Dick said. "They don't know anything else. They don't

178

know it's about Nazi POW escaped criminals. We can talk all we want about thieves, but leave what we know about the Nazi thing out of it until we figure it out."

"We've been hoping to catch them. I think they know enough not to talk about it, but I'll tell them," Jerry said.

Dick reached in his pocket, pulled out a piece of paper and set it on Jerry's desk.

"Here's another one. Copy it and get it to me tonight. I'll put it back under the bridge. Wake me if you have to."

Jerry swallowed. "Another one from under the bridge?"

"I check under there every day. Copy it fast. Wake me when you're done."

"It's a list of words again," Jerry said.

"Make two copies, just like they appear on the paper," Dick said.

"Okay. But you have to drive me to work in the morning, so I can get the copy of it dropped off to Mary to send to Eisenhower, Special Delivery."

"I will," Dick said.

Jerry turned his desk lamp on, pulled his pencil and pen out and carefully copied the German and traced the drawings. He woke Dick and gave him the original back. Dick walked the dark creek, saw the coast was clear and returned the note to the ledge under the bridge.

In the morning they drove to the hamlet, Delphi. Jerry stepped out of the car at Bases's house and walked to where Mary parked her popsicle cart behind his garage. He put the copy in an envelope marked SD for Special Delivery and taped it to the handle of her peddle cart. She would see it and know what to do.

Dick drove to Syracuse, taking Jerry to his last day of work before school started.

The Saturday hayride night at the Barber's was under clear skies speckled with stars and a bright full moon smiling down. The atmosphere was like a happy circus.

All my life ole Charlie here ain't never seen anything quite like a Barber harvest hayride celebration. The bonfire sparked high up into the heavens, touching the stars and enjoyed for more than a mile or two away. Farmhands would keep her burnin' proud and tall throughout the night while wives helped in the kitchen. Kerosene lanterns lit and strung up all around the lawns, drive and porch. When I was alive, I would hitch Nellie up and ride my buckboard down Pompey Hollow Road to spinster Nettie's cabin. Nellie would settle down in harness rig, lift her hoof to rest. I would set with Nettie and pull a chaw, sit and watch the bonfire from up on the Hollow's hill every year.

This time ole Charlie here was on Barber's porch roof. I could take it all in up close and not miss a thing.

Two tractors had two hay wagons attached to each of them. Farmer Parker's team of horses, Sarge and Sally, were hitched to a single hay wagon. All the wagons were bedded down with golden straw that glistened in the moon's glow. The hayriders came from as far as Tully and Lafayette—even DeRuyter Lake, I expect. Cars were lining up and parking along the side of the road as far back as Delphi hamlet one way and down toward the Cherry Valley the other side of the road. Folks were walking and holdin' hands, stoppin' and kissin'. Others were coming alone, hoping to find that special someone. The happy, sad, worn and weary, young and old, all coming for the music, singin', dancin', good food and a nice break from a summer of hard work.

Carl Vaas pulled into the driveway in his Dodge milk can hauler, brakes squealing to a stop, him slapping the outside of his driver's side door with his hand, looking for a little help.

"Can't stay, folks. I have routes to make, but I brought a few to the party," Carl yelled out his window.

Randy stepped down from the truck, and then Mayor climbed down. They asked Carl to wait until they got instructions from Mr. or Mrs. Barber on what to do with Alice. They followed their noses into the kitchen, smelling the brisket, where most of the action was. Mrs. Barber came out walking over to the passenger side of Carl's truck, drying her hands with her apron. She reached up and pulled the door full open. Sitting on the seat was Alice. Carl had picked her up at her place on Ridge Road.

"Will you lookie here! Welcome to the hayride," Mrs. Barber said. "What a pleasant surprise! Alice, we're so happy you came."

"You sure I won't be in the way?" Alice asked.

Mrs. Barber ignored the thought.

"Awful nice of you to fetch Alice, Carl. Care for cider?"

"Sure enough," Mr. Vaas said.

"Randy, go fetch your daddy a wax paper cup of cider from the kitchen. Go on now, run."

"I don't want to be a bother," Alice said.

"Nonsense," Mrs. Barber snipped. "Why a hayride isn't a hayride lest everyone comes, dear. Isn't that so, Carl? That's the tradition."

"I've got my milk can route tonight, Gerty. Save a piece of pie, for sure," Mr. Vaas said.

"Maybe I can sit on the porch. My wheelchair is in the back," Alice said.

"There ain't any bumps on any logs allowed at a good old-fashioned harvest hayride, Alice."

"I don't understand."

"If you do that, set up there on the porch all alone, what on earth will the children do for storytelling?" Mrs. Barber asked.

"What do you mean?"

"Why, we hooked a team of horses to the hay wagons special just for the kids, hoping you'd come. Horses are quieter than tractors, you know—not as smelly, neither. Kids everywhere like to hear stories on hayrides, especially this close to Halloween. Who on earth can we get better than you to tell them?"

"Really?" Alice asked.

"Why, my goodness. They love your stories, Alice," Mrs. Barber said.

Alice beamed a smile warm enough to light up a room.

"I can sure tell them stories," she said.

"We just knew you could, and here you are, answering our prayers that you would come," Mrs. Barber said.

Carl gulped down his cider, crushed the paper cup in his hand and tossed it on the floor of the truck. He clutched his Dodge and started backing out, waving. Why, it weren't but two minutes when Alice was carried over and sitting all comfortable on a bed of straw in the horse-drawn hay wagon, saying hello to the kids climbing on. Young Bobby crawled over the straw and sat next to her, held her hand and waited for the fun to start.

It wasn't long when a car pulled in the drive and Marian got out, wearing her leg braces. She stood up on her own, smilin', her hair in a fresh curl with a pretty pink ribbon in it. She tucked a crutch under each arm and started workin' toward the hay wagons. A nice lookin' young man, the Bruce Gary boy, it was, from up the hill in Berwyn saw Marian making her way on the crutches and stepped out of the crowd. Without catching her eye, he bellowed a hello.

She paused, as if she recognized the voice. She caught his eye and smiled the warmest smile you could imagine back at him. She hadn't seen Bruce in near half a dozen years. They'd known each other from high school. He stepped up and reminded her of their dancing together at their senior prom. She was his prom date, long before she came down with polio. He'd been drafted and away to serve in the army.

They stood and talked a bit, and then he leaned down and lifted her up, her back in his arms, her legs and leg braces in the other raising her like he was carrying her across a threshold, and then setting her gently on a hay wagon. He stowed her crutches, poking them in under the straw, and climbed up to be at her side for the ride.

Tall Jerry, Barber, and their friends walked about, looking properly starched and scrubbed for the occasion. Holbrook had used his brand-new Remington electric razor for the first time and shaved his stubble clean off. The pretty girls they knew—Judy Finch, the Cerio sisters; Mary Margaret Cox, the Holbrook and Bradshaw girls, the Cooks, and a bunch of others at all ages, one as pretty as the next—promised a festive and starry-eyed evening for the men and boys.

The older boys circled in on the Halton girl, Linda Sipfle, and a bevy of lovely girls more their age, all with the same thoughts in mind, to sing along and dance the night away; the older boys lookin' to oblige them on the barn dance floor and to be kissin'.

When Dwyer and Conway parked and walked in the drive, they weren't but maybe fifty feet in when Conway froze up and couldn't move a lick. First thought was he had a muscle spasm from too long settin' in a tractor seat. Then the thought turned to maybe the green apple he munched in the car on the way over wasn't doing him right. It wasn't until a more perceptive Mrs. Barber looked out the kitchen window and saw how the lad was holding up foot traffic and fidgeting when she decided to make her own understanding as to why. Most women would have known it right off, she would say later.

She walked out and stepped behind Conway. She turned him and pointed him like a wheelbarrow and gave him a push over to the girl that had made the lad freeze in the first place—pretty Judy Clancy. Oh my, but he was smitten. Judy had smiling Irish eyes. They were both in a gander at each other, dreamy eyes to dreamy eyes, and without so much as a word spoken, Conway took Judy by the hand and walked her over to the lead hay wagon, where they crawled up, sat, and waited. The two were in love at first sight and ever since. Ole Charlie here saw it with my own eyes.

Eventually the tractors started, the horses, Sarge and Sally did a giddy-up, and the wagons pulled away onto the back fields

183

for a couple of hours of moonlight, singing, quiet romance, and storytelling.

"Shine on, shine on Harvest Moon,
Up in the sky
I ain't had no loving
Since January, February,
June and July…"

The night was filled with dancing music, song, food, fun, and games. Fire pits steamed from husks of corn and raw potatoes thrown on for roasting; a roast pig for carving turned on a spit. Conway won the milk can spin-a-twirl contest. The lad could twirl two at a time. Marian and young Bobby won the Halloween pumpkin carving contest. Dwyer could spit a watermelon seed the farthest, sure enough. Farmer Parker had the best cow call.

Dick and Duba walked by Tall Jerry and Holbrook with corn-cobs in their craw. Dick stopped Jerry and pulled him out of the way of prying ears.

"I have an idea," Dick said.

"What?" Jerry asked.

"We know those two are the escaped Nazis from Pine Camp, right?"

"Right."

"Bobby's dad gets out soon, right?"

"Yes."

"What if we make him a big hero; we help *him* catch the two crooks?"

"He'd be a hero, then," Jerry said.

"You mean us help him catch them instead of him helping us?" Jerry asked.

"Yes."

"In Bobby's eyes, he'd be a hero for sure," Tall Jerry said.

"It could save the kid a lot of fights growing up, trying to explain his old man," Dick said.

"You're a good guy, Dick."

"Don't say a word about it. Duba and I'll figure it out. We're going to Auburn to meet him."

As soon as Dick was finished talking, he and Duba disappeared into a night of fun. Tall Jerry was proud he had him as a big brother.

With people shuffling about eating, talking and laughing, Mary grabbed hold of Duba's younger brother Donny, set up the phonograph player in the hay barn and people square-danced for hours to her special mail-order record that promised many evenings of fun and friendship. Ladies and gents sat around the walls on hay bales, stomping their feet, up on the hayloft, clapping to the music, enjoying every *do-si-do*, *allemande left*, and *twirl*.

Alice sat up, beaming a smile from her wheelchair, clapping her hands, keeping time to the music. The children loved the stories she had told, and sitting around her. Her soul was right with the world tonight.

Mrs. Barber and the ladies were in chairs on the lawn under the big oak humming and singing gospel, thanking the Lord for their families, friends, and the good crop of pumpkins and apples this season.

Holbrook and Tall Jerry walked to the main house and set on the stoop a spell, taking a break, sizing up the evening. They were speculating as to who they might work up the nerve to ask to dance, or did they manage to get any kissing in on the hayride.

It was then Jerry started.

"Hold still. Don't look up," Jerry said.

"Huh?" Holbrook grunted.

"Don't move. Wait until they pass by. Don't let them see us looking up at them," Jerry said.

"The Nazis?" Holbrook mumbled.

"Yes. Okay, come on, they've gone by."

The lads rushed out to the first car on the side of the road and slowly peered over it. Sure enough, the '42 stake-bed with one side door was idling past cars on its way toward Delphi hamlet, as if they were looking for goodies with a flashlight in the front or back seats of cars they passed by.

"We have to tell Dick and Duba," Jerry said.

The older boys were nowhere to be found, so they would wait until morning to tell them. As the evening wore on, the bonfire began to smolder and the crowd thinned. Tall Jerry and Holbrook started walking to Jerry's. Holbrook didn't have to be at the Tully Bakery the next day.

"Hey!" A shout came from behind them.

They both turned.

"Mary said tomorrow, noon, the cemetery," Barber said, before he took a bite from a roasted corncob.

He turned to go back up his drive. He looked back. "Don't leave now," Barber said. "They're getting the fiddles out. Ray Randall's going to put on a show."

The lads walked toward the Delphi Falls, talking about pretty girls, Holbrook's new Remington razor, Nazi escapees, and awkward square dance steps. To be safe, they didn't turn to walk up Cardner Road at Maxwell's mill this night. It would have meant crossing the bridge. In case the Nazi POWs were under it again, they climbed the Delphi Road hill up by where my old place was, and cut through the woods to their camp over the falls. They climbed partway down the cliff, sat on the big white rock, looked at the moon, and discussed girls at the hayride.

"I wonder how many of them wear brassieres," Holbrook said.

"What?" Jerry squirmed.

"The girls we know," Holbrook said.

"We know Mary wears one," Jerry said. "Did you ever apologize to her about that?"

"I tried, but she wouldn't let me."

186

"Why not?"

"She said she knew I was only being protective of her because I have so many sisters."

"True?"

"She said I didn't have to apologize."

"Mary's nice like that."

"Did you see her and Donny Duba hugging on the hayride?"

SECRET CODE

A = D	1 = O	N = G
B = S	2 = 9	O = B
C = M	3 = 1	P = W
D = I	4 = 3	Q = J
E = Y	5 = 4	R = T
F = A	6 = 2	S = P
G = R	7 = 6	T = N
H = Z	8 = 5	U = C
i = O	9 = 7	V = L
J = U	O = 8	W = H
K = Q		X = K
L = E		Y = F
M = X		Z = V

CHAPTER 15

FROM THE CHIEF AND
SUPREME COMMANDER

"I got these two letters," Mary said.

"Open one at a time," Duba said.

"This one is in code," Mary said.

*IBGBNMDNMZ—TYWYDN—IBGBNMDNMZ—CTRYGN
—DTXF SCPOGYPP—MDXW ITCX*

Dick and Duba stepped back and leaned on the car deciphering.

Ole Charlie here followed them and sat on the hood to listen. They walked back to the group.

"Here's what it says:

"'Do not catch—repeat—do not catch—urgent—army business —Camp Drum,'" Duba said.

"Oh, Jeeze," Mayor moaned. "We're in so much trouble."

"What do you make of it, Dick?" Mary asked.

"If this is for real, and it smells like it is," Dick said. "I think they already checked these two guys out and think they aren't dangerous."

"What makes you think that?" Mary asked.

"They would never let us go near it."

"I don't get it," Tall Jerry said.

"They said 'do not catch.'"

"So?" Mary asked.

"They didn't say to drop what we're doing."

189

"We don't want to get in trouble," Mary said.

"They just said it was army business, do not catch."

"I think he's right," Duba said.

"Maybe they're just two old desperate crooks who never wanted to be in the German army in the first place," Dick said.

"Two guys who escaped Pine Camp's prison when no one was looking and have been hiding out since 1944, living off their wits," Duba said.

"That note said Camp Drum. What's Camp Drum?" Holbrook asked.

"It's the same army base that used to be Pine Camp during the war," Dick said. "They changed the name from Pine Camp to Camp Drum."

"We should tell someone at Camp Drum our plan," Mary said.

"No," Dick said.

"Why not?"

"First off, we don't have a plan. Mary, you just keep telling David Eisenhower what we're up to."

"We saw them driving past the Barbers last night," Tall Jerry said.

"You did?" Dick asked.

"They were looking in cars with a flashlight," Holbrook said.

"Who's laughing at my pen pal now?" Mary asked.

"Mary, if we pull this thing off, I'll personally save up and send that Eisenhower kid a pocket watch. The kid is all right. He's got guts," Dick said.

"I already told him he's a member of the club," Mary said.

"Here's the other note." Mary said. She opened it and handed it to Duba.

GYWNCGY 9 BWYTDNOBGP SBIFRCDTI REOXXYT NDKDSEY SCTG NZOP OQI

Duba walked with Dick back to the Willys. This time Dick lit a cigarette, letting Duba do the deciphering work.

"Look at this," Duba said, turning his back to the club members.

"What?" Dick asked.

"Go on, read it," Duba said, holding it out for Dick.

Dick took the piece of paper Duba had scribbled on.

Neptune 2—Operations Bodyguard—Glimmer—Taxable— burn this—Ike

Dick turned a pale white.

"Burn this?" Dick asked.

"Look who signed it," Duba said.

"I can read," Dick said.

"It's signed 'Ike,'" Duba whispered.

"This can't be for real," Dick whispered.

"But what if it is real?" Duba asked.

Dick covered his mouth with his hand.

"What's the chance this is from Ike himself—the president?"

They read it again.

"It's got to be a clue," Dick said. "It's either from Ike, or it's something David heard him say and wrote it like it was from his grandfather."

"I don't even know what it says," Duba said.

"We'll know if we figure out the message," Dick said.

"It has to have clues in it somewhere," Duba said.

"We have to burn it," Dick said. "It says to burn it."

"You think we should?" Duba asked.

"We're not taking any chances," Dick said.

He grabbed Duba's ballpoint pen and wrote *Neptune 2* on his palm. He wrote *Operations Bodyguard*, *Glimmer*, and *Taxable* on his wrist and handed the paper back to Duba.

"Hold it steady," Dick said.

191

He struck a match and lit the message and the translation papers on fire. They watched them burn and crushed the ashes on the ground.

"Mum's the word on this," Dick said. "Tomorrow let's get to the school library and figure this out."

Duba got the chills. He followed Dick back to the group.

"Tuesday, after Labor Day, is the meeting set up at Shea's—noon?" Dick asked.

"I called everybody," Barber said.

"If not, set it up," Dick said.

"What did that note say?" Mary asked.

Dick gave her a look, as if not to ask.

"Tuesday," Duba said.

Everyone knew not to ask. They were mesmerized by the word *army* in the first message and knew they were in for an adventure.

The next day the school was empty, but the school doors were unlocked. Duba and Dick made their way up the stairs and to the hall corner and library, turning the lights on.

"Pull out any books or LIFE magazines you can find about World War II." Dick said, "Anything on Eisenhower, Patton, maybe the Normandy invasion."

"We could get in trouble if we got caught in here," Duba said.

"No kids get in trouble for reading in a library," Dick said.

"What's on your mind?" Duba asked.

"We have to find a clue in that message from Ike. It might have clue words we can't see yet."

"It could be from him, or something he could have said to David, playing army," Duba said.

"I'm thinking this David kid is pretty smart. My guess is he hasn't spilled the beans on us and has been making it a game with his dad and his grandfather."

"Why would the one be signed 'Ike' with special instructions to burn it?" Duba asked.

"You have me there," Dick said.

"It could be David signed it like that, but if Ike signed it, then I'd go back to what you thought originally," Duba said.

"That they checked the two guys out, and they aren't any big threat—just old thieves stealing enough to live on and get back to Germany as soon as they figure out how to change their identities and make false passports," Dick said.

Duba carried a stack of magazines over to the table, the top magazine open to a picture story.

"Take a look at the pictures I found in this one," Duba said.

"What of?" Dick asked.

"Rubber army tanks and trucks."

"Rubber tanks?" Dick asked. "Let me see."

"Look, they're all life-size. Even the rubber landing craft here is life-size. They're all phony. Says here they were made of papier mache or rubber. Even blown up like balloons," Duba said.

Inflatable rubber decoy tank

"Look what it says," Dick said. "General Eisenhower had an entire top-secret division of tanks, jeeps, and planes all built out of rubber and set up on the banks of England to decoy German spy planes."

"Now why would he do that?" Duba asked.

"Here it is on a map—Operation Bodyguard, in Maidenhead, England," Dick said.

A rubber troop carrier.

"A rubber troop carrier decoy," Duba said. "According to this, General Patton was headquartered there as a decoy. One of the most famous generals of the war was stuck in the middle of a rubber tank and plane division doing nothing, just to make it all look real."

"Operation Bodyguard was Ike's phony army in Maidenhead," Dick said.

"It's making sense now. Neptune must have been a code name for something else Ike dreamed up," Duba said.

"Look here," Dick said, turning a page. "They even called it Patton's 'pretend Army'—well I'll be."

"Why do you think Ike built a whole rubber army?" Duba asked.

"It was genius," Dick said. "He wanted Germany to think we would be attacking Calais in western France all the while he was going to attack Normandy."

"That was genius," Duba said.

"It says here they invented wire recorders and had loudspeakers going twenty-four hours a day in the middle of the dummy army to make it sound real, in case Germany had spy planes," Dick said.

"That's it, then!" Duba said.

"What?"

"That's the big clue. Ike wants us to fool the Nazi POW crooks," Duba said.

"By fool, you mean decoy?" Dick asked.

"He wants us to let them get close enough so we can make them think we know about them and who they are," Duba said.

"And then scare them off," Dick said. "Ike wants us to create decoys, just like he did in England. Noises and sounds, too. He wants it all."

"I think you're right. Look at this," Duba said. "It says here the army broke the code of German spies that were hiding and working in England and Ike's pretend troops retransmitted messages to them to tell them places where the attack would start, just to throw the Germans off. That must have been code word *Neptune*."

"It is. Look at this," Dick said. "This says Ike used small boats and aircraft simulating invasion fleets talking to each other over radios with made-up conversations. Code words *Glimmer* and *Taxable* kept stringing the German Nazi spies along, backed up by the original Operation Bodyguard rubber-armored decoy division."

Duba stood. "The Nazis fell for it hook, line and sinker, and believed the main Allied invasion force would attack and land in the Calais region of France. It worked. The ghost army idea—it all worked. They never figured out we were going to attack Normandy. Amazing."

Dick set the magazines on the table and turned to Duba.

"Know what I think?" Dick asked.

"What?"

"I think Ike is calling the shots for us. I think it's a war game for him. He's having fun. He's planning this through his favorite person in the whole world, his grandson, David."

"Just so David can learn tactics and strategy," Duba said. "How lucky is that kid to have a grandfather like that?"

"He's given us big clues," Dick said. "Bodyguard, Neptune, Glimmer, Taxable. It's up to us to come up with a good plan."

"Do you think Ike wants us to build a phony diversion, like his ghost Army?" Duba asked.

"Something that appears out of nowhere," Dick said.

"So we can fool the Nazi guys after we trap them," Duba said.

"I think you're right," Dick said. "Grab a dictionary and look up a word."

"What word?" Duba asked while lifting the large dictionary to the table.

"Look up *asset* or maybe *assets*. They use it a lot in this story about their mission," Dick said.

Duba paged through the book of words.

"It says here a useful or valuable thing or person," Duba said, pointing to a word on a page.

"That could mean anything," Dick said.

"That's all it says," Duba said.

"See if there are any synonyms for the word *asset*, something that can give us a clue," Dick said.

"It has a bunch of synonyms."

"Read them."

"There's *benefit, advantage, blessing, good or strong points, strength*, and there's more," Duba said.

"That's all we need. I get it now," Dick said.

"Get what?"

"We'll come up with a plan, but after we list our assets, just like they did before the Normandy invasion on D-day," Dick said.

"Now I'm lost," Duba said.

"Let's go to the chalk board. I'll explain what Ike's clues mean," Dick said.

They walked to the board where Dick picked up chalk and jotted reminder notes as he thought of them. He drew figures when he had to do that.

"Duba, we play chess, right?"

"Yep."

"We know chess is a war game…"

"Yes."

"It's tactics and strategy. Short-term and long-term objectives, right?"

"Right," Duba said.

"Well, this is Ike's game, a game of chess."

"I gotcha," Duba said.

"What are our assets and what is our strategy?" Dick asked.

"Keep talking," Duba said.

"Asset—we know who the Nazi crooks are; asset—we know where they hang out; asset—we know they smoke a lot; asset—we know they steal; asset—we know they aren't afraid of crowds; asset —now we know we aren't supposed to catch them, just run them off." Dick said.

"I'm not following you," Duba said.

"Those are our assets. Everything we know or have is an asset," Dick said.

"I think I get it," Duba said.

"We need to lure them in—lure them in someplace where there's a crowd," Dick said. "We need to lure them to where we have the advantage of knowing the terrain better than they do, and when we do that, we can be in complete control."

"How about your place at the Delphi Falls?" Duba asked.

"Good idea. It's surrounded by cliffs, hills, and woods they won't know." Dick said.

"Let's have a square-dance in your barn garage," Duba said.

"That's good," Dick said. "We need to figure out how we can get them to want to make a fast getaway, not just be snooping in cars, like Jerry and Holbrook said they did at Barber's hayride."

"You mean we come up with a kind of bait—bait so big it would make them want to steal it and run."

197

"Yes."

"And if that doesn't make them run, have some kind of backup something to scare them into running out of there," Duba said.

Dick erased the chalkboard.

"From now on, all anyone outside of you, me, Dwyer, and Conway will know—at least until the Nazi crooks are chased out of the area—is that they're just a couple of old guys stealing rubber and iron and selling it for scrap."

"You're right," Duba said.

"Nothing more," Dick said.

"But we plan it just like Ike is hinting we should plan it—with a ghost army that pops up and sends phony messages," Duba said.

"And if we jump out of nowhere at them, let them know we know who they are and what they look like, they'll run like the cowards they are and never come back," Dick said.

"Should work," Duba said.

"If we can pull all that off, it'll work," Dick said.

"Should we be calling him Ike?" Duba asked.

"From now on, he's General," Dick said. "Let's put the books back—the magazines, too. Be neat about it. We don't want to leave any evidence of what we were looking at."

Dick paused. "There's one more thing we should do," he said.

"What's that?" Duba asked.

"Monday let's drive to Auburn and see if they'll let us talk to Bobby's dad. Let's tell him what we're up to and ask if he wants to help us run the crooks off when he gets out."

"Don't they listen in on conversations in prisons?"

"If they do, we'll just say hello and tell him how Bobby is doing, and he can't wait for him to be out. We'll play it by ear. This is his chance to be a hero, for a change. Locals will respect him for helping us run off the Nazi guys and their stealing."

They left the school, drove to pick up Conway and Dwyer and headed to Manlius.

Pulling into Suburban Park and parking, they piled out, gathered in a circle and joined hands in the middle.

"Code name for the operation we're setting up is Neptune 2, just like Ike's clues hinted it should be," Dick said. "Neptune was the secret code for his decoy messaging operation for the Normandy invasion. So our code name is going to be Neptune 2. It's official."

They shook hands on the name for the project. It had the highest priority. They were planning to entice the crooks with a lure, catch them in the act, and then chase them off for good.

An inflatable rubber truck—decoy in Ike's Operation Fortitude

CHAPTER 16

IT'S OFFICIAL—THE S.O.S. IS CALLED

Labor Day crawled into the crown on sails of chilled breezes crossing Lake Ontario from Canada. It reminded folks that fall colors were not far behind, and it was time to pull the sweaters and long johns from cedar chests and moth balls—time to tuck summer away for a couple of seasons.

First day back at school after Labor Day, halls smelled like moth balls and cedar. It reminded ole Charlie here of my footlocker aboard ship in 1916.

With the first SOS meeting approaching, noontime at Shea's store, the book club members were finding it hard to concentrate on teachers' back-to-school announcements, much less do any first-day schoolwork.

The message about the crooks got out to the crown, and rumors and gossip flew about for the week, and volunteer prospects were growin' in numbers. An autumn adventure was more fun than football. Dick, Duba, Dwyer, and Conway had come through for them before, and everyone was confident they would again.

High schoolers could leave school during lunch hour. Some sit and eat their sack lunches on the front lawn. After the lunch bell rang Dick and Duba walked to Shea's store and waited for kids to show up. Mr. Ossont, the agriculture teacher, was leaning on a maple tree nearby. Dick and Duba took position on the top step, reading plans to themselves, whispering through small details, getting ready to speak. As the crowd grew into the street, Mike Shea stepped out of the store with a smile and an opened box of shoes in his hands.

"You kids are always welcome. I don't mind you having your meetings here. Just leave room so my customers can get in or out of the store."

"Sure enough," Dick said. He and David moved to one side of the steps.

Dick saw Mr. Ossont in the middle of the growing crowd.

"Mr. Ossont, should you be here?" Dick asked.

"Boy and howdy!" Mr. Ossont shouted back. "If you're talking about the crooks, those varmints—they tried to steal a compressor we had outside the school shop while we were waiting on the lacquer to dry on a wheelchair we're fixing. Just try to stop me from being here!"

Mr. Ossont was different than most teachers. He taught Agriculture and Mechanics. Most kids in the school were farmers. He had a special bond with them.

Dick got down to business. He wiped his glasses on his shirt, lifted them toward the sun to inspect them, and put them on. He signaled Duba to begin.

"Listen up," Duba shouted. "You know the rules—you can join the Pompey Hollow Book Club just by showing up to meetings."

"They know," Mary said.

"This is an SOS meeting—we don't belong to their club but when they call an SOS we help them…and they called an SOS," Dick said.

"Two old guys have been driving around our hills. We know they're stealing scrap iron and rubber," Duba said. "They've been seen pretty much everywhere in the area. If we want to stop them, we have to work fast, or they could get wise before we have a chance to trap them and catch them or whatever we're going to do with them."

With nothin' more than that to go on, Dick stepped up. "Who wants in on the SOS?" he asked.

Every hand went up. One hundred per cent of the crowd volunteered on the spot, including Mr. Ossont.

"You all know the rule," Dick said. "No talking about it."

Dick and his boys suspected kids had gossiped sufficiently and pretty much knew what was going on. They'd say good gossip could save a lot of time, unnecessary conversation, and, if the gossip and rumors were suspenseful enough, they might draw the proper crowd. They were right.

"Listen up!" Duba shouted.

"What do we know?" Dick asked.

"We know they aren't afraid of crowds," Duba said.

"We know they've been seen in the daylight," Dick replied.

"They were checking out cars at the hayride," Tall Jerry added.

"So, they work nights, too," Holbrook said.

"The code name for our operation is Neptune 2." Dick said, "Memorize that code name—Neptune 2."

"Neptune 2 is going to be a trap for them," Duba said.

"A trap?" came a voice from the crowd.

"When?" came another voice.

"Halloween night," Duba said. "But, from here on out only call the operation Neptune 2—never hint to it as having anything to do with Halloween."

"We gotta' keep the date a secret," Dick said, stepping forward with an opened almanac in his hand.

"A surprise attack," Duba said.

"According to this almanac, Neptune 2 will be happening under a full moon," Dick started. "If we work smart and fast, the crooks won't suspect a thing, and they won't know what hit them."

"Why Halloween?" Holbrook asked.

"It'll be another night, but just like Halloween does for everybody, the crooks' imaginations will have them believing anything they hear and everything they see that night."

"Imaginations are a wonderful thing," Mr. Ossont observed.

"We'll use their imaginations to our full advantage," Dick said. "Halloween is a ways off and gives us time to get ready."

"He's smart…Did I tell you how smart Dick is?" Tall Jerry whispered to Holbrook.

"Listen to things we're going to need," Duba said. He unfolded several wrinkled sheets of paper, pressed them against his T-shirt, and handed them to Dick.

"We're going to need a good horseback rider," Dick said.

"What do you mean?" came a voice, knowing pretty much everyone there could ride a horse.

"We need somebody who's not afraid to gallop in the dark of night with or without a moon."

"Where?" Marty shouted.

"Down near the Delphi Falls," Duba said.

"The gallop would be three, maybe four hundred yards in the dark. Any volunteers?" Dick asked.

Marty Bays, the red-headed boy who helped the club investigate and catch the store burglars in Groton years back, raised his arm. "I'll do it."

"You live on the Ridge Road, Marty," Duba said.

"Is there a problem with that?" Marty asked.

"That's 5 miles, Marty. Will your folks let you ride to the Delphi Falls in the dark?" Dick asked.

"Horses can see in the dark," Marty said. "Tell me where to be and what time to be there. Sandy and I'll be there and ready to ride." Sandy was Marty's palomino.

Dick started reading to himself from the paper.

"Who knows Alice, the story reader, or Marian Cook?"

"The girls with polio," Mayor said.

"Yes," Dick said.

Most hands went up.

"While we're planning what we're going to do, think of something they can do, regardless of their wheelchairs." Dick said.

"Make them a part of the action," Duba said.

"We're going to need a decoy built, a big one," Dick said.

"What're you thinking?" Mary asked.

"We have to make it look real. Something that will hide two people behind or underneath."

"We're thinking something we can maybe stack hay on top of, eight or ten feet up, so it'll look like regular tall haystacks and no one will suspect what's underneath it," Duba said.

"Done!" Mr. Ossont barked. "Barber, Dwyer—you boys meet me at the shop on your study break or recess, and we'll come up with a sketch of something. I have ideas."

"You thinking a haystack, Mr. Ossont?" Dick asked.

"A tall one with a room under it," Mr. Ossont said. "Boy and howdy."

"We could use two," Dick said.

"Once we design it, two's as easy as one," Mr. Ossont shouted.

"We're going to need pineapples," Duba said. "Whole and ripe, skinned, and dripping juicy."

"With faces carved on them like pumpkins, you know, hollowed out and filled with red food coloring," Dick said.

"Cut off heads and blood," someone shouted.

"I'll have them for you," Mike Shea said through the screen door.

"Juicy and dripping ripe by Halloween night," Duba said.

"I'll have them for you, no charge," Mike Shea promised.

"We're going to need forty old boots and five or six shovel or broomstick handles," Dick said.

"Forty boots?" Holbrook asked.

"We'll need a record player. Does anybody have any square-dance records?" Duba asked.

Mary raised her hand. "You know I do."

"Thirty-three RPM or forty-five RPM?" Dick asked.

"Thirty-three," Mary said.

"Good. We'll need a record player, long playing, you have one?" Dick asked.

"I have a phonograph, too. You can use it," Mary said.

Dick didn't miss a detail, checking them off on the paper as he read them.

Mr. Ossont piped up. "I'll put a box by the door of the shop to throw in old boots you have for the cause. If you need them back, put your name in them on a slip of paper."

"Anybody think they could figure out how to rig up either a line of rope or a wire from a treetop on the top of a hill down five, maybe six hundred feet to a fence post down by a road?" Dick asked.

"What's that for?" Dwyer asked.

"It has to be plenty strong. Taut," Dick said.

"What's it for?" came a voice.

"I'm thinking we hook something on it and slide it down the length of rope from the treetop all the way down."

"You mean it would ride down the hill, over the trees," came a voice.

"Yes," Dick said. "We'd need it strong enough to guarantee it'd go all the way without stopping and hit a post by the road at the bottom of the line."

"What's it going to weigh, the thing sliding down?" Dwyer asked.

"About the same as a medium-size pumpkin," Dick said.

"Five, six hundred feet is longer than a football field," Dwyer said. "I don't know."

No one else spoke up. Dick turned to Duba and asked if he and Conway could get with Mr. Ossont and help Dwyer think up something.

"With Mr. Ossont's help we can get it done," Duba said.

"This is getting good," Barber said.

"What's sliding down the rope or wire?" a voice asked.

"Not sure yet," Dick said. "We're thinking a pumpkin."

"Maybe a carved pumpkin, but whatever it is, we want it to explode when it hits the post," Duba said. "We want to scare them."

"Just hold on," Mr. Ossont barked. "I can't be any part of kids playing with explosives."

"Too bad Mr. Ossont couldn't be with us today. But if you see him, don't tell him what we're going to do with the Zippo lighter fluid and pumpkin, okay?" Dick asked.

Mr. Ossont grinned at Dick's cover-up attempt. He knew every kid in school had his back, and he knew lighter fluid wasn't a TNT or dynamite explosive.

"We're going to need eight or ten cars to turn into the Delphi Falls driveway and park at the barn garage."

"What for?" Mayor asked.

"Like they're going to a big Halloween harvest moon hoe-down and square dance in our barn," Dick said.

"How many have a driver's license?" Duba asked.

Six kids raised their arms.

"How many know how to drive, have a farm permit and can 'arrange' to get a car after dark and get there if you had to?" Duba asked.

Near every kid raised an arm. Those days in the early fifties there wasn't hardly a kid living in the country whose folks hadn't sent them to the store a time or two using the family car or truck from age fourteen up. Everyone pretty much took it for granted. There wasn't all that much traffic to worry about. Farm kids had permits at twelve and thirteen to haul milk from the dairy barns in the farm pickup daily. A tractor on open country roads didn't need a license.

"We need a tuba. Who can get a tuba?" Dick asked. Duba was grinning, knowing full well Tall Jerry was still stuck playing tuba for the school band. Jerry looked around, hoping someone else played. He had to raise his arm.

"Can you sneak it out of school for a couple of days?" Duba asked.

"A tuba?" Jerry snorted.

"From the band room," Dick said.

"Have you seen one up close? It's huge. Sneaking it home? I have no idea how to get it out of the school without getting caught."

"If Jerry can get permission from Mr. Spinner, can someone help him get it home?"

"My dad could," Randy Vaas said.

"Mine, too," Marty said.

"What time is it?" Dick asked.

"Five minutes before the bell," Duba said.

"Everyone coming to the barn dance on Halloween night wear a costume, a mask or something," Dick said.

"Make it believable," Duba said.

"That reminds me," Dick said. "I need an outfit. I need a costume that will make me look big, like a giant with no head."

"The headless horseman?" a voice shouted.

"We can do that," the Bryan twins yelled. "We have a sewing machine."

"What'll you need?" Dick asked.

"If anybody has any spare felt, or throw-away sheets, if you'll put them in Mr. Ossont's box. We'll pick things up there. We'll dye it black."

"Don't bring good. Only throw-away material, if you can spare," Mr. Ossont said.

Dick turned to Duba, covering his mouth with the paper sheets in his hand.

"I think we could use the Bryan twins. They're identical. We need to come up with something."

Duba looked at his watch.

"Last thing," Duba said, "we need bait…and a way to hook them."

"Hook them?" a voice asked.

"Bait isn't bait unless it's a prey our hunter wants," Duba said. "We have to figure out bait, and then we have to make sure the hunter knows about it, or it's no good."

"Be thinking what bait we might use and how we can get them to know about it, so they want it," Dick said.

"Don't be coming to us with any fool ideas without thinking them through. See you Friday noon, right here for our next meeting," Duba said.

"Remember, no talking," Dick barked.

He leaned down to Barber. "Call a meeting at the cemetery for tonight. Eight o'clock, just the regulars."

He stood back up.

"What's the name of the operation again?" Dick shouted.

"Neptune 2!" the crowd answered.

"Who can we talk to about Neptune 2?" Duba shouted.

"Nobody!" the crowd answered.

"And what do you do if you see the crooks driving around in their stake-bed?" Dick asked.

No one answered.

"We don't want them getting suspicious. Don't look at them. Let them go about their business," Dick said.

"Who thinks they can get Alice and Marian to help us?" Duba asked.

"Like what could they do with polio?" Mayor asked.

"You ever see the fire in those two girls' eyes, Mayor?" Conway said.

"You're right," Mayor said.

"They could do anything they set their minds to. I'll even make it official," Dick said. "Dwyer and Conway—Alice and Marian are now your assistants, if they want to volunteer. Will you ask them?"

"We both will," Dwyer said.

"Swear them to secrecy," Dick said.

The lads nodded approval.

"Dick, your folks know about any of this?" Randy asked.

"No," Dick said, "but they know Alice."

The meeting broke up; a few jumping into the store with their nickels and dimes, others heading back to school before the bell rang. Everyone walked taller, looking forward to an adventure of a lifetime.

For the club meeting after school, cars were parked on the cemetery drive when Dick drove in with Tall Jerry. Mr. Crane was sitting in his car, waiting for the meeting to be over so he could drive Mary and Holbrook home. Jerry lifted his lantern from the floor of the car, stepped out and lit it.

"Mary, any more letters from…?" Dick started.

"I got one in today's mail."

"Is it coded?"

"No, it's a regular pen pal letter."

"What's it say?

"It only said, 'Be careful. Write soon,'" Mary said.

"The Bryan sisters. It's almost impossible to tell them apart," Dick said.

"They're identical twins," Randy said.

"Does anyone know what an optical illusion is?" Dick asked.

"Isn't that when you think you see something, but you really don't see it?" Barber asked.

"Like a mirage?" Mary asked.

"Something like that," Dick said. "What if we had Jane Bryan made up in a costume like maybe she had a sword or a spear stabbing through her, blood and guts spilling out?"

"Yuck," Mary said.

"Do we know anybody who could make her up like that with make-up and costume and props, the works?" Dick asked.

"If Mrs. Coco, the art teacher showed us what to do, what to use. We could make her up to look like that," Mary said.

"Good. She could be the 'before'—then we'll make the other twin the 'after'. Make Janet up to look like her own ghost—maybe long cheesecloth wavy robes and sleeves, skull-white face, black eyes and black teeth. We'll have a *before* and *after*," Dick said.

"Randy, can you take that project with Jane and Janet?" Mary asked.

"We'll get it done," Randy said.

"Randy, have them at our house by three o'clock on Halloween? Try not to let anyone see them in costume," Dick said.

"I can get my dad to drop them off," Randy said.

Dick and Duba wanted to break up the meeting.

"That's all we have. Make the costumes and makeup good, like we're doing a play at school."

"Anything else to talk about?" Mary asked.

"How about Bobby?" Barber asked.

"Bobby who?" Dick asked.

"Bobby, the kid staying at the Barbers," Tall Jerry said.

"What about him?" Duba asked.

"You know what Neptune 2 day means for him?" Barber asked.

"Same as Halloween for any kid, right?" Dick asked.

"His dad gets out of Auburn," Tall Jerry said.

"That's right," Duba said.

"I forgot," Dick said.

"Mary, ask your dad if he can go to Auburn and find out what time he gets out and if he can pick him up and bring him to our house?" Dick asked.

"I'll ask him," Mary said.

The group wasn't aware that before Neptune 2 began, Dick and Duba were planning to go see Bobby's father several times, clueing him in secret about the Nazi crooks and were including him in on the plan to scare them off.

"Mary, can your dad bring him to our place first?" Barber said. "My mom and dad are expecting him. Then we'll take him over to Tall Jerry's."

"Maybe there's something Bobby's dad can do on Neptune 2," Dick said.

Dick and Duba kept mum. They knew it was already planned for Mr. Crane to bring Bobby's dad to them first.

The meeting broke up. The next was set for the following Friday at Shea's store.

CHAPTER 17

LUCKY FRIDAY AND A BRILLIANT IDEA

"Listen up!" Duba barked.

"Here's the deal," Dick said. "We don't want to capture these guys, we want to trap them."

"After we trap them, we want to scare the pants off them—and then run 'em off and out of the crown for good!" Duba said.

"Won't they just come back?" a voice asked.

"Not if we catch them red-handed," Duba said. "If they know we can identify them, and they know we've seen them stealing, they'll never come back."

"Concentrate on luring them into our trap," Dick said. "Let's talk about bait. Anybody come up with ideas about bait we can use?"

"Explain bait again," Barber said.

"What do you mean?" Dick asked.

"Can you explain bait again?" Barber asked.

"I don't understand the question," Dick said.

"We know they showed up at the hayride, right?" Barber asked.

"Right," Dick said.

"We know they were looking in cars with a flashlight," Barber said.

"Yes," Dick said.

"Doesn't that make a hayride bait? Why don't we just have another hayride?"

"The hayride, that's a decoy, not bait. Another hayride would be a good decoy," Duba said. "We plan to do something like that, make noise to distract them."

"Like what," a voice asked.

"It'll be a Halloween masquerade barn dance," Duba said. "At the Delphi Falls."

"That will be the noise we'll need to lure them into snooping around—the decoy—but we still need bait," Conway said.

"Bait is what will get them to want to get out of their truck and snatch something. That kind of bait. We need them to want to steal something so valuable they'll make a run for it, trying to get away," Dick said.

Mike Shea came out of the store on the top step behind Dick and Duba for a breath of fresh air.

"We've got old tires," a voice came from the crowd.

"Duba, write these down," Dick said.

"We have fencing," another said.

"How about a roll of barbed wire?"

"A keg of nails?"

"Box of horseshoes."

"How about milk cans?" Conway asked. "They seem to favor milk cans."

The suggestions were coming from the older kids—the kids who seemed to grasp the concept. Other than the barn dance idea, the club had blank, frustrated stares on their faces. They were about to give up when Jerry started wriggling.

"Gold?" Tall Jerry shouted.

The word *gold* went over the crowd's heads. These mates mostly came from modest to poor country homes and farms. It got quiet suddenly, folks discounting it as Tall Jerry's lack of common sense.

"Gold!" Tall Jerry repeated, this time with conviction.

Still no one said a word. Kids turned and looked at him like maybe he was touched in the head and didn't understand the economic climate of farming in the crown.

"Gold?!" Duba repeated, almost with a spit.

"Gold, I tell ya!" Jerry shouted again. "Gold!"

Duba and Dick were staring down at the lad like he had better make this good or there would be serious consequences.

Jerry stepped up on the first step, turned and as fast as he was able without stammering like he usually did when he got nervous, he said his piece.

"Doc Webb uses gold to fill teeth, right?"

Weren't a soul there could deny it.

"What if the crooks learn that a shipment of gold was being sent to the doc?"

The crowd began to rumble.

"And, let's just say, it was going to be left in our mailbox on October 31st—you know, Halloween night?"

"It could be left there as a matter of convenience, because we can pretend the doc and Mrs. Webb were going to be spending Halloween in Syracuse overnight," Holbrook said.

"They are going to a party up there," Tall Jerry said. "The doc told me."

"Then wouldn't we have both," Mary asked. "We'd have a lure of the barn dance to decoy them to the Delphi Falls driveway and the bait—gold—to get them for sure to get out of their truck and look in the mailbox that night, steal it, and take off running."

"What crook won't do anything for a handful of free gold…and then run like all hell broke loose after they stole it?" Holbrook asked.

The crowd hushed, letting the proposition sink in.

Tall Jerry stepped down. Holbrook slugged his arm, calling him a genius. Mike Shea smiled and turned back into the store.

Dick and Duba smirked approval down at Jerry. They began to clap. Slowly at first, but then louder and faster; soon the crowd was clapping, then applauding until a cheer filled Shea's corner like Tall Jerry had hit an out-of-the-park home run. His idea was brilliant!

"We'll come up with a plan," Dick said. "Duba and I'll hand out assignments to anyone who signs up on a sheet in the store marked

Neptune 2. The sheet is behind the counter; ask Mike Shea for it, sign it, and give it back to him."

"Everybody read the notes we give you, memorize them and tear them up. Swallow them if you have to," Duba said. "No talking about this to anyone, swear?"

"Swear!" came the shout-outs.

"Mr. Ossont, how soon can your team be ready with the haystack frames?"

"Less than a week, me and the boys will have them ready."

"We're going to need hay to make the haystack piles on top of them." Dick said.

"Farmer Parker will give us all we want," Tall Jerry said. "Tell me when, and he'll haul it down."

The meeting broke up, kids heading back to school and kids bombarding Shea's store to see how far they could stretch the penny, nickel, or dime they had in their pockets.

As Dick and Duba walked toward school, a car pulled up and onto the edge of the sidewalk, getting their attention. It was Bruce Gary, the boy who had started courting Marian at the harvest hayride. Marian, in her leg braces, was sitting next to him.

"Somebody told me you want me and Alice for something," Marian said. "We're both ready for excitement. Thank you."

"We'll come up with something for you to do," Duba said.

Marian grinned.

Dick leaned on the car, peered in the window.

"Marian, are you afraid of horses?"

"Heck no. I could still ride if my leg braces got secured somehow to the stirrups. I could ride. I'm not afraid of horses."

"We'll come up with something, Duba will keep you posted."

"How about Alice?" Marian asked. "What could you have her doing?"

"I don't know," Dick said. "She's a bit frail; we'll give it thought."

216

"Don't you be thinking frail, Dick," Marian said. "Please come up with something fun Alice can do to help. I'll get her in leg braces. The girl may look frail in the legs, but weak and frail her spirit sure isn't."

"We'll think up something, Marian," Duba said.

The two turned and walked to school as Bruce and Marian drove off.

When Jerry got home, he handed the tuba mouthpiece he had pocketed to Missus, who lifted it to her nose to smell it.

"I'll boil it."

Then it happened. It was after a supper only Missus and Tall Jerry were at the table for when the telephone rang.

"Hello," Missus said.

"Honey, the Y's on fire," Big Mike said.

"What?"

"Get here as soon as you can."

The Cincinnatus "Y", the dancehall pavilion Big Mike and Missus owned, was ablaze—twenty miles away.

Missus dropped the phone and got her coat.

"Jerry, put your coat on," Missus shouted.

"What happened, Mom?"

"Get in the car, hurry. The 'Y' is on fire."

"Who was that, Mom?"

"Just get in the car. A farmer up near the Pryor's called your dad at the bakery. Dick is on his way. Mike's driving from Syracuse."

They drove the twenty miles without saying a word to each other. As Missus started up the long hill toward Cincinnatus, they could see flames billowing high in the sky from miles away, lighting up the night.

Jerry had never seen a house or barn on fire before. He had only heard of my house and barn being burned to the ground after I died. Just the thought of it made the lad weep.

Missus parked on the side of the road. Stepping out of the car, Jerry felt the heat from the flames on his face. The air smelled of smoke.

It was awful. A simple dance hall alone on a hilltop was all it was. This was a one-story, wooden building, built by area farmers years ago as a place to get together with neighbors. The place spent time as a roller-skating rink. It was up on stilts several feet off the ground with large, four-foot by eight-foot wooden tilt-flap shutters all around it to be opened for summer dances. They were closed and bolted when the hall wasn't in use.

Jerry saw Dick walking down the road with a flashlight, looking on the ground.

Bursts of fire belted out from under the structure, chomping into the breezes of air going by, feeding their appetites. Jerry stood staring at one small, red tongue of fire seeping out through a crack from inside—out through a crack of the closed shutters. It'd spit like a snake's tongue out and up to a roof shingle. It would jump out and up and withdraw, tagging the shingle and dropping back down. It was like a cat playing with a mouse—until the shingle sparked and burst into flames.

The fire raged.

The sounds of a fire roaring and the intense heat pounding out frightened Jerry. Noises from things not supposed to be burning in his wildest dreams making last sounds, before giving up, succumbing to darting red and yellow tongues of flames.

Jerry stood, thinking of the campfires—how a campfire was a friendly fire, started from wood that had fallen from trees, to give warmth and light.

This fire was a nasty, mean fire from hell, destroying a simple dance hall that never caused anything but smiles and good memories.

Dick was standing on the side of the road, about fifty feet from the fire. Jerry walked down to him.

"Check this out, but shut up about it," Dick said.

He pointed his flashlight to the roadside gravel. There were twenty or thirty cigarette butts smashed out in a circle. Dick leaned down and picked one up.

"They're Pall Malls," he whispered, "the same cigarettes that are under our bridge. The same lengths when snuffed out."

"You think it's them?" Jerry asked.

"Maybe. But it could be just a coincidence."

"What are you going to do?" Jerry asked.

"We can't talk about it yet. Not here, anyway. Not one word that there might be a connection."

"I won't say anything."

"Our plan could blow up," Dick said. "Mom would stop us for sure. Besides, cigarette butts aren't evidence."

Jerry's earlier Hardy Boys mystery book reading told him to agree with Dick. This find of smashed-out cigarettes was circumstantial. There was no law against smoking.

"I know you, Dick. You're thinking they set this fire, aren't you?" Jerry asked.

"Maybe," Dick said.

"How would they know about the place so far away from the Crown where they've been doing their stealing? It's more than twenty miles," Jerry said.

"They could be reading people's mail," Dick said. "Like ours at Delphi Falls and they saw something in it about this dancehall in Cincinnatus. They could have seen a bill or something for the 'Y'."

"And if it had this address on the bill, they broke in the back here and stole stuff they thought they could sell and set the fire to cover it up," Jerry said.

Dick walked to the center of the road in front of the flames, Jerry at his side.

"We've got to figure out how to surprise them, to corner them to be sure," Dick said. "We have to think it out, or we'll mess it up."

"What do you mean, corner them?" Jerry asked. "I thought we were going to catch them stealing and run them off."

"I'll explain it later," Dick said.

"Tell me now. I'm not a kid."

"We know they're the Nazi POW escapees from Pine Camp."

"Right."

"We know we're going to scare them enough so they'll hightail it down Pompey Hollow Road on Halloween night."

"Okay," Jerry said.

"None of that is any good if we don't let them know we saw them do it, and they know we can't identify their faces," Dick said.

"I get it," Jerry said. "If they don't know we know who they are, they could come back."

"If we corner them so they know we see them and get a good look, they will be scared off forever," Dick said.

Something crashed to the floor inside the burning building. Ole Charlie here could tell in Jerry's eyes, he was trying to imagine what it was. Was it a beam, a wall? He walked away from Dick and stared at the lone corner post, standing tall, ablaze, being pelted by tongues of fire, daring it not to burst into flames like the walls that had fallen around it. Even after the roof fell in, the corner post stood, like it was trying to hang on, trying to help. It was doing its job as corner post. Tall Jerry was looking at the post as if it were a lone soldier.

There were explosions, a tank of gas, chemicals, various battles going on inside. It was a lost cause, a fireman said, and it couldn't be put out.

Dick walked over and stood by Jerry.

"Why do things have to die?" Jerry asked.

"Ride home with Dad," Dick said. "He needs company."

The boy walked to Big Mike's car. Big Mike looked somber as he came over and got in.

The two—father and son—didn't say anything to each other.

Missus was going to drive the other car, with Dick following her. Gourmet Mike headed back to Syracuse.

Tall Jerry lay on the rear seat with his knees up, not knowing what to say, thinking about the corner post standing like a soldier, while everything was falling and burning.

The post was burned into Jerry's memory. He promised himself he'd remember it as a symbol for being brave.

Big Mike started the car and put his arm over the seat. His hand squeezed the lad's knee.

"You okay, son?"

"I'm okay," Jerry said.

Ever since Big Mike forgot and left him in the grocery store when the lad was a small boy, he'd check to see whoever was supposed to be with him was in the car.

He pulled onto the road and started slowly, passing the burning old friend with his car window up. The flames still lit the night. Big Mike gazed through the window, his head turning as they passed by. The car rolled down the long hill from the "Y", he clicked on the radio for the news, turning the dial.

Jerry watched the half-moon following them. The car smelled of smoke.

221

A song came on the radio with Hank Williams singing. Big Mike turned up the volume.

Hear that lonesome whippoorwill
He sounds too blue to fly
The midnight train is whining low
I'm so lonesome I could cry…
I've never seen a night so long
When time goes crawling by
The moon just went behind a cloud
To hide its face and cry.

Jerry sat up. There was a reflection off the inside of the front window from the glow of the radio light on the dashboard. In the reflection the lad watched his dad blotting his nose with a handkerchief, wiping his eyes. This was the saddest the boy had ever seen him.

Ole Charlie here knew it weren't the dancehall burning down what got to Big Mike. It was the memories near everybody got just driving by and seeing the place. It was a quiet drive home.

Big Mike didn't turn the lights on inside the house. He told Jerry he was going to sleep in his clothes on the couch, in case someone called and needed him. Jerry got two pillows, one for his dad. The lad lay on the floor in front of the couch. He watched his dad's silhouette, sitting tall and still on the couch, the moon behind him. In the background was the roar of the Delphi Falls. The lad remembered the tall corner post soldier, being just like his dad, and how brave he imagined it was, and how lonely it must be now.

They were asleep when Missus and Dick got home.

CHAPTER 18

THE HOOK IS BAITED

The telephone rang.

"It's for Dick," Missus shouted from the bedroom. She stepped out into the dining room.

"Is Dick here, honey?"

"He's out riding Molly," Jerry said.

Missus went back to the phone, then returned.

"Jerry, it's Mike Shea."

"For me?"

"He's asked to speak with you."

Jerry jumped up.

"Is there trouble?" Missus asked.

"Dick probably left his books at the store. He goes there after lunch sometime."

Jerry went into his mom and dad's bedroom and picked up the receiver.

"Hello?"

"It's Mike Shea."

"Hi. Dick is across the way, riding horse."

"Tall Jerry, those two men you're hunting, they kind of scruffy looking? One old with a white beard and one maybe forty or so?"

"Yes."

"What are they driving?" Mike Shea asked.

"I think it's a '41 Chevy," Jerry said.

"With a stake-bed?" Mike Shea asked.

"Yes."

"This truck has a raccoon tail on the antenna and it's missing the passenger side door."

"That's them," Jerry said.

"Okay, good. So hang on son, don't go away. I've got to do something here and now," Mike Shea said.

"I'll wait."

"I'll be right back to the telephone, understand?"

"Well, no."

"Just don't talk or make any noises into the telephone that could be heard through the earpiece until I come back."

"Oh, okay."

"The younger is about to come in the store. I'll be right back. I'm setting this phone down. Don't talk."

"I won't."

Jerry stood motionless. He was snap-dab in the middle of a Nazi mystery, and he stood at attention, holding the telephone receiver, not talking—barely breathing—his heart pounding, not knowing what was happening on the other end of the wire. After a while, through the telephone earpiece, the lad could hear the store front door's bell ting-a-ling. It jingled again after minutes, and then he could hear a door slam and then footsteps.

"You still there?" Mike Shea asked.

"Yes, sir."

The lad was confused as to why he had to stay on the phone quietly and wanted to get his details straight.

"I don't understand. I heard you talking like you were on the phone. Do you have two telephones, Mike?"

"We have the store telephone and we have the nickel pay phone for customers," Mike said. "I called you on the pay phone and kept you on it so it would be busy and couldn't ring in if someone called it. Then I made a make-believe call to the telephone booth from the store telephone. Of course, I got a busy signal, but I pretended I was talking with somebody."

"That's smart," Jerry said.

"Tall Jerry, you can tell your brother Dick and his friends that the bait is on the hook."

"I can?"

"Yes, young man, tell Dick that the truck with only one door stopped at the store. The younger one came in looking for soda pop and cigarettes."

"Pall Malls?" Jerry asked.

"You boys have done your homework. Tell him those bad guys overheard me as I pretended to call Doc Webb on the other phone. I was making it up, loud enough for him to hear me clear."

"This is so neat," Tall Jerry said.

"I went on and on, telling the doc that his full ten ounces of gold would be in on the thirty-first of October."

Tall Jerry got goosebumps.

"I said out loud I knew he and Mrs. Webb had plans to be in Syracuse that evening, so I would put the gold in Big Mike's and Missus's mailbox at the Delphi Falls…"

"Holy Cobako," Jerry mumbled.

"Right after dark, where it would be safe. I made a point to say it was the mailbox just up from the bridge and alfalfa field, and no trick-or-treaters ever walked the long, dark drive at the Delphi Falls on Halloween, so the gold would be safest in that mailbox."

"Perfect," Jerry said.

"I said into the phone like I was talking to the doc, I'd do it on my way to the square dance in Big Mike's barn garage Halloween night. Tall Jerry, he thinks I told the doc he could pick up the gold out of that mailbox on his way through from Syracuse the next morning."

"Amazing," Jerry said.

"The scoundrel believed me."

"This is perfect," Jerry said.

"I could see his eyes sparkle with just a hint of the glitter of gold. He believed it. He believed every word."

"Holy Cobako. This is so great," Jerry whispered into the phone.

"Yes-siree-bob," Mike Shea continued. "I managed to get the word *gold* in about eight times, and that younger one nearly swallowed his chewing gum every time I said gold. I know the bait is hooked. The only place in the area where there's a bridge and an alfalfa field side-by-side is at your place. The trap is set."

"Everybody knows that alfalfa field," Jerry said.

"The scoundrel knew exactly where I was talking about. I could see it in his eyes."

"Thanks, Mike. Thanks a bunch," Jerry said.

"You kids are on your own from here on out. You have to leave my name out of it. I'm on the school board, and I wouldn't want loose ends on this thing flapping around and pointing back at me, understand?"

"You and Mr. Ossont, we know for sure," Jerry said.

"Good night, son, and good luck," Mike said.

Jerry hung up the phone and ran over to the alfalfa field. He waited for Dick and Molly to come full circle and then told him what Mike Shea had done.

"All right!" Dick said. "That's perfect. Let's go, Molly."

Molly circled the field again, the ground shaking with her hooves pounding. As Molly galloped back by the base of the hill, partridges flew from a bush she nudged, flew under her legs, over her, but the flock raised to get clear.

As Molly came back around, Dick pulled her up for a rest and pointed to a spot down Cardner Road about fifty feet.

"Walk down the road until you see the cigarettes."

Jerry didn't question him; he started walking.

"Let's go, Molly."

Flump, flump, flump—off they went again.

Jerry found the place on the road. Scattered about were twenty or thirty cigarette butts in a circle, just where Dick had pointed. The lad picked one up.

"Pall Mall," he said to himself, dropping it. When he got back to the field, Dick and Molly were full circle again.

"They're Pall Malls," he shouted. "It's them for sure."

"Do they look familiar?" Dick asked.

"Same as under the bridge?" Jerry asked.

"Doesn't it look like the circle of cigarette butts where the 'Y' burned?"

"I bet they set the fire," Jerry said.

"We've got to run them off, or they could be setting more fires," Dick said.

"Any new ideas?" Jerry asked.

Molly stretched her head out and down for Jerry to scratch under her chin.

"We know we can lure them with the barn dance," Dick said.

"Yes," Jerry said.

"Thanks to Mike Shea we know we can get them out of the truck with the bait, the gold," Dick said.

"Yes," Jerry said.

"We have a pretty good idea they'll run like the wind after they get their hands on the gold," Dick said.

"Once they have gold they'll take off. All they have on their truck is junk," Jerry said.

"We have to come up with a way to see to it we run them down Cardner Road and guarantee we point them left, up the hill and then a right on Pompey Hollow to Cherry Valley and out of here," Dick said.

"Why down Pompey Hollow Road, so long as we chase them away?"

"There'll be kids walking around the hamlet on Halloween. If we ran them on Delphi Road into the hamlet, someone could get hurt. Pompey Hollow Road will be straight, empty and dark."

"You're right."

"We've got to chase them down there."

Dick told Molly to go around again. As she turned, Dick looked over at Jerry.

"Get word to Mary to write David Eisenhower and tell him that Neptune 2 will be driving the Nazi crooks down Pompey Hollow Road to Cherry Valley sometime after dark, maybe an hour after dark on Halloween."

"Why does he have to know?" Jerry asked.

"Just do it," Dick said.

"Okay."

"Do you have a pencil?" Dick asked.

"Yes." Jerry pulled a pencil stub from his back pocket.

"Got any paper?" Dick asked.

"I have an envelope."

Dick dug in his pocket and threw down a piece of paper for Jerry to catch.

"Copy this here and now, so I can put it back under the bridge."

"Is it another list?"

"It has five words. Duba found a translation dictionary. We're going to see what the words say."

"I bet that's all the others were—just lists," Jerry said.

"Nobody's translated them for us. We don't know. We're translating them from now on. At least we know they're in German."

Jerry squatted to copy the list. Then he raised his arm up, holding the original for Dick to grab and return under the bridge.

"Want to ride with me to Duba's?" Dick asked.

He jumped down from Molly and walked to his Willys.

"Lock the gate behind me and hop in," Dick said.

"When we're done with those two, they'll wish they never escaped from Pine Camp."

Driving out from the alfalfa field, Dick pointed to the cigarettes on the road.

"That spot, right there, is where they sit in their truck and smoke every time they come, and it's where we're putting a post. Twenty or thirty feet back from it into the field over there we'll put the two dummy haystacks."

"Two?" Jerry asked.

"Two of them, stacked maybe ten feet high with hay. You'll be under one with Holbrook," Dick said.

"The other?"

"We're thinking Bobby and his dad. Not sure yet."

"That would be great for Bobby," Jerry said.

"It'd be an adventure for them to share. It would bond them good," Dick said.

"You're a nice guy, Dick, anybody ever tell you that?"

"Don't let it get out. Could spoil my image."

Jerry had no idea why Holbrook and he would be under the haystacks, and he didn't care. There was a job to be done and most were happy just having a part in it. When they got home, Dick parked in the barn garage and walked the creek bank to return the list.

Waiting for the school bus the next morning, Dick asked Jerry, "Did you give Mary the time and place?"

"It's all set."

"What did you tell her?"

"I told her we're chasing them down Pompey Hollow Road to Cherry Valley after dark. She's writing David tonight," Jerry said.

After school Jerry jumped off the school bus and ran to Farmer Parker's house and told him what Dick had coached him to say and to fill him in on what they were up to.

"Farmer Parker, you know what SOS is, right?"

"Sure do, son. Three dots, three dashes, and three dots."

"We're going to run the crooks off for good."

"When?"

"On Halloween night, but keep it secret."

"What do you need? I'll help."

229

"The older guys need you to signal up to the top of our hill behind the alfalfa field that night if the crooks stop their truck where we think they'll stop it and start smoking."

"They park down past the alfalfa field and then hide under the bridge," Farmer Parker said.

"That's right. But we found out sometimes they sit in the truck and smoke."

"Just like late-night vermin," Farmer Parker said. "Those rats."

"You'll have to hide where they can't see you, and Dick says you have to wait until they turn the truck motor off."

"I can hide. But why do they have to turn their engine off? What if they don't?"

"We can surprise them better if they do. Do you have a flashlight you can signal with?"

"I have a good one and depending on which tree I got to signal to, I can sit by my upstairs bedroom window for the best angle, out of sight and be ready."

"Good. I'll tell Dick," Jerry said.

"I can see near everything from there. Anything you boys need, just tell me."

"Could we borrow hay for our haystacks where we hide? Just until after it's all over."

"Whatever you want. I'll load the hay wagon and have it ready for hauling."

The nights working their way to Halloween seemed to have a spell over most in the know that month of October in 1953. It wasn't often something this big happened in the Crown; weren't a kid could sleep without tossing and turning in anticipation. Halloween and Operation Neptune 2 was a week away. After school Dick and Duba would drive to the Ag shop where they worked on school buses. They'd carry out burlap bags filled with old boots, sheets and bolts of felt fabric kids had donated for the cause, and never stop to talk. They'd come, get the bags, and leave, so they wouldn't draw attention.

One day as Jerry got off the school bus, he could see Dick and Duba down past the alfalfa field. He stuffed his books in the mailbox and walked over to see what was going on.

Off the road, maybe four feet from the circle of cigarettes, they had a tall wooden fence post pounded into the ground, and they were scattering the dirt they had dug up to make the post look like it had been there all along. They drilled a small hole through the top of the post and had the rope pushed through and double-knotted on the back side, holding it secure. The rope knot and the fencepost were stained a dark creosote to hide any signs of the rope.

Dick shouted across the field, up to the top of the hill.

"Give her a yank!"

Nothing happened.

He reached in the Willys and pushed on the horn a few times…

BEEEEEEP. BEEEEEP. BEEEEEEP.

"Yank her up!" he shouted.

A line of grease-blackened rope slowly popped up, appearing from under the tall pasture grass that hid it. It began to lift off the field from the post by the road over to the base of the woods, and then, in one big leap it bounced up as straight and taut as a violin string—all the way to the top of the hill. The rope strung over the treetops up to the tallest tree. Just as straight as an arrow, it stretched from that pine tree right down to the fence post Dick, Duba, Conway and Dwyer had just pounded in.

Jerry stood there.

"I don't have a clue how you did it," Jerry said.

He was plumb in the middle of the adventure of a lifetime, and it only promised to keep getting better. Dick reached up and plunked on the rope like a bass fiddle string. She was taut and strong.

"Drop her down!" Dick shouted, waving his arms. The rope soon rested on the ground. Duba and Dick leaned down in a

231

scramble, following the rope from the post by the road all the way back through the field, checking to make sure it was hidden again and tucked under the field grass and couldn't be seen from the road.

Mr. Vaas pulled up in his milk-can-hauler truck with Mr. Ossont in the cab seat beside him. When they came to a stop, Holbrook, Barber, Mary, and Randy jumped out of the back and wasted no time lifting out the first of the two metal-pipe framed cages shaped like a large igloo.

"Tell us where you want it," Holbrook shouted.

Dick ran out to where he wanted it. "Here, put it here."

They took it to the exact spot and gently set it down.

"This first haystack is code-named *Glimmer*," Dick shouted.

They went to the truck for the next metal-pipe igloo. Dick went over and stood where that one should be.

"This one is code named *Taxable*."

The bases for the haystacks were in place.

"Looks perfect," Mr. Ossont said.

Hearing horse hooves up on Cardner Road, they looked up. Coming down the hill around the curve by his house, Farmer Parker was on his hay wagon with Sarge and Sally, hauling a load of hay to the lads.

"I thought it best we hide those things right off, in case someone starts wondering what they are," Farmer Parker shouted.

There were grins all about at the electricity and excitement of how it was coming together in perfect harmony. Farmer Parker said "whoa" and Barber, Holbrook, Mary, Randy, and Tall Jerry each grabbed armload after armload of hay and carried it back to cover the cages. Farmer Parker brought his barn ladder so the boys could climb up and completely cover both stacks, making them look like normal, ten-foot-high hay stacks out drying in the field.

"Jerry, did you ask Farmer Parker about the flashlight?" Dick asked.

"He did," Farmer Parker said.

Dick handed up the binoculars he bought out of a comic book advertisement.

"Farmer Parker, can you see the pine tree up there in the woods on top of the hill? It's the tree left of the elm and right of that sugar maple. Can you see it?"

"I can make it out," Farmer Parker said.

"Is there a place you can get up without being seen?"

"I'm certain there is," Farmer Parker said.

"Maybe up on your rooftop or by a window? It will all start just before dark Halloween night."

"I can see that pine from our upstairs bedroom window. I'll be in there."

"We'll get your cows milked if you need us to."

"My cows get milked before dark. I'll get it done."

"Can you wait up there for as long as it takes and see if they park here, by this post?" Dick asked.

"I surely can."

"Now, and this is important. If they park here by this post like we hope they do to smoke, you keep your eye trained on them, but don't do anything until after one or both get out of their truck and walk back to our mailbox, reach in and take a package out of it," Dick said.

"I can do that."

"After they open the mailbox you have to wait for them to get back here and climb into their truck."

"Gotcha. I don't signal until after they get back in their truck."

"They'll think they stole something valuable and we hope they'll want to make a run for it, which is just what we want them to do," Dick said.

"What'll be in the mailbox to give them that idea?"

"They'll think it's a gold shipment for the doc."

"That'll do it. Ha!"

"Farmer Parker, the second they're climbing back in the truck, is when you SOS with your flashlight, up there to that pine tree."

"The second they get in the truck I send the SOS signal. Got it."

"Keep signaling and don't stop until they signal you back with a light flashing on and off twice that they got your message. Can you remember all that?"

"I sure enough can."

"That's when we have to let the Nazi crooks know we've seen them steal the gold and we can identify them," Dick said.

"Count on me. I bought new batteries for my flashlight just in case," Farmer Parker said. "Let's go, Sarge." Farmer Parker slapped the reins down gently.

As the wagon pulled away, people scattered. Mary, Holbrook, and Tall Jerry jumped on Dick's running boards and rode to the house.

"Dick, you think Mary and Holbrook can stay over tonight, so they're here for the midnight meeting?" Jerry asked.

"If you all keep your mouths shut at supper, don't see why not," Dick said.

He drove through the gate and up to the barn garage. Filled burlap bags were piled in a corner.

"Boots," Dick muttered, and motioned for the kids to get in for supper and not give any secrets away.

They were almost ready.

CHAPTER 19

SAVED BY PROVIDENCE

Having Mary, Holbrook and Jerry there together at supper was providential for Dick. It brought up a subject—one small detail even he had overlooked. Despite all their secrecy, their planning, and strategizing, he and his cronies Duba, Conway, and Dwyer plumb forgot about Missus and Big Mike being at Delphi Falls on Halloween. They forgot his mom, who would hardly tolerate any part of this lunacy they were planning.

People at the supper table were passing around pleasantries along with a meat platter and bowls of vegetables when ole Charlie here felt something good was about to happen. Angels do that.

At this here supper with Big Mike, Missus, Mary, Tall Jerry, Holbrook, Dick, and their Aunt Kate, —all enjoying conversations and good food—was when the heavens seemed to open an opportunity for Dick. It was almost like a miracle, it surely was.

"Boys, your father, Aunt Kate, and I have been invited to an early supper in Cortland," Missus said.

"When, Mom?" he asked.

"It's a social at Mrs. Vunk's home on Friday."

Dick about had a seizure. "Are you going, Mom?"

"We thought we'd stay over and visit old friends on Saturday."

"All night, Mom?" Dick was counting his chickens, as be said, hoping they'd hatch.

"There's no school Friday because of the teacher's conference. Ever since the fire, this will be the first Saturday we're able to take a break in years."

Then came the eleven-million-dollar question Dick was praying for.

"Would you two be okay with that?" Missus asked.

Dick took his time. He couldn't afford putting a foot in his mouth now.

"It'll be Halloween, I know, and if you would rather we stay here with you, we would," Missus said.

Ole Charlie surely stepped up this time and did my part. To roll back the clock and make this happen like it was natural from the Delphi Falls down to Cortland, I called in favors over two counties. But as guardian angels know, it was no telling what the rascals, God love 'em, would do now. The next move was in their hands.

You should know it was pretty much a known fact that the gravel drive to the Delphi Falls house was so long and spooky dark at night, with racket from the waterfalls, no kid dared walk it, looking for treats on Halloween. That's why the crooks would believe gold would be safe hidden in the mailbox, especially on Halloween.

Dick led the response to Missus dropping hints like breadcrumbs for Tall Jerry to follow.

"I should be studying my Latin for the Regents exams, Mom. I'll probably just stick around the house."

Ole Charlie here wasn't certain, but my guess was Dick wasn't passing Latin. Come to think of it, I wasn't sure he was even taking it. But it's mystery, just the mention of the word *Latin* was so lofty high it could scare respect into most anyone.

Missus lifted her salad fork and smiled. Big Mike knew better than to give an endorsing smile. He smirked but covered his mouth with his napkin.

"Jerry?" Missus asked.

Missus looked at the lad, waiting for his Halloween plans. This could determine whether they would stay or leave. It was on Jerry's shoulders. This was pressure.

Mary saw the pain Tall Jerry was in and knew how he stammered when he got nervous, so she stepped in to help.

"I'm teaching Holbrook, Tall Jerry, and a bunch a new square dance," Mary said.

And that she was. It just wasn't going to be on Halloween. A small detail. The club president was good at leaving out small details in times of national crisis.

"Wonderful," Missus said. "That settles it. Your father, your Aunt Kate, and I will go see old friends in Cortland, comfortable in knowing that you're both safe and not in harm's way."

Jerry could never keep a good straight face. Mary gave him a look to leave the table. He excused himself, said he had to go to the bathroom, jumped up and took off. Missus and Mary stepped in the kitchen to start scraping and stacking dishes. Holbrook was eating pie in the kitchen. Big Mike looked for his evening newspaper.

Aunt Kate was still sitting at the table holding her cane, staring over at Dick while he spooned his pie. She had an inkling he was up to no good.

Suspecting this, Dick put his elbow on the table, pulled his glasses off, dangled them, rolling them with his fingertips, and looked up at the ceiling while mumbling to himself, like he was a Harvard professor. "*Amo, amas, amat, amamus, amattus, amant.*"

He put his left hand to his chin, reflecting on each Latin syllable's enunciation.

Missus listened from the kitchen to his conjugations, unaware it was the only thing he had learned taking Latin.

Aunt Kate wasn't buying it. Her eyes rested on Dick like claws on a trout. He looked back at her and thought of another strategy. This time he put his elbows on the table and folded his hands in front of his face, like the picture of Jesus on her bedroom wall.

"*Dominos vo biscum,*" he muttered. Then he made the sign of the cross.

Aunt Kate made a quick sign of the cross, stood and shuffled away with thumps of her cane.

Oh, what scoundrels the tepid torments of battle do sculpt. Ole Charlie here learned this at my graduating ceremony while getting my guardian angel wings. We had to memorize it. It meant that it was natural that kids like Dick could be scoundrels at times, when the situations arose. And they were allowed to be, when needed. We just understood we had to nudge them on occasion to know the difference between good needs and bad needs.

Back in Dick's room Tall Jerry, Holbrook, and Mary asked if he thought Missus and Big Mike believed them. Dick looked out his window, thinking about it.

"Mom did. I'm not sure about Dad. Dad knows Mike Shea and Doc Webb too well," Dick said.

"They don't keep secrets," Tall Jerry said.

"He probably knows what we're up to," Holbrook said.

"The thing is, he would have stopped us tonight if he thought we were up to no good," Tall Jerry said.

"I bet he even arranged their going to Cortland," Mary said.

"Everybody, go to bed. I'll wake you for our meeting," Dick said.

Mary was sleeping in Gourmet Mike's empty room. Holbrook was bunking with Jerry.

At midnight a warm, clammy hand covered Jerry's mouth as Dick whispered in his ear.

"Wake up. You guys get out to the barn garage. No lights and don't make any noise. Go wake Mary, but be quiet about it."

Missus and Big Mike were asleep with their door closed.

When the four got to the barn garage the night inside the barn was a starless pitch black. The sounds of the waterfalls filled the night air. There were no flashlights on, and no candles in use.

"Duba, are you in here?" Dick asked.

"Yeah," Duba said.

"Who else is here?" Dick whispered.

239

One-by-one, voices announced themselves.

"This is Barber. I've got Bobby with me."

"This is me, Bobby."

"Mary."

"Holbrook."

"Randy."

"Carl Vaas."

"Donny," Duba's brother said.

"Bases."

"Judy Finch."

"Cox, Mary Margaret."

"Mayor."

"Marty."

"Marian."

"Alice."

"Linda Sipfle."

"Conway here."

"Judy Clancy."

"Parker."

"Dwyer."

"Jane Bryan."

"Janet Bryan."

"Paul Shaffer."

"Tall Jerry."

"Ossont."

From that point on it was only voices-in-the-dark.

"We have pineapples, and they're peeled, carved and wrapped in wax paper, so they don't dry out?" Dick asked.

"That's a check," Duba said.

"Are they dripping ripe?"

"Juicy ripe, yep. That's a check."

"Got two bottles of red food coloring?"

"Four bottles. That's a check."

"Marty, can you get here riding Sandy, say between three and four o'clock?"

"I can."

"Ride right up to the barn garage."

"We'll be here," Marty said.

"Farmer Parker, can we borrow Sarge and Sally Halloween night?"

"You can."

"Can they trot?"

"Pulling a load?"

"No, just running with horses."

"They can run with the best of them," Farmer Parker whispered.

"Can Marty take them?"

"I'll have them over here at three."

"Jerry, you put the halters on Jack, Major, and then on Sarge and Sally when they come," Dick said.

"Sarge and Sally will already have halters," Farmer Parker said.

"Okay, good," Dick said.

"They'll be here and ready," Farmer Parker said.

"Marty, at four, lead the horses down to the Maxwell mill on the corner."

"How many?" Marty asked.

"Jack, Major, Sarge, and Sally, and you on Sandy."

"I'll get them there."

"Put them in their stable. It's empty and will hold them."

"Gotcha," Marty said.

"Now listen up, Marty—and this is important."

"I'm here," Marty said.

"Take the pineapples and the food coloring with you. They'll be wrapped in wax paper, so they won't be dripping until you need them. When you have the horses in the stable at the Maxwell place, go ahead and take all of their halters off."

"You sure?" Marty asked.

241

"We want them to look like wild horses," Duba said.

"They'll look wild with no halters on, but be sure they don't get out of the stable until you're ready, because the minute they get out…"

"Oh, I know exactly what they'll do," Marty said. "They'll hightail it up Cardner Road in a blind run home to a familiar barn, lickety-split."

"They surely will," Farmer Parker said.

"Your horses will come to this barn and Parker's will probably follow them," Marty said.

"Exactly," Dick said. "So, you have to make sure you do three things."

"Name them," Marty said.

"First, just about dark, tie the pineapples on the ends of two six- or eight-foot ropes."

"I will."

"You think you can twirl them around your head in full gallop?"

"We'll know tomorrow night, but it shouldn't be a problem."

"Good. Then, number two, pour the red food coloring all over each of the pineapples so they get blood red. Use all the bottles of it. Soak them good."

"Done," Marty said.

"I wouldn't wear anything you don't want stained with red food color," Mary said.

"I won't be wearing my leather chaps, then."

"Don't start swinging the rope until you get close to their truck or at least within eyesight of them."

"Gotcha."

"Good. Number three is critical."

"I'm ready."

"From the Maxwell corner, just at dark, it's important that you keep a sharp eye on the post we've set in the ground by the road down in front of the haystacks."

"I know the post. I helped you hide the rope," Marty said.

"If we figured it right, the crooks should be parked beside that post, smoking cigarettes. When you see the pumpkin explode, that will be your signal."

"Explode?"

"Yes."

"Where?"

"At the post by the road."

"A pumpkin will explode at the post. A ball of fire. Got it," Marty said.

"The second that happens, the second you see it, that's when you let the horses out of the stable. Mount Sandy and ride like the wind, all the horses stampeding together up Cardner Road."

"I'll be ready to mount and ride," Marty said.

"Scream your loudest, Marty. Give it your best 'Yip yip yipeeeeeee kyaaaaaaaa.' Scream that rebel war yell all the way up the road."

"I can do it," Marty said.

"Try to stare 'em both straight in the eye as you get close. Don't stop screaming or twirling the pineapples until you get through our gate, up the drive and to this barn garage, or Farmer Parker's barn, whichever barn the horses run to."

"Will do."

"And try your best to get that warm, blood-red pineapple juice over them on your way by them, screaming like all get out."

"I can do it," Marty said.

"With the pumpkin and that fence post in flames, there should be enough light for them to see the red and think it's blood," Duba said.

"It's Halloween, they'll believe anything they see!" Mr. Ossont said.

"Duba, Conway, and Dwyer—are you ready with the rope and hoisting it up high and taut enough to carry the pumpkin down the hill over the trees, all the way across the field to the post?" Dick asked.

"We've tested it. It works perfectly," Dwyer said.

"The pumpkin smashes into the post time after time," Conway said.

"Everybody, we strung the rope covered in creosote oil loose along the field like a snake, camouflaged by the field grass," Dick said. "No one will see it in the dark from the post up over the branch on that pine on top of the hill."

"It's about three hundred, sixty feet back in the woods from the base of the hill," Conway said.

"That's a long rope," Dick said. "How are you pulling it up off the ground and getting it that taut all the way up the hill?"

"The rope goes to the top branch of the tree at the top," Conway started.

"I get that," Dick said. "But—"

"On that tree we have rope stirrup loops tied at the end of it. The loops are about eight feet apart. When we want to lift the rope up off the field and tighten it to the top of the tree, three of us will climb the tree and we'll each put a foot in a stirrup loop."

"And you ride it down the height of the tree?" Dick asked.

"Just like that," Dwyer said.

"We all push away from the tree and just ride the rope down to the ground. By the time we land at the bottom, our weight pulls the rope straight and taut from the post to the treetop. A tight-rope walker could walk it without a quiver," Conway said.

"Last one down ties it off around the base of the tree to hold it secure," Dwyer said.

"That'll be me," Conway said.

"I like it," Dick said.

"That's when Conway climbs back up the tree again, this time carrying the pumpkin and he hooks it to the rope for its slide down to perdition," Dwyer said.

"That's a long climb. Be careful," Dick said.

"When I get to the top of the tree is when I fill the pumpkin with the lighter fluid."

Murmurs went through the barn.

"We need you to make a change in that if you can," Dick said.

"A change?" Conway grumbled. "At this late date?"

"Like what?" Dwyer asked.

"We've been practicing all week. This ain't no time to be changing anything," Conway barked.

Dick ignored him. "Can you make a kind of pulley that'll lift someone to the tree top without their having to climb it?" Dick asked.

There was silence.

"A pulley?" Conway asked.

"Yes."

"What kind of a pulley?" Conway asked.

"Can we use Molly?" Dwyer asked.

"Yes," Dick said.

"A barn loft hayfork and pulley would do it quick with Molly pulling it," Farmer Parker said.

"Where do we find a hayfork pulley?" Conway asked.

"In my barn," Farmer Parker said.

"Alice, you and Marian want to get out of those wheelchairs Halloween night and be two of the three that will be floating down that tree, tightening the rope for the pumpkin ride?"

There was silence in the room.

"Marian?" Dick asked.

"Yee-haaa," Marian said in a loud whisper. "Alice, you'll need a set of leg braces on your legs."

"I don't have any," Alice said.

"I have an extra pair. You can use them. Will you do it with me, please, please, please?"

"Why the heck not?" Alice whispered.

"So, let's do this then, Dwyer. Get Marian and Alice up the hill somehow," Dick said.

"We'll use the stone boat," Conway said.

"Good idea. Then you'll have Molly up there ready to pull Conway, Alice and Marian, all three of them up to the top of the tree with the hayfork pulley."

"That'll sure make it easier than climbing it," Conway said.

"The hayfork pulley will make it happen," Farmer Parker said.

"What keeps you from hitting branches and getting hurt coming down?" Duba asked.

"We already cut the back half of the branches off, all the ones on the back side," Conway said.

"After they push off and ride down the tree and the rope is tied off at the bottom, that's when you'll put Alice and Marian on Molly's back and lead them down to the alfalfa field," Dick said.

"Leave the stone boat up there?" Conway asked.

"Leave it up there," Dick said. "I'll be in the alfalfa field in my costume ready to mount Molly. I'm hiding in my Willys over in the corner of the alfalfa field by the woods where you come out. It's covered with hay. They can both ride with me. Marian, in front and Alice in back. It'll be easy for you both to balance and hold on. Molly has a wide back."

What a wonderful moment it was in that dark barn garage. Two bright minds with beautiful eyes and big hearts were not going to be bystander witnesses on project Neptune 2 just because of any polio, leg braces, or wheelchairs.

"Be sure you strap their feet and leg braces secure in the rope's stirrup loops. See that they have safety harnesses attached to the rope, so they can't come loose during the drop down to the ground. How tall is that tree, anyway?" Dick asked.

"Sixty feet, maybe seventy," Dwyer said.

"Will you have stories to tell the kids after this, Alice?" Mary asked.

"Yippee," Marian said. "Thank you, thank you. Thank you all."

"Polish the leg braces so they sparkle, ladies. Let's scare the pants off those crooks," Dick said.

"With the hayfork lift and Molly, Conway wouldn't have to climb back up the tree with the pumpkin. We'll lift him back up with the hayfork," Dwyer said.

"How much lighter fluid we got?" Dick asked.

"We'll have six cans emptied into a canteen. We'll pretty much fill the pumpkin," Duba said.

"How do we light it? Anyone come up with an idea?"

"We have four boxes of kitchen matches—three or four hundred—the kind that light by being scratched on something hard. We stuck the matches in backward with the heads out for striking, each one less than an inch apart all over the pumpkin. The second the pumpkin hits anything hard, like the post, it should spark, bust open, and the lighter fluid will do the rest," Conway said.

"What's to keep it from hitting a tree or something else before the post?" Dick asked.

"A full moon guiding our aim and prayers," a voice said.

Little did they know ole Charlie was here to answer their prayers and would see to it nothing got in the pumpkin's way on Halloween night.

"Let's wrap the post top with sandpaper, so it's sure to strike the matches," Mary said.

"Good idea," Dick said.

"Tall Jerry, you have your tuba?" Duba asked.

"Yes."

"Get it under the haystack code-named *Glimmer*, the one on the left at four o'clock," Dick said.

"Holbrook, you be under the same stack as Jerry," Dick said. "When you're under it just be patient and quiet. People outside will be able to hear you talking."

"And have four sandwiches," Holbrook said.

247

"Sometime after dark when you hear a voice shouting out the words, 'Let the tiger loose!'" Dick said, "get ready to make a roar, a loud growling sound through the tuba and don't stop. Got that?"

"Tiger?" Jerry asked.

"Let the tiger loose!" Dick said.

"Who's going to be saying that? The *let the tiger loose* thing?"

"Bobby, you and your daddy will be under the other haystack, the one on the right, code-name *Taxable*."

"We will?" Bobby asked.

"Your dad will be working two peepholes. He can see Farmer Parker's window through one. When he sees Farmer Parker's flashlight SOS signal, your dad will turn and start looking up the hill for another signal."

"From me in the tree," Conway said.

"That will be the signal that they're sending the pumpkin down. When the signal comes, that's when your dad will yell out in a growly voice "Let the tiger loose!" Then he'll count to ten and yell "Let the tiger loose, now!" Dick said. "Just as loud as he can."

"You want to help your dad remember to do that, Bobby?" Jerry asked.

"Sure, I do," Bobby said, with trembling excitement in his voice.

"I'll rehearse him when he gets here," Barber said.

"My dad can do that," Bobby said. "But can I ask something?"

"What?" Dick asked.

"Why does he shout that?"

"Good question," Dick said.

"It's so we make sure they'll run," Conway said.

"With their truck missing a door, they won't want to hang around thinking there's a tiger loose," Duba said.

"Have him shout it as loud as he can," Dick said, "but remember to have him count to ten after the first time he shouts it."

"I'll remember," Bobby said.

"And Jerry, it's after you hear the second shout that you make the loudest tiger growl and roar you can come up with through that tuba. Keep growling until you hear their truck start up and drive off. Can you do that?" Dick asked.

"I can do a loud growl all night if I have to."

Ole Charlie here could feel the tension in the dark. The plan was coming together—in all its complex and ingenious detail.

"Who is either driving or has a ride here tomorrow night for the masquerade barn dance?" Duba asked.

Voices came back from the dark.

"Me."

"Me."

"Me."

"Me."

"Me."

"Me."

"Me."

"Me."

"Me."

"Me."

"Who has the phonograph player and square-dance record?"

"Me," Mary said.

"Good, listen up," Dick said. "Everybody, when you come, come the back way around the doc's and Farmer Parker's—not up from the hamlet."

"Why?" Carl Vaas asked.

"That way you're not passing their truck if they're here already."

"That makes sense," Carl Vaas said.

"When you get to our drive, slow down and look to see if the crook's truck is down past the alfalfa field. If it is, stop at our mailbox and pretend you're putting something in it before you turn in. Open the front and stick your hand in it. Put on a show. They will think it's the gold. There will be an important-looking package already in there with a yellow-painted rock in it. Leave it there."

"Just reach in and pretend?" Mary asked.

"Yes, then close the mailbox," Duba said.

"This is important, hear me good," Dick said. "Once you get to the barn garage, turn the lights on with the breaker switch on the wall by the door. By then the boots we have will be rigged up on long broomstick handle poles and sitting in the middle of the floor waiting for you. Mary, starting at dark, you play the square dance record over and over as loud as you can get it. Don't stop it. The others of you in here each grab a broomstick loaded with boots and keep stomping them up and down on the wood floor like it's a lot of people dancing and having fun. Got it?"

Ole Charlie here was amazed at the amount of thought Dick and Duba had put into this. I sure could help, sure enough—as a ghost. Their prayers that the pumpkin not hit anything on its way down the hill would be answered. I'd ride the pumpkin to its inferno. It's a little-known fact an angel on a mean-spirited mission can double, maybe triple, a burst of a scary fire of flames, scaring the devil out of most anybody.

Then Dick added, "Molly and I, along with Alice and Marian, will have our own surprise."

"The headless horseman's ride," Duba answered.

Kids started to clap, three of them said, "Shhh," "Quiet!" "Shhh."

"Will they be able to see you with Alice and Marian on the horse, too?" Conway asked.

"My costume stands two feet over my head, with wide shoulders and no head on top. It's Halloween. They'll see us all right. Me headless, and the girls in leg braces," Dick said.

"Oh, that reminds me," he added. "The twins, Jane and Janet, do you have the costumes yet?"

"Your costume is at Mary's house. Ours are at Randy's house— the makeup, too," Jane said. "Mrs. Coco dropped them off today."

"Which will have the sword stabbed through you, all bloody, and which one is the white ghost with the black eyes, face, and teeth?" Dick asked.

"We're not sure yet. We haven't decided," Janet said.

"We need the bloody one crouched behind a haystack, out of sight. After the pumpkin explodes, do a fast count to twenty before you stand up, stagger, best you can, around to the front of the haystack like you got stabbed, maybe twirl or something and fall back down dead, not moving a muscle. Got it?"

"Got it," Jane said.

"Whichever plays the ghost, you stay down at Maxwell's place with Marty. When Marty sees the pumpkin explode and takes off galloping up Cardner Road, that's when you walk up Delphi Road hill and stand at the corner just above the Pompey Hollow Road turn. We're wanting to scare them into turning right on Pompey Hollow, just where we want them," Dick said.

"Stand with your arms out, looking ghostly, your veils flowing in the wind. Sneer with your black teeth," Duba said. "Be careful of the traffic. Don't stand in the road, but there shouldn't be much, if any."

"We'll be careful," Janet said.

"Did you say how Alice and I are going to get up to the top of the hill by that pine tree?" Marian asked. "We'll be wearing our leg braces."

"The stone boat. Have Bruce bring you by around three o'clock, and we'll haul you and Alice up then," Conway said.

"I heard that," Marian said. "I'm not sure we could ride down that steep hill on Molly's back, though."

"On her back down the hill or in the stone boat and then mount up with Dick. We'll decide all that when the time comes," Conway said. "We'll do the safest."

"There will be bikes here," Dick said. "Five maybe, more if you bring them, when they begin to hightail it out like we're hoping they're going to, the fastest peddlers grab a bike and follow them. Not

251

too close. Let them think they're being chased. Follow until at least they're down Pompey Hollow far enough to be at Cherry Valley and out of the area. They'll think they've gotten away with the gold, but knowing we saw their faces they sure won't be coming back."

"Marty, when you get back to the barn garage, could you saddle up Major for Bobby and his dad?" Duba asked.

"Of course," Marty said.

"Then you ride Sandy and lead them on the chase. Try to keep the lead, but stay back, in a trot, just to be safe with Bobby on board."

"You on the bicycles," Marty said. "Wait on us down at Maxwell's corner to catch up. Then we'll follow them in more of a formation."

"That's a good idea," Dick said.

"Does everyone know what to do?" Duba asked.

The group mumbled a *yes.*"

"Go home and get some sleep. See you tomorrow. Oh, and Bobby…"

"Yes?" Bobby asked.

"Make sure your dad knows which horse Major is. He's the chestnut," Dick said. "He'll need to know, for when we chase them, can you tell him?"

"Okay."

Dick didn't say another word to the boy. He wanted his plan for the boy's dad to be a hero of the night to be a surprise.

Cars started up in the dark with lights off and drove away slowly and quietly.

Ole Charlie here could sense there was a lot of tossing and turning that night. Young bright minds, scattered over the crown, were in a freefall tailspin, thinking about all that was about to happen tomorrow night.

Alice dozed off and dreamed of running and jumping in a playground.

Marian dreamed of her high school prom, with no crutches or leg braces, dancing a jitterbug with her boyfriend Bruce.

252

Bobby imagined his daddy being fancied up and smart in a navy dress uniform like on a billboard, with a brand-new gold star and ribbon for being a hero. The lad cracked an eye from his happy dream, smiling up at the stars. He caught one star blinking back at him just before he closed it again.

"Night Mommy, I love you," the lad said, dozing off.

CHAPTER 20

A FULL MOON WILL BECKON

Big Mike, Missus, and Aunt Kate drove off to Cortland at dawn. That was so early, Dick felt Big Mike had an inkling what was going on and wanted to give the lads breathing room— leaving them space to do their thing. About the time they drove out was about the time Mr. Crane drove in, pulling up to the barn garage. He and another man stepped out of the car.

Dick recognized the man Mr. Crane had with him as Bobby's dad from their visits in Auburn. He and Duba walked over and shook his hand.

"Hi, Harold," Dick said.

"Hey, Dick," Harold said. "Duba, how are you?"

"Happy to see you, Harold. Have you been over to Barber's or did you come right here?" Dick asked.

"Not yet," Harold said. "Can't wait to see my boy, but thought it best to come here first and hear what's going on. Meantime, call me Hal. My friends know me as Hal."

"You have coffee going?" Mr. Crane asked.

"Let's go perc some," Dick said. "Won't take a minute. Jerry, Holbrook, and Mary are still asleep. It was a late night. I think we met in the barn garage until two this morning."

A box of assorted Danish pastries on the kitchen counter showed Dick his notion was right about Big Mike knowing what was going on. With no school because of a teacher's conference, his dad likely suspected there'd be morning guests at the house.

254

Dick, Duba, Hal, and Mr. Crane sat at the table and talked about the plan—how it came about by Missus first seeing the crooks at the fence line. Dick was sparing greater detail until the men had coffee in them. He made pleasantries.

"Prison time wasn't right," Dick said.

"All that jail time, just for busting a guy in the beak," Duba said.

"And you with a kid," Mr. Crane said.

"There was a war on," Hal said. "They made an example of me."

"But why you?" Duba asked.

"If it wasn't wartime, I'd probably have been put on report, is all. They would have put us in the ring with boxing gloves. A world war is different. Submarines in the Pacific were dangerous."

"It stinks," Duba said.

"It's okay. I had served most of my time when it happened. I served my country and learned farming in stir."

"It's all over now," Duba said.

"Are you ready to help us catch some crooks?" Dick asked.

"I've been listening to you two, thinking about it. This is going to be fun," Hal said.

"And your Bobby right at your side," Dick said.

"That will make it special," Hal said.

"There's a new wrinkle, Hal—one we haven't told you about."

"Uh-oh," Hal said. "Here it comes."

"Actually, we haven't told anyone."

"Doesn't sound good," Hal said.

"We need to hear what you have to say about it before you go volunteering," Dick said.

Hal took a bite of his cherry Danish.

"Let me have it," Hal said.

"You know there are two crooks."

"Two crooks. Right. I knew that."

"What you don't know is about Mary's pen pal…"

"You never mentioned a pen pal, no."

255

"And the Nazi escapees from Pine Camp."

"Huh?" Hal blurted.

"You know Pine Camp?" Duba asked.

"Of course, I know Pine Camp. I was in Pine Camp—the brig there in '46 for a while—before they moved me to Auburn."

"The crooks we're after were POWs who escaped Pine Camp in '44," Dick said.

Dick took his time, telling the story in full detail. Hal savored his first cup of homemade coffee in years, taking in every word. In time, Mary, Holbrook, and Tall Jerry stepped into the dining room with pastries and milk and sat with the four. Dick told of the coded messages, about the Cincinnatus 'Y' burning, and the Nazi POW's hideaway station under the bridge.

"We took a vote, Hal," Dick said.

"What'd you vote?"

"We voted you should lead us in chasing these two Nazi crooks down Pompey Hollow Road and out of here."

"Me?"

"It was unanimous," Mary said.

"Why me?"

"We thought you should be the one to do the crown the honor of leading the chase and running them off."

"But why…?"

"It might go a way to making you and Bobby feeling good again, after all the years of bad times and nightmares this has been for you and the kid."

"I found Bobby sleeping in an alley," Tall Jerry said.

"It could make him and you heroes," Holbrook said.

Hal pursed his lips. A tear welled. His mouth tightened and clenched, a single drop rolled from his eye. His fingers trembled so, a morsel of cherry dropped from his Danish onto the plate. He stood up enough to reach in his pocket. He pulled a folded-up piece

256

of paper from it and sat back down. Looking around at the faces, he unfolded the paper and murmured the words written on it.

"Dear Daddy,
    A nice boy found me a place to live until you come get me. You don't have to worry about me. I love you, Daddy. Bobby"

He looked up from the letter at Tall Jerry.

"You're the one?"

"He was sleeping behind the hotel I worked at," Tall Jerry said.

"I don't have the words," Hal said, wiping his eyes. "Thank you."

"Bobby's a good kid," Dick said.

"You'd have done it for us," Mary said.

"Can I ask a favor?" Hal asked.

"Anything," Dick said.

"Can Bobby be at my side when we run those bums off?"

"That was our plan," Duba said.

"Better than that, you and he will be on horseback," Dick said.

"On Major," Tall Jerry said. "He's a good horse. Won't buck."

"Chasing them to Cherry Valley," Holbrook said.

"Does this mean you're volunteering officially?" Dick asked.

"Count me in. Bobby, too. We're both in."

"Mr. Crane, can you take Hal over to the Barbers? Mrs. Barber will want to start fattening him up with a good breakfast."

"Be my pleasure," Mr. Crane said.

"Bobby needs to hug his daddy," Mary said.

"Mary, you go, too," Duba said. "Be back just after noon—at least before one. Bring Barber with you."

Hours later, at high noon on Friday, October 31, Operation Neptune 2 began with Mr. Crane returning to the Delphi Falls. Dick and Duba stepped from the house to meet them. Barber and Mary got out of the front seat. Bobby and Hal climbed from the back seat. Mr. Crane poked his head out the driver's window.

"I'm off to work. Good luck."

"Thanks, Mr. Crane," Dick said.

"The Barbers want you to come around eleven, Sunday," Mr. Crane said.

"For church?" Duba asked.

"For a breakfast celebration," Mr. Crane shouted from his car window.

Dick waved at him while he was backing around.

"Bobby, I bet you are a happy kid," Dick said.

"The Barbers are nice people. Dale has been rehearsing me all morning," Hal said. "What a Halloween this is going to be!"

"Barber or Bub," Barber said. "No Dale."

"Are you ready for some fun?" Dick asked.

"You know I am. Been stir-crazy for most of my boy's life. We're both ready!" Hal said. He put his arm around Bobby. "By the way, Mrs. Barber wants all to come to a late breakfast Sunday."

"That's what Mr. Crane said. We'll pass the word," Dick said.

Mary handed Dick a cardboard box with his Headless Horseman costume.

She handed Duba a letter from her pen pal, David Eisenhower. "I got this today," she said.

Duba opened and read the letter to himself.

"Dear Mary, Thank you for your letter. Good luck with Neptune 2. Write soon. PZYYWABEI 00 Your Pen Pal, David Eisenhower."

Duba handed the letter to Dick.

By this time Duba had the translation code memorized. He leaned over and whispered into Dick's ear the translation.

"It says '*Sheepfold 11*,'" Duba whispered.

258

"*Sheepfold 11?*" Dick whispered. "I wonder what it means? Did you see it in any of the books or magazines we went through in the library?"

"Could be a password. No time to figure it out now," Duba said.

"The word 'sheepfold' mean anything to you, Hal?" Dick asked.

"Sheepfold…sheepfold. It rings a bell." Hal said, "Can't place it, though."

Farmer Parker, Barber, and Tall Jerry tied ropes to the halters on Sarge, Sally, Jack and Major, getting them ready for Marty. Just at three o'clock Marty came riding in, sitting tall in the saddle. His western hat was rolled to a near point in front, shading him from the sun. He rode in a steady cavalry canter up the drive. When he pulled up to the barn garage Jerry handed him two of the halter ropes. Holbrook handed him the other two.

"Leave the halters at Maxwell's tonight," Farmer Parker said. "I'll fetch them tomorrow."

"Yo," Marty said. "Anybody have rope? I couldn't find any at our place I could use."

Holbrook went into the barn garage and came out with rope and baling twine. He handed it up.

"You need a knife?" Holbrook asked.

"I've got one," Marty said. He reined Sandy around slowly and led the four horses down the drive on the first leg of his mission. He held the ropes of the horses following, two on each side. Sandy's reins were looped over his saddle horn; Marty knew Sandy would mind his voice. His saddle bags bulged with the carved pineapples wrapped in wax paper.

Once he reached the gate and turned onto Cardner Road, the horses began a trot. Sarge and Jack whinnied when they passed Molly in the alfalfa field. Molly looked up at the caravan of horses, saw Dick wasn't with them, and went back to grazing.

Jerry put the tuba under his arm and grabbed sandwiches. He wanted his bike, so Holbrook and he walked to the gate, Holbrook pushing the bike.

Farmer Parker waved at them from his upstairs window. He'd be ready, right after milking. He pointed at Dick's binocular strapped around his neck and the flashlight in his hand. Tall Jerry and Holbrook got comfortable under their haystack, Hal and Bobby under the other. Dwyer hitched Molly to the stone boat and hauled Marian and Alice in their leg braces up the hill to the tall pine. Duba and Dwyer walked about, taking care of last-minute details. They made certain the rope from the top of the hill to the post was secure. They walked the field, tucking rope under field grass, so nobody could see it.

Hal pulled hay and made a small sight-hole through the side of the haystack until he could make out Farmer Parker sitting by his window. He put another hole on the other side, so he could see the Maxwell place, where Marty was, and one in the back, so he could see the pine tree, where the signal to him would be coming from.

They were ready. At least the decoy haystacks were ready, and it looked like most everything else was, too.

Jerry put the tuba mouthpiece in his pocket to keep it warm and lay down to rest until it was time to do the "tiger roar." The lad made roaring sounds over and over in his head until he found the one he liked and would use when the time came.

Holbrook watched through the hole he had made so he would know when it got dark, which was when things would begin to happen. They could hear cars coming down the road and driving by. None slowed like they were curious; the camouflage was working.

After what seemed like hours, it started.

Holbrook peeked through his peephole.

"Here they come," Holbrook whispered.

Jerry sat straight up.

"It's not even dark, yet," Holbrook said.

He could see the truck rolling down around Farmer Parker's hill and past Big Mike's front gate and mailbox. They were driving slowly, looking out through the missing truck door, checking things out, making their way over the bridge and past the alfalfa field.

"No talking," Holbrook whispered.

The nerves raised goose bumps on the boy's arms.

As Dick expected, the Nazi crooks parked their truck in front of the post where they had found the circle of cigarettes.

Those under the haystacks only had to wait for the chain of signals setting Neptune 2 into motion.

Neither team in the haystacks, or Jane Bryan, hiding behind one, could see the Nazis in their truck parked in front of them. They couldn't hear anything with the truck motor idling. They could only wait.

Then it happened.

The Nazi POWs turned the engine off. It got so quiet, those under the haystacks imagined two thieves sitting in a truck smoking and getting the lay of the land.

This was about when ole Charlie here got to remember the German I learned back in 1917, fighting in World War I. What little I knew was to come in handy this night, it surely was.

"*Lass uns das Gold, Rolph,*" the younger one said.

Well, that sure enough meant *let's go get the gold,* and it also meant the older one's name was Rolph.

Holbrook and Tall Jerry bolted up with a jolt at the sound of the voice, the German accent. They looked at each other, eyes bugged out. With the missing door they were amazed how clearly they could hear the talking.

"*Nein, nein, wir müssen warten,*" Rolph snorted.

The old one wanted to slow down. He was greedy, and he was saying they should wait to be sure the gold was there and that nobody was watching. He was mumbling to Hans, the younger one, to be patient, and then he added something like, "*let the Americans dance. There is a dance, like you said?*"

"*So sitzen und ruhig sein,*" grunts Rolph. "*Wir werden sicherstellen, dass das Gold ist zuerst da. Dann werden wir es nehmen.*"

"*Ya, Rolph.*"

"*Iff sie tanzen, gibt es keine Falle.*"

Rolph said the more they danced, the less likely it was a trap for them.

Under their haystack, Hal tapped Bobby on the shoulder to get his attention. He indicated he was going to start his lookout through the peephole. It was getting darker outside.

In their haystack, Jerry lifted his tuba and rested it upright on the ground between his legs. He pulled the mouthpiece from his pocket.

Under his haystack, Hal got in position. He could keep an eye on Farmer Parker's window and not miss the signal. He reached his arm around, holding up one finger. Bobby tapped him on the shoulder. When Hal turned around, Bobby shrugged his shoulders.

Hal leaned in and whispered. "One car came in the driveway for the barn dance."

Minutes later he held up two fingers, then three, then four, then five.

No one was talking in the truck in front of the haystacks. Holbrook and Tall Jerry, Hal and Bobby thought the crooks were watching people drive into Delphi Falls, pretending to put something in the mailbox, like the gold.

The night air began filling with sounds of loud fiddles and plunking banjos strumming square-dance music from the barn garage. A caller shouted in tune.

"Form four couples
and swing around
Ladies and gents,
Let's go to town."

Music blared out of the brightly lit barn garage, echoing off the shale cliffs. Shortly after, came the pounding of dancing feet, stomping in rhythm.

"Alamande left and alamande right.
Swing your lady with all your might
Now doe si doe and around we go."

The boots pounding and scuffing the floor could be heard at the bridge and past the alfalfa field. It sounded like it was supposed to—like dozens of dancers at a square dance.

"All hold hands and circle around...
Take your lady right into town."

One Nazi stepped out of the truck.
"Beeilen Hans, holen das gold," Rolph said.
He was telling Hans to "Hurry, but be careful, run get the gold. Don't leave any of it."
Hal peeked through his peephole. He could see the younger Nazi, Hans, walking quickly toward the front gate and the mailbox. He passed the alfalfa field, then crossed over the bridge. He was nearing the gate.
"I feel like I'm in my old submarine," Hal whispered to Bobby.
He was not to take his eyes off Farmer Parker until the SOS signal was given. He didn't.
Through their peephole, Tall Jerry could see lights down at Maxwell Corner, where Marty was.
Then it came, it sure enough did, a flash of light.
Dot dot dot—dash dash dash—dot dot dot.
Farmer Parker flashed his signal.
It came again...
Dot dot dot —dash dash dash—dot dot dot.

263

After seeing it, Hal turned and saw the answering light signal come down from the top of the pine—on and off. It repeated four times, signaling they were letting the pumpkin slide the length of the hill and officially start Neptune 2 off with a bang.

He turned and got into position.

It was time.

Hal grabbed Bobby's hand and squeezed it for good luck. He sat up, took deep breaths, flexed his chest, and shouted in the lowest, meanest, and gravelliest voice he could muster.

"Let the tiger loose!"

Hal counted to himself in the dark—one, two, three, four, five, six. That's when he heard the older German talkin'.

"*Was ist das für ein Geräusch, Rolph?*"

The Nazi crook was asking, "What was that noise?"

Nine, ten…

"LET THE TIGER LOOSE, NOW!" Hal shouted, as loud as he could.

Tall Jerry timed the signal in his head and blasted a tiger roar through the mouthpiece of the tuba that would make a zoo keeper proud.

"RRRRROOOOOOAAAAAARRRRRRRRRRR!" the tuba growled.

"*Was zum Teufel ist das, Hans?*"

That's when Rolph started yelping, "Start the engine, Hans. Start the motor."

Hans sat up straight.

"I think it's loose, zat tiger, und we have no door!" Rolph shouted.

On top of the hill, Alice and Marian got their hayfork-lift pull to the treetop and, along with Dwyer and Conway, made the jump of their lives, dropping the full seventy feet down to the ground. Dwyer tightened and tied the rope to the base of the tree while the hayfork-lift hoisted Conway and the pumpkin back to the treetop.

"Were you scared, Alice?" Marian giggled.

"It took my breath away. Whooosh!"

"Was that fun or what?" Marian asked.

"It was exhilarating." Alice's grin glowed in the dark.

Ole Charlie here floated up the tree, following Conway. Once the pumpkin was attached to the rope, I sat cross-legged square on top of it.

It was those torments of battle moments ole Charlie was telling you about. I intended to make the loudest, shrillest, scariest, whirring and whistling, ghostly screaming sounds ever heard in the hollow.

The rope, now taut as a piano wire in the dark air, stretched unseen from the post by the road to the pine tree up here near heaven. Soon the rope was vibrating good and proper. Down we screamed, rippin' the night air open, making that rope smoke in our wake.

"RRRRROOOOOAAAAAARRRRRRRRRR!" the tuba growled again.

"*Hans, erhalten das Fahrzeug gestartet—ich werde nicht erzählen Sie wieder*. Start the truck and go."

The truck engine cranked.

Nothing.

"Now, Hans."

"I think it's flooded, Rolph."

"RRRROOOOOAAAAAAAAAAAARRRRRR!" the tuba growled.

The pumpkin took wing over the treetops and screamed down across the field below.

"*Es ist ein tiger, ein tiger.*"

There's a tiger loose, Rolph. and the truck won't start. What are we going to do?"

He slammed his foot on the starter pedal.

Nothing.

Both feet at once, this time.

"Nothing."

The pumpkin, with ole Charlie here, slammed full force into the post, busting the pumpkin open on impact.

Caaaaaaarash!

And it exploded into flames.

KAABOOOOOOOOOOM!

"Yaaaaaaaaaaaaaaaa!" Hans screamed. The burst of flames was giving Rolph chest cramps.

"*Mein Gott!* he shouted, "I think we're caput. We die tonight, Hans...*Mein Gott.*"

Cardner Road began to rumble and shake. Marty and Sandy were off and running from the Maxwell place at the corner, surrounded by four wild-eyed horses galloping and pounding in a blind run up the road, with Marty screaming.

"Yip, yip, yippee kaiiiiiiyaaaaaaa."

Louder their steel hooves clattered.

"Yip yip yip!"

Five horses, cracking and sparking the pavement from twenty steel horseshoes, galloped the canyon like runaway wild stallions.

"*Heiligen Geist—es ist die apocolypse.*" Rolph screamed, "Look down there, it's the horsemen of the Apocalypse."

"Our judgment is upon us for certain, Rolph."

Square dance music blared, boots pounding the floor back at the barn, shaking the night like marching ghosts. Wild eyes and frightening hooves charged at them through the night. Marty and his horses reached the old truck, just as the engine coughed.

"*Achtung! Achtung!* Move it, Hans, we don't have all night!"

"*Hilfe, Hilfe.* Hey, look, Rolph! He's got heads on those ropes. They're heads."

Marty screamed another war cry as he swung the ropes full circle, the pineapple heads with them, blood red and juicy.

"Ahhhhhgggggggg! Rolph, that's blood on you and on the seat. It's on me, too. Those skinned heads. I saw the eye holes, Rolph. They're gonna get us. They're gonna get us!"

20 steel hooves sparking in the dark

Marty and the horses thundered by, disappearing up Cardner Road into the driveway.

The Nazis' eyes popped as big as half dollars when they saw Jane Bryan staggering around the haystack, holding a sword stabbed through her chest, her guts hanging down. Using a needle, she popped the balloon hidden under her blouse filled with tomato juice. She twirled about, blood gushing as she plopped dead as a doornail on the ground.

Rolph jumped from the truck and ran around to the driver's side, his English improving.

"Move over, you idiot, there's no time, We got to move."

Hans sat behind the steering wheel, wiping pineapple blood on his jean legs.

"Put the gold under the seat. Slide over. Now! Move, before I leave you here for that tiger to eat. *Sie lamebrain Entschuldigung für nichts gut.* You lamebrain, sorry good-for-nothing."

Rolph got the truck started and rolling just as the sounds of new hoofbeats flooded the night air.

FLUMP, FLUMP, FLUMP, FLUMP

Molly was down from the hill and crossing through the alfalfa field. The hoofbeats soon stepped onto the road and became the brassy sounds of lightning striking pavement as Molly trotted on the pavement.

CLIP CLOP, CLIP CLOP, CLIP CLOP

Dick was in his black costume regalia, looking ten feet tall and headless, sandwiched between the two girls wearing leg braces reflecting the moonlight.

Marian, Dick, and Alice were riding bareback.

"Go get 'em, Molly," Dick snorted.

Louder and closer, Molly crunched down the road, gaining on the truck.

Occupants of both haystacks punched front peep holes—this they couldn't miss. Jane squinted one eye open to watch the action.

Rolph looked through the back window at Molly.

"*Heilige Geister*, Hans. Holy crap, Hans, it looks like an elephant. The headless horseman on top. I know headless horseman, Hans, I heard it on the radio. We have to go, fast. *Wir müssen wieder zu entkommen.*"

Hans was on his knees on the floor of the truck, his head on the seat, praying for the Lord to spare him. "Not my head, God, please, not my head. *Nicht mein Kopf, Gott, bitte, nicht mein Kopf.*"

Molly caught up, towering over the truck, as it started to pick up speed.

Tall Jerry remembered Mr. Lance's original introduction to Molly.

"*TIMBER!*" he shouted at the top of his voice from under the haystack. Noises from the waterfalls, the loud square dance music and boot stomping drowned out his voice.

Dick swung his arms out with the long black sleeves and cape and no head. Rolph stomped on the gas pedal to go faster.

Remembering Tall Jerry's story of how he had first met Molly, Holbrook leaned over, grabbed the tuba, put his mouth to the mouth piece and with all his might he repeated Tall Jerry's yell, but this time through a big brass tuba.

"TIMMMMMMMMMMMBERRRRRRRRRR!"

Molly bolted, stopped short, kicking a firework of sparks back near a foot from each of her four hooves. Her head went straight up, almost smiling; she jumped full circle, looking for a tree to fall, making her rump bump the side of the truck, lifting it up to a tee-ter. Marian was holding on to Molly's mane, Alice was holding on to Dick and both were screaming their best dead zombie screams while Dick gurgled like a headless horseman.

"*Helfen Sie uns. Helfen Sie uns. Helfen Sie uns, Herr,*" yelled Rolph.

Ole Charlie here had no idea what that meant, but I imagine it was Rolph's prayer that wasn't about to be answered, given the side of the Lord he was on. His face was as white as a ghost. This I know.

The truck tires bounced down on the road, popping a rear spring. The spinning back tire screeched against the pavement, belching puffs of burned rubber as the truck jerked and chugged on down the road, Rolph and Hans, covered in blood from the pineapple and shaking in terror. Rolph's beady eyes stared at the road ahead, praying there were no more bloody heads to contend with.

Near down to the Maxwell Corner the Nazi crooks were when Holbrook and Tall Jerry lifted the *Glimmer* haystack and crawled out. They went over and lifted haystack *Taxable*, so Bobby and Hal could crawl out.

Marty trotted up on Sandy, Major in tow, saddled and ready for Hal and Bobby to mount up.

"He's a police horse, Hal," Marty said. "Just give him the rein, he'll know what to do and you'll be safe."

Hal mounted and Holbrook lifted Bobby up behind him. Bicycles were whizzing down the road, following the crooks. Jerry carried his bike to the road, jumped on with Holbrook balancing on the handlebars, legs dangling out front.

Farmer Parker came walking down from his place.

"Wasn't that something?" he guffawed.

People gathered on Cardner Road in front of the alfalfa field, savoring the victory after scaring the tar out of and running off two bad people.

"Conway, you and Dwyer go get the Willys," Dick shouted. "It's hidden under that pile of straw in the corner. Give anybody a ride who wants one. Follow us. Giddy-up, Molly."

"Jump in, let's go!" Conway shouted.

"Marty and Hal, you lead the way!" Dick shouted.

After they took off, a group ran back to the barn garage where the square dance music was still blaring, and the boots were still being stomped. They unplugged the record player, bringing the night to a still again, with only the sounds of the Delphi Falls roaring behind them. They jumped in cars or raced on foot to meet at Maxwell's Corner.

When Holbrook and Jerry got there, bicycles were waiting for them. Marty and Hal on horseback were there. Barber and Mary were on the bikes in front. Barber motioned for Tall Jerry to stop and stay quiet.

"What's up?" Jerry asked.

Barber pointed up the hill on the left, where the second twin, Janet Bryan, was acting the ghost.

"She scared the pants off Rolph," Barber whispered. "He forgot to clutch and gear down going up the hill."

270

Hans was behind the truck, pushing it the extra few feet it needed so they could turn on to the level Pompey Hollow Road and make their getaway.

"Let them get ahead before following them," Marty said.

"We don't want those crooks to give themselves up; we want them to keep running on out of here," Dick said.

The truck turned onto Pompey Hollow Road and rolled about three, four hundred yards down past the scare of the dead ghost they saw on the corner, when it jerked to a stop while Hans was running, still trying to catch up.

Rolph jumped out with a package in his hand, leaving his door wide open. He stomped a foot on the ground and began hollerin'.

"*Dumkopf, du dummer kopf, du Arschloc….*"

He would have gone on and on, but Hans stopped him.

"*Was habe ich getan, Rolph*? What did I do?" he pleaded.

"This *ist nicht* gold. There never was gold. *Gab es nie einen gold*," Rolph snorted.

It went something like, "This is a painted rock, nothing more, a stupid stone."

"Huh?" Hans whined, perplexed and confused and panting from his pushing the truck and running behind.

Rolph flung the rock to the ground and marched back to the driver's side, climbed in and stomped on the gas pedal.

As the truck pulled away, Hans picked up the rock and examined it. The closer he stuck his nose to it, looking at it under a moonlight, the madder he got. It wasn't gold at all. His nostrils flared, he spared a German curse word or two, kicked a leg in the air, hauled off and pitched the rock as hard as he could.

"Uh oh…"

The rock crashed through the back window of the truck, missing Rolph's noggin by inches.

The truck started rolling faster.

"I'll pay for it, Rolph," pleaded Hans, running alongside the truck, trying to hop in. "I'll pay for the window."

"*Jawohl*, like you paid for the door," Rolph grunted.

The group assembled at Maxwell's Corner, with Hal and Bobby riding Major in the lead. Off they rode, peddled, drove, and walked, close enough to follow the Nazi crooks without being seen.

It was down Pompey Hollow Road a way, right on the back side of the Barber farm and just above the creek, when they could hear Hans through the broken window.

"Rolph, I gotta pee."

Must have been Rolph had to pee, too, because the truck came over to the left side of the road and pulled to a stop.

Horses, bikes, people on foot and in the cars with lights off pulled onto the grassy edge, staying still, crouching to hide.

Barber whispered, "Watch this."

"Watch what?" Holbrook asked.

Barber grinned.

"Just watch," Barber said.

Hans and Rolph stepped around cautiously, looking about to be sure there were no tigers or elephants anywhere. They moved to the edge of the road's shoulder, standing side by side, to do their business. What they didn't know was they were about to do their business down a slope into the back side of the same pasture Barber and his dad put their old bull in just a week ago.

They unbuttoned their pants and stood there on the embankment above that new electric wire fence below. They were both waiting for nature to drain their tanks, as be said, when, as nature does, two golden streams flowed out— glowing a sprinkled sparkly under that big full Halloween moon. Rolph's was slow, in ole man spurts. Hans's stream curved out and down the side of the bank until it splashed on Barber's electrical fence wire below, sending a current full upstream.

Hans let out the bloodiest scream.

"AAAAAARRRRRGGGGGHHHHHHH."

He jolted off the ground near a foot and flipped like a flapjack down flat on his back.

Rolph knelt beside him.

Opening his eyes and looking up at stars, Hans's voiced cracked. "What happened, Rolph, was I in hell?"

Rolph's looked down the road and he was startled at the motion he thought he saw behind them.

"Get in the truck, *dumkopf*. Hurry."

The POWs jumped in the truck.

"Now!" Dick blurted.

"Now!" Duba shouted.

The stake-bed truck pulled away, picked up speed, distancing the chasers.

"Everybody! Let's go!" Dick shouted. "Make sure they know we're behind them. Don't stop chasing until they're at Cherry Valley!"

It was just before the cutoff on Tracy Road when the truck began slowing, swerving back and forth on Pompey Hollow Road, nearly going over the embankment.

"Hold up," Hal shouted.

"They're going to kill somebody," Marty shouted.

It slowed to an idle, puttered and chugged a few feet and stalled out.

Hal reined Major around in two circles looking at the truck.

"Why, that truck is empty," Hal barked.

"What?!" Dick barked.

"They've jumped out."

"They've escaped again," Conway blurted.

"God damnit," Dick shouted.

Hal jumped off Major and lifted Bobby down. He handed the reins to Bobby.

"Hold the horse still, son."

"Where you going Daddy?" Bobby asked.

"Stand here and don't move. I'll be right back."

Hal moved cautiously to the stalled-out truck and looked inside. He took the keys from the ignition, pocketed them and picked up a baseball bat from behind the seat. He carried the bat and stepped back to the stunned and waiting chasers.

"Marty, do you have any rope?"

Marty turned about on his palomino reaching into a saddlebag. He tossed a small ball of twine to Hal.

"Here."

"What do you think, Hal?" Dick asked.

"Who can tell me what's on the left of the road?" Hal asked.

"Limestone creek and our cornfield, but there's a pen wired with electric fence and a bull is in there," Barber said. "One of them peed on the electric fence. That's why he jumped."

"The Tracy Road cutoff is about half a mile up," Conway said.

"On the right or left, and where's that go?" Hal asked.

"It's on the left, it goes down to Oran Delphi Road," Barber said.

"They know that road, that's where we saw them looking in cars," Tall Jerry said.

"At cars on Tracy Road?" Hal asked.

"No, on Oran Delphi," Tall Jerry said. "The night of the hayride and dance."

"Who here knows the woods on the right?" Hal asked.

"I do," Tall Jerry said. "Holbrook and I know it. It's mostly apple orchard."

Taking command Hal turned to the waiting chasers.

"Everybody," Hal shouted. "You in that first car, keep your eyes peeled and drive up ahead and turn down Tracy Road and see if you can find them."

"Now?" Conway asked.

"Go ahead and take off."

Conway pulled away slowly in Dick's Willys.

"Lay on the horn if you see them," Hal shouted.

Hal pointed diagonally, almost as if he was pointing toward Cazenovia.

"Tall Jerry and Holbrook, see where I'm pointing?" Hal asked.

"We see," Holbrook said.

"You cut exactly that direction and look for them in the trees. They know camouflage and they know how to hide."

"They've been hiding for ten years," Marty barked.

"That's right," Hal said.

With that, Tall Jerry and Holbrook stepped off the shoulder of the road and entered the wooded area.

"They're old and it looks like it's mostly hill, so they won't be going too fast on foot," Hal cautioned.

"Watch out for a surprise jump at you," Marty said.

"Grab sticks and be careful, but keep moving and looking best you can," Hal said.

"What about us?" Dick asked.

"Bobby and I are going to look around here by the stake bed," Hal said. "They may come back to it. All you on foot, bikes and horses and the other cars, charge up Pompey Hollow Road to the crossing you mentioned."

"Cherry Valley," Dick said.

"Yes, keep moving and don't stop until you get to Cherry Valley," Hal said. "If you see them, don't lose them until they're all the way out of here."

"Will do," Dick shouted. "Everybody, follow us!"

"Be careful, you two," Mary said to Hal and Bobby.

"We'll be careful," Hal said. "Everybody just keep making noise all the way."

Three horses, a dozen bicycles, the remaining four packed cars and a flock of kids on foot moved quickly, marching down Pompey Hollow Road, growling and threatening, hoping to see the two escaped Nazis who had disappeared.

It was then the big thing happened.

It was like a frightening, glowing volcano.

They were almost to Cherry Valley—old Route 20—when bright white lights flashed on like a giant wall of light.

"What in hell?" Dick shouted.

It was a blinding light blocking the entire width of the road.

"Damn," Duba shouted.

A wall of lights stood thirty foot up if it were an inch. Bright enough it was to make eyes, back near a quarter mile, water and squint. It was headlights from US Army trucks. A huge tank and Army jeeps were lighting up the entire end of Pompey Hollow Road like it was the Fourth of July.

Fifteen soldiers in fatigue battle gear lined the width of the road, aiming their M1 rifles at the crowd.

"Halt!" a sergeant ordered.

"Don't shoot, don't shoot. It's only us!" Dick shouted.

"Who is us?" a voice came from a megaphone.

"We were chasing crooks," Duba bellowed.

"We lost them," Marty added.

A voice echoed through a megaphone, filling the night's air.

"Stand down, men," the voice said to the men aiming the M1 rifles. They stood at ease.

Marty on Sandy rode up first, holding Major's reins. Molly with Dick and the ladies in their leg braces were close behind, followed by the crowd. The cars pulled to the side of the road and parked with lights off.

A lieutenant stood up in his jeep.

"You're a long way from any villages for trick or treating, aren't you?" the lieutenant growled.

"We weren't trick or treating," Mary sparked.

"Honest, sir," Dick started.

"It's still a long way out," the lieutenant said.

"We were chasing two Nazi POW guys that escaped Pine Camp in the war."

"The war has been over eight years, son," the lieutenant said.

"They've never been caught," Mary said.

"And you saw these two, you say?" the lieutenant asked.

"We saw them all right," Duba said. "We were chasing them."

"We lost them back a way," Marty said. "We screwed up somehow."

"It's because they saw us," Barber said. "They stopped their truck and saw us crouching by the side of the road and took off."

The lieutenant looked at Dick and the women in braces on Molly's back.

"It'd be hard to miss you three on that giant horse," the lieutenant said.

"We screwed up," Dick said. "All our planning, up in smoke."

"And them two know the lay of the land better than any of us," Marty offered.

"They've been hiding out for years all around here," Duba said.

A loud shout came from the wooded area.

"It's us!" Tall Jerry shouted. "Holbrook and me. Don't shoot!'"

Holbrook and Tall Jerry made their way to and over a roadside fence and walked into the crowd.

"Who are these guys?" Holbrook barked.

"What's it look like?" Mary asked.

"Did you see anything?" Dick asked.

"They're long gone by now," Tall Jerry said.

"They probably already stole another car," Holbrook said.

Behind the wall of lights came a short honk of the Willys's horn and a shout out from Conway.

"Is it okay if we walk around all this?" Conway shouted.

"You know the voice?" the lieutenant asked Marty.

"We know it," Marty said.

"Come about," the lieutenant ordered.

Conway and the others stepped around in the bright lights.

"We didn't see them anywhere," Conway said.

"Where were you looking?" the lieutenant asked.

"We've been all down Tracy Road, took Oran Delphi over to the Cherry Valley and up here where we saw your lights. We found no trace of them. They've caught a ride or are hiding out somewhere, but they're nowhere near here."

"They're not in the orchard," Holbrook said. "We walked all eight rows of apple trees."

"I think they made it across Cherry Valley from somewhere up the hill through the orchard," Tall Jerry said.

"Can I ask what you are doing here, sir?" Dick asked.

"Like with tanks and guns?" Duba blurted.

"You never said why you are here, Lieutenant," Mary asked.

It was then when they heard the beeping of a vehicle horn from the distance on Pompey Hollow Road.

"Stop or we'll shoot!"

278

"Everyone move to the side of the road, move it now, quickly!" the lieutenant ordered. "Men, stand ready."

The rifles were pointed again.

Distant headlights were approaching quickly, horn honking.

"It's them," Marty shouted.

"It's the POW guys," Dick shouted.

"That's their truck," Tall Jerry shouted.

"They're going to ram us," Barber shouted.

"Everybody, get back!" a sergeant shouted.

"Stand ready, men," the lieutenant barked, with a '41 stake-bed speeding its way toward them. The soldiers were ready to shoot. The truck skitter-bounced, screeching ten foot of rubber, and came to a full stop.

"Get out with your hands up," the lieutenant barked through the megaphone."

"Keep them high in the air. We will shoot!" a sergeant ordered.

Young Bobby stood on the seat and leaned out the passenger side where there was no door.

"It's us," Bobby shouted.

"We know them, Lieutenant," Marty shouted.

"Stand down, men," the lieutenant ordered.

"We caught them. Daddy and I caught the crooks."

Hal stepped down from the driver's seat, walked around and climbed into the truck bed, helping Hans and Rolph to their feet. Two armed troopers approached with handcuffs.

"Fellas, I used a sailor's bowline knot on their legs, a cinch on their wrists. You'll need a knife to untie their hands," Hal said.

"Where were they?" Marty asked.

"Anyone know the Beckers?" Hal asked.

"The Becker girls go to school with us," Mary said.

"Well Mr. Becker nearly got us with his shotgun."

"He was more scared than you were, probably," Mary said.

"We found these two hiding under a tarp in the old man's fishing boat. He thought we were trying to steal his boat."

Hans and Rolph promptly obliged the troopers, who helped them from the truck bed, most likely figuring they would be safer back in a POW prison than they would be in Delphi Falls after tonight. They were handcuffed, loaded into an army truck with four armed guards, and driven away toward Camp Drum.

"At ease, men," the lieutenant ordered.

Hal stepped off the truck and got back on Major, pulling Bobby up behind him.

The lieutenant stood in his Jeep, holstered his revolver, snapping the leather covering closed.

"I don't know who had a hand in organizing this operation, but whoever it was, Camp Drum and the US Army want to congratulate you. You did one hell of a job!" the lieutenant said.

"You'd be surprised who had a hand in it," Dick yelled.

"You'd be astounded!" Mary affirmed.

"What's going to happen to those two?" Marty asked.

"Hell, we don't want them," the lieutenant growled. "We were just following orders to wait here and grab them after dark tonight."

"Orders?" Mary asked.

"We were to wait here at the corner of Pompey Hollow Road and the Cherry Valley."

Mary turned to Dick. "They had orders," she said.

"Most wartime POWs we sent back to Germany and Italy in '46 are probably good citizens today. These two guys are bums in our country, and they'll be bums in their country. We'll ship them to Berlin tomorrow and let the Germans deal with them."

With the army so convenient and with a little nudge from a guardian angel, Dick ripped the top of his costume off and threw it to Conway to catch. Thanks to ole Charlie here, the last clue that came that day, *Sheepfold 11*, started ringing in his brain. I got behind

Dick and the girls on Molly's back. With another nudge from me, and the US Army's wall of bright lights to read by, Dick reached in his pocket and pulled the list of words he and Duba had translated. He edged Molly in closer to the front, towering over Hal and Bobby, sitting on Major.

"Lieutenant, would you know what *Sheepfold 11* might mean?" Dick asked.

"Say again, son?"

"*Sheepfold 11.*"

"Can't say I do," the lieutenant said. He turned and yelled to his troops behind him.

"*Sheepfold 11.* Mean anything to anyone?"

No response. He turned around.

"Anyone. Know what *Sheepfold 11* might mean? Anybody back there?" he shouted again.

The lid of the tank next to his jeep rose up and a trooper lifted himself out to his waist.

"Lieutenant, there's the Sheepfold cemetery. It's the old cemetery the army used for burying POWs in World War II. It's down by the Remington Pond, you know, Lieutenant, near Black River, sir. The men fish the banks there," he said.

"Thank you, Corporal. Well, now you know, son. Sheepfold is a cemetery. Why are you asking?"

Dick and Duba looked at each other; they looked at the list in Dick's hand. Their hearts began pounding in anticipation, as their brains were about to bust.

"Sir," Dick said, "we have reason to believe those two crooks are burying valuables somewhere, and we think it could be in that cemetery, *Sheepfold 11.*"

"What would make you think that, son?" the lieutenant asked.

Mary knew they should keep the coded notes secret.

"We're just guessing, Lieutenant. Those guys escaping from there and clues," Mary said. "It only makes sense it's up there."

"And why is that?" the lieutenant asked.

"No one in Camp Drum would ever suspect they'd come back to Camp Drum, ever."

"Well I'll be…" the lieutenant started.

"Can we go dig it up and see?" Dick asked.

"It could be a lot of valuable stuff," Duba said.

"Young fella, cemetery graves would be on sacred ground. Why, it would take an Act of Congress to get permission to dig one up."

Hal stepped Major up to the front.

"Maybe not, Lieutenant."

"Excuse me, sir?" the lieutenant asked.

"Maybe not this grave, *Sheepfold 11*, sir."

"And who might you be?" the lieutenant asked.

"Sir, my name is Hal Grumman, Chief Petty Officer. I served time in Pine Camp during the war, waiting for my dishonorable discharge. I just finished my time in Auburn—released today."

"You've done your time, citizen. The army holds no grudges. What would you know about *Sheepfold 11* that the army wouldn't already know?"

"During the war, sir, although Pine Camp held thousands of POWs, there were only eight POWs who died there all during the war. Only eight of them were buried there, in Sheepfold, the whole time. It was six Germans and two Italians died to be exact."

"And how would a navy man, a sailor come to know this sort of detail about an army base, Mr. Grumman?"

"I was in the brig there after D-Day. I remember. I was ordered to dig the last POW grave just before VJ Day. It so happened I dug it as the war ended. It was right after that burial the prisoners were sent back home to Germany or Italy or wherever they came from."

"So, what's your point, Mr. Grumman?"

"Sir, it's impossible for anyone to be in grave number 11 in the Sheepfold cemetery."

"And why is that?"

"Sir, I dug the last grave there and it was number 8. I'm certain of it. It was number 8, I dug it. Grave 11 is an empty grave."

"This is interesting," the lieutenant said.

"It has to be an empty grave if Sheepfold was only used as a POW cemetery in WW2," Hal said.

"We'll have to check into it, see what paperwork we'll need."

"When?" Mary asked.

"We'll do it first thing in the morning. Once we do, we'll maybe be able to see what treasures those two may have buried there, or if there are any records or rewards."

"Thank you, Lieutenant." Hal said.

"It may take a day or two," the lieutenant said.

"We'll be patient," Hal said.

"How can we find you, Mr. Grumman?"

"Sunday," Barber shouted. "We'll all be at our place, the Barber farm. North of the hamlet, about a mile up on Oran Delphi. It's a celebration breakfast. You're invited, Lieutenant. Your men are, too."

"Tell you what, folks. We'll check this Sheepfold business out and we'll do just that. We'll come by the Barber farm Sunday and share any news there may or may not be at that time."

"Bring your appetites," Barber said.

"You'll get the best breakfast, Lieutenant," Bobby said.

"You have your daddy's smile, son," the lieutenant said.

Bobby beamed.

With that, the army turned its tank, jeeps, and trucks around, loaded up and headed north to Camp Drum. One army truck towed the crook's stake-bed off as evidence.

The SOS crew went the other way and headed to the falls and turned the music back on. They would be up most of the night, setting out by the waterfalls, square dancing, telling stories. Some

283

were smooching. One thing was certain. Many of them branded their memories with the best adventure they ever had.

They would stare up at the moon from time to time, hear an owl through the noise of the Delphi Falls and smile.

CHAPTER 21

A SIGN OF THE DOVE

Aurora is the goddess of dawn. The night was aglow, like a Milky Way dancing for the moon. The trees atop of both cliffs tapped their leaves together in the wind like applause.

The party started just at midnight, Halloween at the Delphi Falls. If you've ever seen an aurora borealis, the northern lights doing jigs in a setting horizon, you'd have a feel of the time I had on the roof of Big Mike's barn garage that night, setting on the roof enjoying the celebration below. I had good reason to celebrate.

Happenings all around showed what hoping and dreaming can do and how easy helping someone else can be—how opportunity to lend a hand is another occasion to rise to.

As for angels, it keeps us alive.

I felt I owed something back for feeling so good I could bust, so I spent the night in front of Delphi Falls, conjuring on Big Mike's barn garage rooftop.

Nudging is what us guardian angels do best, and I figured I still had powerful nudging left to do. They ain't no better clock than a Halloween night's timepiece. There's good reason. Halloween is the one night of the year when the devil is beside himself, hiding out, nowhere to be seen. With young'uns running about in scary devil masks and ghostly getups scaring him, it's a perfect time for a guardian angel to take advantage of his blind side.

I let the young be young down below, dancin' the night away and sparkin' a kiss or two, fallin' in love and reveling as they might

285

in the barn garage. I gave them space. Same time as their square-dancing strummed and stomped, ole Charlie here prayed.

On Sunday Mr. Barber woke Hal long before the rooster crowed. The two climbed in the pickup with mugs of coffee and circled the farm's acreage, touring fields and fence lines, gabbin' about things like the best mix combinations for silage; whether or not steer or beef cattle would eat up too much pasture and milk profit; and could they pay for themselves with meat prices being what they were; if the hog shed needed to be by the creek a bit more downwind; and what they would have to do to keep wolves out.

Pastor promised to come give Sunday blessings at the farm during breakfast, and as the sun peeked up Mrs. Barber already had a kitchen filled with busy church ladies. With mixing spoons and bowls; beating eggs; whippin' flour and cream; frying bacon; but all praising the Lord and prayin' the clouds overhead would pass on by. They were expecting sixty. If more than a dozen guests come any thoughts of table-eating at Barber's were dashed and gave way to using the table as the serving buffet for vittles and people's laps or knees being the trays holding the paper plates.

Weren't long before people started coming in the drive to the farm breakfast—about eleven o'clock. It was with their first coffee or sip of orange juice, the morning started on the right foot, thanks to my prayers to the Lord. I first asked without bragging about my year, could He give thought to this Sunday late breakfast at the Barber's and giving the morning a sign of sorts? Ole Charlie here knew fallen soldiers had a special place in the heart of heaven and might have the keys to a few secret tricks.

Wouldn't you know, as Mrs. Barber stepped out on the porch for a first ring on her dinner bell, a white dove fluttered down and landed on the triangle, sitting there bobbing its head up and down looking all about? Both hands went to the sides of Mrs. Barber's cheeks. She didn't say a word, but knew it was a sign— that it was going to be a blessed day and figured folks wouldn't need a bell to come get food. She had a sense the morning would come together on its own, and she went back into the kitchen.

Alice and Marian were setting together on the porch, each in their leg braces, sipping coffee with notice of the dove. Marian had mastered her braces and could get about with crutches under her own steam. She'd given Alice walking lessons with her new crutches and braces, and Alice was taking to them and using less of her wheelchair. Despite their polio, they both knew they'd been blessed living in the crown. Seeing the dove, they breathed in the fresh morning air, feeling contentment with all their friends about.

Big Mike and Missus stopped by on their way home from Mass in Manlius to say a proper hello and to drop Tall Jerry and Dick off. Missus had a piece of toast with marmalade and sipped tea, listening to Mrs. Barber talk of the many blessings happening all about. They walked out to Alice with news that there were fourth-grade teaching jobs available in the county, and she was highly recommended by them both for the one of her choice. The beam in that girl's eye was a whole other song.

About that time was when Bruce Gary, the boy Marian danced with at her high school prom all those years ago before the war and she just rode the hayride with, stepped up on the porch."

"Good morning," Marian said.

Without a word, Bruce knelt on one knee in front of her, took her by the hand and asked her to marry him.

"You want to be thinking this over?" Marian asked, pointing down at both her legs strapped in metal leg braces.

"Marian, I'm asking for your hand in marriage—and anything that comes with that," Bruce said.

"He loves you," Alice said.

Marian squeezed the lad's hand and said yes, which seemed appropriate. They were still as much in love as they'd been since their high school prom dance. They just didn't know about it until the hayride.

Mr. Barber balanced a plate of scrambled eggs and cantaloupe slices when a parade of seven army ambulance trucks with big red crosses on their sides, led by a troop carrier and a jeep, rolled in the driveway. The lieutenant stepped from his jeep and waved for the ambulances and the two troop carriers to park between the two barns in the back. He walked to where most of the crowd was sitting on the lawn and side porch or on the empty hay wagon, eating and talking about their Halloween.

"Is Mr. Grumman here?" the lieutenant asked.

Hal was standing next to Bobby and Mr. Barber, holding a paper plate of food.

"Over here, Lieutenant," Hal said.

"I have our report on the two escapees and of *Sheepfold 11*, Mr. Grumman. Would you like to step inside to hear it?"

"Right here will be fine. There's not a person among us who didn't have some kind of a hand in chasing those two off. The news belongs to them as much as me, even more," Hal said.

Mrs. Barber offered coffee to the lieutenant and his men.

"Thank you, ma'am. Let us do our army business first, and then we'd be honored to join you," the lieutenant said.

He stepped back and onto his jeep and stood.

"Camp Drum and the US Army would like to thank all you citizens who came forth and risked your necks making it possible for us to capture two German soldiers who have been a nuisance since their escape from Pine Camp in 1944. They may be older, but it doesn't seem they're much wiser for all the years that have passed. We've made a complete study on this and the army is pleased to tell you, Mr. Grumman was correct that no one was buried in the plot *Sheepfold 11*. We're also happy to tell you that there was treasure of sorts buried in that grave."

Cheers went up.

"Now the good news is, these two Germans kept meticulous records. We all know how detailed and thorough their nature is for detail, German folk. In the grave were nearly four hundred lists of exactly what they had stolen over the years."

"Four hundred?" Dick asked.

"There was a complete inventory on separate handwritten lists, right down to milk cans and tire rims. The bad news to those who lost items, is that they sold them and converted the cash into gold coins."

"That's how we trapped them, with gold," Holbrook said.

"Best we could figure is they used the lists they wrote to shop the items around at pawn shops without the chance of being caught with the goods on them. The grave had gold and silver coins buried in it."

"It did?" Mary asked.

"There wasn't much. Not near the real or sentimental value of what they stole."

"Is there any reward money?" Mary asked.

"There was no reward for the capture of the two escapees. Seems the army was too busy in 1944 fighting a war in Germany and in the Pacific to be thinking of the detail of offering a reward and since the war the escapees just fell through the cracks."

"How about a reward for the gold and silver?" Holbrook asked.

"I'm certain you all could use gold or silver. It could help, I'm sure," the lieutenant said.

"We sure could use something," came a voice from the crowd.

"I could use me some new teeth," came another voice.

"I'd give any reward I get to Bobby and his dad to get a farm," Dick said.

Everyone who was involved in the running off and capture of the POWs applauded at the thought.

"Am I to understand some of you would forgo a reward, if there was one, so Mr. Grumman and his son might get started farming?" the lieutenant asked.

"Most of us, probably," Mary shouted.

"You're fine folks."

"Well I could have told you that, Lieutenant," Mrs. Barber said with a guffaw. "We may be poor but we believe in the Almighty."

"The army made decisions with what we had to deal with."

"Can't hear ya' back here, Lieutenant," a voice shouted.

The lieutenant stood on his jeep.

"Ladies and gentlemen, the army had a dilemma and came up with a solution."

"Any reward?" a voice asked.

"We know what was stolen from parts of the state, they listed each item. Our dilemma is we have nothing to show for it but a pittance of gold and silver. We can't return items stolen. Wished we could, but we can't."

"You found gold, Lieutenant – we'll take that," a voice shouted.

"Like I said, there wasn't all that much gold and silver and it'll take a military tribunal to determine what to do with it."

"So, there ain't no reward," came a voice.

Mary bristled. She stepped over by the jeep.

"We didn't catch these crooks for any reward," she snapped. "We caught them to keep them from stealing more and from setting fires."

"We apologize for the interruptions, Lieutenant," Mrs. Barber said. "Please continue."

"What we can do, however, is benefit all the citizens of the areas who helped us catch them."

"You mean the Crown," Barber shouted.

"I stand corrected," the lieutenant said, "in the Crown. We're giving the towns of Cazenovia, and villages and hamlets of Pompey, Pompey Center, Delphi, Shea's Corner, Apulia Station, Tully, and Lafayette their own fully reconditioned and fully equipped medical ambulances, fresh out of retirement. Every town gets one. Ladies and gentlemen, they are 1942 Chrysler diesel truck ambulances, fully equipped, rebuilt and running like new. They have many years left in them and should be welcome additions to your volunteer fire departments."

Mr. Barber walked over and stood on the porch.

"Lieutenant, I know I can speak for our communities when I say thank you. Ambulances are expensive items and we will treasure them. We all benefit from your gifts."

"With our compliments, from the army and the soldiers at Camp Drum, Sir," the lieutenant said.

"That's reward for sure," Mary said. "Thank the army for us Lieutenant."

"Now with your permission we have something for Mr. Grumman for telling us about *Sheepfold 11*."

"Why me and not everyone, Lieutenant?" Hal asked.

"Ambulances aren't cheap, son," a voice in the crowd said. "We sure can use them."

"Without your knowledge, Mr. Grumman, that grave would have never been touched in a thousand years."

Mr. Barber walked over to Hal and brought him forward a few feet to hear what the lieutenant had to say.

"Mr. Grumman, in the lead army truck over there between the barns is an old 1938 Allis Chalmers tractor and plow. They've both been in a US Army Quonset hut at Camp Drum and unused since 1946. We had them completely reconditioned in our motor pool and they are as good as new."

"Why me?" Hal asked.

"Our best guess is that you were the last person to ever drive that tractor before it was put in storage when the war ended, the time you dug the last grave in Sheepfold."

"We wouldn't have the ambulances if Hal didn't know about the empty grave," Mary said.

"Mr. Grumman, the tractor and plow are our gift to you and your son for your new farm when you get one."

"He deserves it," Dick said.

291

Cheers went up.

"That's mighty generous, Lieutenant, but it'll be a time before we have a farm. Thank you for the courtesy, though. Thank you, everybody, for your kind generosity and caring for my boy the way you have," Hal said.

"Now hold on, Hal," Mr. Barber said. "Gert and I bought the old Toby place yonder in '48. There's been a for sale sign there ever since, and not a bite. The house is a shack, but it's fixable, has a wood burning stove and a handpump water well. Ninety-two acres go with it, good soil. It hasn't been plowed since '47. Too short-handed. It needs a tractor and plow. You fix the place up and farm it, I'll make you a fair price and you can pay me off with ten percent of your crop each year until it's paid."

"Lieutenant, I guess I'll take that tractor and plow after all," Hal said.

"What a wonderful day for the Crown, for the US Army, and for a boy and his dad who have a whole lot of living to make up," the lieutenant said.

"Lieutenant, you and your men have driven a long way. Is there anything we can get you?" Mrs. Barber asked.

"I smell bacon, ma'am. We might start there and see where that takes us," he said.